T0156669

REEDE
THESE

HOWARD REEDE-PELLING

ISBN: 978-1-4669-9592-5 (sc)
ISBN: 978-1-4669-9594-9 (hc)
ISBN: 978-1-4669-9593-2 (e)

Library of Congress Control Number: 2013909756

Trafford rev. 05/22/2013

 www.trafford.com

North America & international
toll-free: 1 888 232 4444 (USA & Canada)
fax: 812 355 4082

FOREWORD

REEDE THESE
BY
Howard Reede-Pelling

These twenty two short stories are entirely fictitious and no reference is intended to any person alive or deceased, except in the stories which are marked 'A true story'. These stories are very diverse and include true-life experiences mixed with a goodly smattering of reading suitable for children. Tales of the Australian Bush, skin diving with sharks and adventures with a Gem Club, are just a teaser of the feast of reading about every-day events in quite a good range of topics. Children will get knowledge of events of yesteryear in this volume.

Agent:–Rory.

To my esteemed friend

RORY

Rory

Rory and Michael at camp

REEDE THESE
BY
Howard Reede-Pelling

vii

INDEX

Continued

INDEX

Continued

1   Linnie   21/6/78

Part One

It was a crisp, sharp morning high in the ranges of out back Victoria, Northeast of Eildon past the weir. A chill wind cut to the very marrow of Bryan's bones, as he left his fishing gear by the mountain stream and set a mug by the glowing embers of the warming fire. The billy was about to boil and a hot cuppa was just the thing to warm the fingers and put renewed energy into his shivering body. Bryan had been camping at this spot for two weeks now and the fishing had been good, he never failed to catch his breakfast from the clear trout stream, although on occasions it appeared hopeless. Bryan always persevered and usually won out. Already this morning he had one trout, only just of size and decided to make a meal of his efforts and catch another. As he added tea to the boiling billy and placed it beside the mug with a fresh gum-sprig across, he noticed the float at the edge of the bank had submerged. Bryan quickly took up his rod, eying the net to make sure it was handy, then lightly struck. The fish was a good one; he could feel the weight of it as the trout took out the slack and frantically dived for cover. Bryan played it carefully, the tea forgotten as the thrill of the chase took over his whole being. The fish was a trout all right, he knew by its reaction and when the fish rose to gain slack so it could spit out the hook; Bryan kept a steady strain not for one second losing concentration. A helicopter suddenly burst over the hill behind Bryan and came down almost on top of his camp, hovered a while, then disappeared over the tree-tops.

"Damnation!" Bryan growled, as he heard the motor drone quietly into oblivion.

He had not looked up and was still in control of his fish which was tiring. Slowly he edged it to the bank where his net lay, already under the water. As the trout came over it, Bryan raised the net and landed his fish.

"Four pounds at least!" He whispered to himself. "What a beauty!"

He immediately killed and bled the fish, then hung it while he washed and sat by the fire to enjoy his 'cuppa'. He was sitting thus, when the drone of an approaching motor announced the return of the helicopter. Bryan idly watched as it erratically swung from side to side. It half circled left and then to the right, travelled a bit and then repeated the manoeuvre. 'Must be looking for something', he speculated. The craft was almost overhead and had there been a clearing about, Bryan was sure it would have landed. 'Wish they would move on, the wind is cold enough as it is!' Bryan mused. 'Seems to be hanging around for something'. Even as he watched, the answer became obvious, as the door opened and an arm waved after dropping a heavy white object on the small grass clearing, just away from Bryan's panel van near the water's edge. Waving back, Bryan hurried across to the message, for it could be nothing else. The helicopter droned away over the hill. A light breeze began to rustle the tree-tops and Bryan quickened his pace as the piece of paper around the heavy object began to flutter. The object was a spanner and it had bounced out of the paper upon contact with the ground. The paper, barely held by a corner, fluttered off just as he lunged for it. Out of reach upon the surface of the water, the swift stream was taking the paper ever more away. Bryan raced for his fishing net and fruitless efforts were his reward, for the elusive piece of paper floated too far out or reach; to be washed ever further away. Bryan let out a deep sigh, retrieved the spanner, which was placed into his fishing creel; then returned to carry on with his breakfast.

"I wonder what on earth was in that message." He muttered out loud. "Wonder if it was important? Nah! Probably just passing the time of day—may have seen me land the fish and just sent congratulations—yeah; that's it!"

Having settled the matter in his mind Bryan finished his breakfast, packed the gear as was his wont and after checking that the camp was spotless and tidy, locked his van and with well-stocked ruck sack and fishing gear; set off upstream. As it was his intention today to fish a quiet backwater he had found on a previous excursion, there was no need for his water bag, since he would be following the river all the way. However he did take a blanket and a towel for washing; just in the event he was caught out by inclement weather or some other unforseen obstacle. There were a few old gold diggings in the area and they would make very good shelter from bad weather. Bryan could not imagine the weather turning nasty; it was going to be a glorious day.

It was three quarters of an hour later that Bryan arrived at his destination and keeping well out of the way of the little backwater, so as not to disturb what fish may be there, he set his gear down beside a large outcropping. There he would be sheltered from the slight breeze and it was also a good spot to light a fire for his cup of tea; which he was looking forwards to after his long hike. Bryan prepared the chosen site well, clearing away all inflammable materials and gathering a small circle of rocks to house the embers of his fire, then had a lazy search around for firewood. Before long Bryan was comfortably seated upon his rolled up blanket, back against the wall of granite and that refreshing cuppa making him at peace with the world. His idle gaze scanned the stream and he noted that although it was quite wide at this particular spot, there would be no trouble at all in crossing should he desire to try his luck along the bank of the stream on the other side. There was no need to fish just yet, Bryan preferred early morning and evening fishing. It was true, occasionally a good trout could be caught in the middle of the day if one sank a frog and left it awhile, however, Bryan had no intention of having fish three times in one day. He had ample supplies of tinned food and there were still potatoes and carrots left in the van from his supply of fresh foodstuffs. He might even go out and shoot a bunny later and stew it for tea. Tinned food would suffice for lunch, today was to be a lazy day. Just a quiet fossick around the river banks and maybe chase up another old mine tunnel to explore, perhaps even go further upstream and find that waterfall he could hear in the distance. His gaze centred upon the clearing across the river, it appeared to be fairly well used. Here and there an empty can and the odd bit of paper, a cigarette packet was caught amongst the scrub around a tall eucalypt tree.

"Filthy buggers!" Bryan cursed the thoughtless picnickers who would have left it. "Must be an access road away from here on that side of the river" He muttered.

Bryan rinsed his tea-things and with just his torch and a snake stick, he went in search of an old mine; having doused the fire and tidied up. An hour or so later he was back at his small camp-site upstream. There was no sign of a gold workings but he did see the most awe-inspiring waterfall tumbling down some one hundred metres on a gradual rocky decline. The falls splashing and sparkling with rainbow hues, as the warming sunshine glistened where it filtered through the trees and played upon the dancing droplets, were picturesque. Froth and foam eddied in a small catchment area at the base to surge away at first, and then idly meander as the clear mountain waters wound haphazardly down to the meadows a kilometre away. The beautiful picture still in his mind, Bryan rekindled and lit the fire. Soon the smell of sausages and vegetables was wafting lazily across the stream in melodious rhythm to the sizzling of the near boiling billy. Bryan was so engrossed with his cooking, he jumped as if shot when a weary childish voice yelled.

"I'm hungry!"

With startled expression he gazed in awe at the spectacle he was witnessing. There, in the clearing by the water's edge, on the other side of the stream; stood a dirty, unkempt, ragged little girl. Visions of a helicopter and a lost note flashed through his mind. Stunned, he stood staring.

"I'm hungry!" The girl trembled, beginning to cry.

Bryan snapped into action and quickly crossed the stream, reaching out to the girl. Sobbing, she ran into his arms. He held her closely, patting her back gently.

"There, there Sweet pea, it is all over now. You will soon be home. Let me lift you and I will carry you over the water, then we will have something to eat!"

The events of the past few minutes were so quickly over that the dinner on the fire had no time to burn. But it was very hot. Bryan scraped it all onto his plate and left it to cool a bit, while he poured some tea into a mug.

"Don't touch the food yet Sweet pea, you will burn yourself, there will be plenty to eat; just wait a bit."

He went to the stream and got a beaker of cold water with which to cool the tea. The little girl drank a few sips and then placed the mug down, looking hungrily at the laden plate. Bryan sat her on his blanket, put his towel upon her lap and placed the plate upon it. Offering a spoon, he cautioned.

"Now take it easy, it is hot."

The girl nodded and wolfed down the food, blowing occasionally. It was hot but the girl did not care, she was starving. The food diminished rapidly. Bryan studied the little mite as she ate. The clothes she wore had been of good quality and she must have looked cute when first she became separated from her parents, but now—huh! What a dirty little wretch she appeared. Only slight and about eight, he thought, but she was beautiful with her long, dark hair and deep, wide brown eyes. The tear stains had left veritable canyons in the grime on her face and the torn fragments of her clothing, gave her an 'Artful Dodger' look. The little girl finished the plateful and Bryan offered her the mug again. She took it gently, hiding her face behind it.

"What is your name Sweet pea?"

Bryan always called little girls 'Sweet pea'; it had a nice friendly sound to it. The girl gulped, and then answered.

"Linnie"

The voice was calmer now and had a rather deep quality to come from such a wee thing. Bryan gathered that the name was short for Lynne or Lynette but just nodded.

"I am Mister Reynett but everyone just calls me 'Fred', Linnie."

"Mpf." She murmured.

"When did you lose Mummy and Daddy, was it today?" Bryan asked, as casually as he could. She sniffed, a tear trickled down her cheek.

"No," she paused "it was yesterday. I was frightened in the dark, all the goblins was trying to catch me—"

The tears began to flow again and she came over and snuggled into Bryan.

5

"Come now Sweet pea, it is all over–remember? There were no goblins; the noises were just the crickets and the insects that live in the trees at night, probably an old possum or something. Did you have enough to eat?"

Linnie did not answer, she just nodded her head, and then she looked up at Bryan.

"Mister Reynett, I want my Mummy!"

Surprised at her good memory and noting that she did not use the nickname he offered, a sign of good manners and breeding, Bryan soothed.

"Sure, sure, just as soon as I can I will get you back to your parents. Now, how about we give your face a wash, eh? It will make you feel so much better because we have a long way to go back to my car and you will have to be nice and fresh!"

Linnie followed docilely to the stream. Bryan used his dishcloth to wipe her face and brush her hair; he also dusted up her rags a little. For once he did not wash up; a quick rinse in the cold water would have to do. Everything packed and the fire out, Bryan took the little girl's hand and they set forth.

The outward trip took Bryan only three quarters of an hour but he knew it would take almost twice as long to return, as the child was quite small and the path fairly rough. The noonday sun filtered through the trees as the bush was quite thick. A faint splutter from afar and Bryan rejoiced in the thought of the helicopter returning. He knew it was useless to build a smoke fire as there was no clearing anywhere around that Bryan knew of, only the one back at his van. As the helicopter chopped the air overhead, he tried to be noticed amongst the trees. Waving his white towel frantically he hoped they would see the movement. If they saw at all, there was no sign of it for the helicopter moved away.

'If only they had seen' Bryan thought 'at least the parents would have known their little girl was safe'. A heavy silence fell on them; the craft had stilled the normal sounds of the bush, momentarily.

"It's gone!" The child's hopeless words seemed to echo like a cannon shot.

"Never mind, we do not need it!" Bryan reassured his little charge.

They plodded wearily on, the child beginning to stumble but she did not complain. They were halfway by now and Bryan realized it was too much for little Linnie. She had probably been stumbling for hours before she found him and goodness knows from where she started her wanderings. They stopped and Bryan emptied his rucksack, laid his fishing gear beside a fallen log and packed everything in tight as was possible underneath it. As he broke some small scrubby bushes to hide his gear, the little girl just stood watching with tired eyes and heavy lids. Not a murmur escaped her lips. He hated doing it but Bryan cut leg holes in the bottom of his rucksack with his fishing knife and asked Linnie to step into it, like a pair of pants. There was no argument as she did that which Bryan asked of her. Bryan stood her on the log, put his back to her and fixed the straps over his shoulders. As he walked away, Linnie was carried 'piggyback' style. She put her arms around the strong shoulders and fell into a deep sleep. The child weighed little more than his hiking gear but Bryan was glad when the small clearing where his panel van waited, came in sight. Opening the van, he laid the youngster gently in his bed and covered her. She slept on. It was a long way back to any sort of township as Bryan had camped way out on a mountainside in the back of beyond and cursed himself for going so far from civilization—then bit his lip—what would have happened to the little girl if he had not done so? He was sure there was not another living soul up there at normal times, with the possible exception of an odd gold prospector, maybe. Now of course it was probably alive with people searching for Linnie. Bryan had heard no sounds of a search party. Normally in the circumstances the coo-ees would be heard for miles, yet all had been quiet until the advent of the helicopter. His only conclusion was that the little girl had travelled far—and not in circles as the lost are wont to do. No wonder she slept so soundly, the little mite was worn out. Another thought struck him. The wind was blowing off the mountains and down to the plains or rather, across them. Normally an updraught comes from the plains but with the sunny weather and only a slight breeze, it was possible that any sounds of a search were carried away from his camp site. Bryan began to feel the pangs of hunger and yearned for a cup of tea. All of his dinner was given to the one who needed it most and as he took only one mug, he missed out on a cuppa, too; using the remaining tea to douse the fire and so get the little lost waif back quickly. He remembered a block of chocolate he had in the glove box and thankfully ate most of it, keeping some in case Linnie should wake. Bryan doubted it; she was sleeping a sleep of relief and fatigue, and would not wake for some time.

Even the almost nothing of a trail that it took a real bushman to read, and then negotiate in its rough state, would not awaken her; Bryan felt sure. The trail led to a more respectable track made by logging trucks and the going was much easier. After about five minutes of travel on this one, Bryan thankfully noticed a clearing by a small creek. A regular wayside stop, he was most relieved to see police vehicles and a rescue-squad caravan with about twenty people milling about, apparently being briefed. He learned later that they had come in for lunch and to report progress. They were just about to set forth again on the search. Surprised at a vehicle approaching from that direction, all eyes were turned towards him and as he pulled over, a Senior Policeman with heavy dark eyebrows; challenged.

"Hey! Did you–?"

"Yes, she is asleep in the back!"

"Thank God!" He exclaimed, craning his bull-like head over the seat the better to see but Linnie was well snuggled and undercover.

Bryan alighted and as he opened the side door, a very pale-faced lady the image of the girl, barged through the throng as amid a chorus of cheers, word got around that the girl was found safe and well.

"Linnie!" She cried, oh my Dear Linnie!"

The little one woke at her mother's voice and with a shrill scream.

"Mummy!"

They were in each others arms, the mother repeating over and over.

"Oh thank you. Thank God. Thank you!"

Hardened men were hard pressed to hold back a tear. A rifle discharged three shots at evenly spaced intervals–a bush signal–it would call all searchers in. The mother of the child was joined by her husband but the three of them were oblivious of the rifle shots. Bryan had wandered off to the police caravan to help fill in the report and indicate on the local map the point at which he located the child. A Salvation Army lady came in bearing a hot cup of tea and a plate of sandwiches, pushing them at Bryan. His thanks were evident.

"Ah! You are an angel of mercy. I gave my lunch to young Linnie!"

"Not so!" She said. "You are the angel of mercy, you delivered the Dear babe–thank the good Lord!" She smiled as she left, tears in her eyes.

His business with the police finished and the mob dispersing, Bryan closed his van and drove off; returning to his camp site. There was his gear stashed away and he wanted it back, Bryan would not leave his beautiful fishing rod behind. As he tramped back to his van with the gear, he was aware of the helicopter. The same procedure again. The arm, the white message, then off it flew. Bryan was not going to let this one get away, he fairly flew at it. The message read:-

Dear Mister Reynett,

We owe you a rucksack; please let us say our thanks properly.

It was signed and the address clearly written. Bryan recalled the wide brown eyes and good memory of a well-mannered little girl. Yes, he would give her parents that chance.

THE END.

Howard Reede-Pelling.

9

2   Charlie

                        Part One

"The time son—you want to know the time?"
The tall hawk-nosed man in the dark suit peered over his pince-nez spectacles as he addressed the youngster who had questioned him; annoyed at being distracted from the paper he had been reading. Out of wide blue eyes the freckled young lad gazed in anticipation at the man's wrist watch.
"Yes Sir, please!" The boy impatiently craned his neck, trying to read the time upside down.
A quick glance and the man informed the boy that it was seventeen minutes past one.
"Thank you Sir."
The boy was off, to disappear amid the throng of office workers and shoppers who were hustling to and fro during the lunch-break. The tall man "Hrrumpfed" and went back to his reading. The boy hurried to a bus stop and was only just in time to catch the bus that would take him back to his school.
He arose late that morning and after the few home duties were done, had raced off to school. His mum refused to give him a note for the teacher, saying it would teach him to be early next time. When he turned into the street that housed the Technical School he attended, he was much too late. Mister Houston, the Candy man who controlled the school crossing, was just on his way home.
"Hello young Charlie, you are very late, my word you will cop it!"
He cheerily waved as he turned the corner. Charlie knew he was late, he did not have to be told but the telling frightened him. He stopped to think things over. 'Damn! It was not his fault; Mum should not have expected him to do the odd jobs this morning. They could have been done when he returned home that afternoon. Now he was late again—again—jeez! Won't his maths teacher give it to him though, after being late yesterday and getting that final warning off old 'Gabba' Jackson, his teacher? The nick-name

was well deserved, boy! Could HE talk and Charlie's ears were still ringing from the tongue-lashing he got then.' Rather than face 'Gabba' again, he decided to 'wag' it for the morning. He would go to school after lunch and tell the teacher he had to do messages or he was sick or some such. He would think of something, he had to. Maybe if he went to the pictures he would be able to think of a good excuse, yes that's it. There was a picture in town he wanted to see and he felt sure that while watching it, he would get inspiration and think of a powerful excuse for not attending school that morning. So it happened that Charlie was in the City asking the time. Unfortunately the pictures did not come out until a fraction after one and by the time the boy bought a can of drink and a bread roll, it was late. Hence his mad rush to get to school again. 'Gee-whiz I am in trouble' he worried to himself. 'I will never get in there before classes start again!' So engrossed was he with his thoughts that he forgot to pull the cord to stop the bus at the school. It was a stop after that the bus driver halted his vehicle and shouted to Charlie.

"Hey Son! Isn't that your school back there?"

"Huh? Oh! Yes Sir, I am sorry—thank you Sir!"

He rushed out of the bus, flustered and frantic. What to do?

"Damn bloody damn!"

Charlie kicked at a tuft of grass. He felt like crying but as his dad would say. 'Gosh Son, you are a big boy now; big kids do not cry—not eleven year olds!' At his old school he would not have worried. Old man Gabba frightened all the boys, it was not only Charlie.

"Better make a whole day of it now."

Charlie mumbled to himself as he ambled away towards the sports ground across the road from the bus stop. His thoughts hung heavily upon him. He was happier at his old school that is where all his mates were. Gee! Wouldn't it be great to have some of them with him now? Of course if his mates from the State School were here, Charlie would not feel as lonely as he did. That was the trouble with moving to a new school, especially if your mates did not move too, a fellow had to make all new friends. As yet, Charlie had not done so!

Even though he was quite independent, it was nice to have someone to play with or just have around with whom to talk. Dad always seemed to be too busy or wanted to listen to the races, and then on Sundays off he would go to golfing. Charlie often pestered his father offering to be his caddie, but his father usually brushed him aside saying the boy would only get in their way and spoil the game. Charlie was now at the pavilion by the side of the oval. A small open drain trickled around the rough area behind the pavilion; it was a natural attraction to children. They would put matches or sticks in it and race them until they disappeared under the boundary fence at the side of the sports ground. Charlie followed the drain to the fence and decided to climb over. He had always wanted to do it but never got the chance before, there were always other boys or teachers about to either pimp on him or stop him. Charlie had heard the drain had a tunnel about five houses further along and that it emptied into the sea about half a kilometre away. He would explore the drain and see. As he reached the opening of the tunnel Charlie had grave doubts about entering, it looked awfully dark in there although he fancied he could see a faint grey filtering through from the other end. He entered and slowly crept forwards into the darkness.

"Hello Son!" A voice startled him!

Charlie froze, trembling.

"Spooks!"

He whispered to himself, eyes searching the darkness. Thoroughly frightened, Charlie began backing out; too frightened to turn and run in case he was attacked from the rear. He could see the faint silhouette of someone now that his eyes were becoming adjusted to the gloom.

"Hey Sonny, don't get all frightened up; I won't hurt ya. I just come in here to drink me grog, talk ter me; a bloke gets lonely on his own alla the time."

"No! I'm scared, I–I gotta go!" Charlie was still backing out.

"Wait Son, don't go rushing off! Tell ya what, I'll just come to the front of the tunnel an' you can see me in th' light, then you'll know there's no need t' be 'fraid o' ol' Ben!"

The boy was well out into the open drain when the owner of the voice appeared. Charlie screwed up his nose. Never had he seen such a ragged old man, he looked about ninety (he really was only forty five but the mixtures he drank, had taken their toll with be whiskered face, unkempt straggly hair and dirty baggy trousers half hidden under an old gaberdine greatcoat; frayed at the cuffs.

"See Son, I won't do you no harm. Where was you off to?" He sat at the entrance regarding the boy; a huge stain-toothed grin was evident. Charlie stopped his backwards journey when he realized that the man was no immediate threat to him, secure in the belief that he could easily outdistance this frail old man.

"Nowhere, not really. I mean, I was going to see if the tunnel came out at the beach but it does not matter, I–er–I really don't care!"

The old man cackled.

"Heh, heh, she sure does me boy, she sure does. That's how ol' Ben got 'ere. I alwuz come in from th' beach to drink me grog, then I can sleep it orf 'ere an' the fuzz don't catch me. Heh, heh, smart ol' Ben is; smart!"

He looked quizzically at Charlie who was fascinated by this new experience, knowing he should not linger with this strange old man, yet the fact it was a new experience; made him curious.

"Ef yer like" old Ben was saying "I'll come froo with ya, then you won't get inter no trouble. I'll look after yer, I gotta go back to th' beach now anyway. Time ter go to th' Salvo's fer a bit a' grub. What do ya say Son? 'Ere, come on over an' let me 'ave a look at ya!"

He beckoned the boy. Charlie began to go forwards, and then faltered. His parents had warned him about strangers and this one sure looked strange.

"Tha's the boy, I tol' ya not ter be frightened, I won't hurt ya. I like kids." He waved his hand urging the boy closer. "Come on, what's yer name?"

"Charlie." The boy answered, as he slowly came forwards.

The old man had tired brown eyes that still showed a little sparkle and a jolly sort of face that smiled almost continuously.

"My word! You are nice lookin' lad, aincha? I like kids wot 'as blue eyes. My boy 'ad blue eyes but 'e 'ad fair 'air–he died you know–in a car crash. I been on th' booze ever since, s'nice to talk ter 'nother blue eyed boy. Brings back mem'ries."

Old Ben nodded absently as he rose and gazed into Charlie's eyes, then suddenly turned and began walking.

"Well, come on Charlie, we'll head for the beach!"

Apprehensively Charlie followed. He knew he should not but the old man seemed friendly enough and harmless. As they made their way along the tunnel, the boy soon caught up with the old man as he did not like being left alone in the darkness. It was not that way for long. Soon the greyness ahead became lighter and then as they turned out of the curve in the tunnel, the sea could be seen in the opening at the end. Charlie forged ahead of Ben and the old man cautioned him.

"Steady Son, don't want to rush out 'til we see who's out there. Neither of us should be in 'ere ya know!"

He put a hand on the boy's shoulder to restrain him. Charlie stopped.

"Rightoh! Let's go ahead slowly!"

The boy felt a hand on his buttocks as old Ben eased him forward, gently squeezing.

"Hey. Let go of my bum!" Charlie challenged. "You a 'poofy' or something?"

The old man seemed genuinely upset.

"Aw, no Son. I didn't mean nothin'; I was just pushin' ya forward!"

"But you squeezed my bum!"

"Yeah–I'm sorry–forgive me boy, will ya?"

"Don't do it again!"

Charlie raced out of the tunnel, heedless of old Ben's warning and hurried along the sea wall that separates the sand of the beach; from the road; before mounting the parapet. He glanced back. Old Ben was standing at the entrance; shaking his head–sadly–it seemed to Charlie. The boy felt a pang of pity. Perhaps the old man was not really being rude, maybe Charlie was just jumping to conclusions.

As he studied the man, the boy could see his own loneliness in the appealing look old Ben was casting at him. Charlie slowly walked back. As he stopped well in front of old Ben, Charlie noticed a teardrop on the man's cheek. He opened his mouth to speak but the man, eyes dropped in shame, spoke first.

"I'm real glad ya come back boy, believe me I really am sorry. Guess I'm jus' a drunk ol' fool–I promise it won't happen no more–truly! Think yer c'n believe me? Please Charlie, I ain't got many friends."

Charlie sat on the sand, not taking his eyes off the man for a second. The morning sun had warmed up the sand and now in the early afternoon, there was quite a distinct chance of the weather becoming quite hot. Not getting an immediate answer, old Ben raised his eyes to look at the boy. Charlie's gaze held steady, his young mind trying to analyse the man; he remembered his father saying 'think Son, always work things out then make up your mind and stick with it; stand by your decisions'.

"Well Son. We gonna be friends?" Ben worried.

"I s'pose." Charlie smiled fleetingly. "But I prob'ly won't see you anymore. I am not supposed to talk to strangers, 'specially when they are–." He faltered and Ben finished for him.

"When they's dirty unshaven old drunks–eh boy?"

Charlie struggled, not wishing to offend.

"Well–?"

"S'all right Son. Tell you what–" he thought for a moment "tell you what" he repeated, and then burst out "listen boy, I like ya an' as I said, I need a friend. I ain't always been a drunken bum but since I lost me boy I ain't had nothin' t' live for; you remind me of him a lot Charlie boy. Will ya help me Charlie, will you be me friend an' I'll try an' dry out? I'm goin' ter th' Salvo's terday, I'm gonna 'ave a bath n' a shave–see if I c'n get some clean clobber, jus' so you'll be me friend an' ya won't be ashamed of me!"

He eagerly studied the stunned lad.

"Well, what say? Will ya help me, is it a deal; please boy I need someone to live for!"

Charlie could not believe his ears; he thought he must be in another world. Here he was, an eleven year old boy and a grown up old man was pleading with him, as if he–Charlie–was a king and could miraculously change his world. He thought. 'The silly old man must be mad or something.' As he looked for a way out.

"But I can't do anything for you; my Dad'll kill me if he knows I wagged school. He will wonder how I met you!"

The old man pondered awhile.

"Yeah" he said, then "we'll have ter do it right!" He thought a moment longer. "D'yer live far away, Son?"

"No, just a few streets past the school."

Charlie told Ben the address, then wished that he hadn't but it was done.

"All right then!"

Ben was getting eager, the grin again evident and a definite sparkle in his eyes. Charlie fancied the old man was beginning to look younger.

"Tell you what we'll do" Ben continued "you come back here termorra after school–no–that's too far for ya. I'll meet ya at the park where th' drain starts, an' I promise yer; I'll be a diff'rent bloke. All nice an' clean an' I won't 'ave another drink, but ya gotta 'elp me Son. If you ain't there, ya gunna break me spirit. I need ya now Charlie boy; will ya promise you'll be there?"

He eagerly studied the boy's reaction but there was indecision on the youngster's face.

"Aw, I don't know. I will get into trouble."

"Gee Son, don't let me down now I got me faith all built up; I need you boy. I said we'd do it right, you see termorra. I c'n keep me word an' when I 'ave proved that to ya, we c'n go an' see ya dad an' say you jus' met me at the footy oval. I'll tell 'im I want you as a sort a' mascot to 'elp straighten me out. I got a pitcher a' me boy somewhere's, I'll fish it out an' then y'll both know as I am fair dinkum. That sound all right?"

"Yes, I suppose. I–I had better be going now, goodbye!"

Ben reached out and touched his arm.

"Hey boy! Ya will be there?"

Charlie nodded as he walked away.

"Yes. I said I would be your friend but only if I can trust you!"

Old Ben sighed as he watched the youngster wander off towards the pier. Ben was happier than he had been for a long time; he turned and made his way to the People's Palace.

Meanwhile young Charlie was busy with his thoughts. He would be in enough trouble for wagging school but once his father found out he had explored a drain and spent some time with an old hobo, he would really be in for it. There was a distinct possibility, now that he had divulged his address that the old drunk would turn up at the doorstep looking for a handout. Charlie's freckles stood out as his face reddened at the thought. Gosh it had been a rough day. Was the old man a 'poof' or not? One thing for sure, old Ben nearly broke his heart when Charlie accused him. And the old man did apologise. Ah! He is probably a harmless poor old coot!

It was an hour after school the following day and as Charlie made his way over to the fence where the drain ran under, he was conscious of a man walking to and fro. However it was not Ben. This man had a smart suit with an open-necked shirt and only looked middle-aged. Charlie thought Ben was at least seventy or eighty, so he tried to keep well clear of this stranger. The man approached as Charlie tried to avoid him.

"Glad ya come boy, didn't really think ya would, yer dunno as 'ow happy I am as I can trust ya t' keep ya word!"

Charlie was amazed. It was definitely Ben's voice, he could not mistake that; he stood spellbound. Ben pulled a photograph out of his pocket as he reached the stunned boy, who was staring disbelievingly.

"See Charlie, there's a picture of me boy, he was only ten; I–I killed 'im. Was drunk at th' time. Couldn't control the car, it rolled over" Ben sniffed, wiping away a tear "his mum too–my Dear wife–I loved her so, that was years ago, many years–" his voice trailed off.

The youngster looked at the picture, realizing that there was a similarity between the two of them but could not make himself believe that this freshly shaved person with the slicked down hair, was the same old man he met in the drain; the has-been of the previous day.

"What say we sit on th' bench yonder an' 'ave a bit of a talk. Sorta plan t' see y' dad an' all." Ben suggested.

Charlie had other ideas.

"No! I would rather go over there under that big pine tree and sit in the sun!"

Ben glanced over, noting that there was an occupied car in the background.

"Aw, I dunno Son. The sun ain't too hot just now, she's beginning to set an' there's a bloke in that car; he might 'ere us talkin' an' get to wonderin'."

Charlie shrugged.

"There is a seat we can sit on."

He made towards the seat in question. Ben had no recourse but to follow. After all, it was he who was relying upon the boy for friendship and so had to tread water for a while. They settled themselves, Ben casting a suspicious glance at the motorist but he appeared to be engrossed in reading the evening paper. Charlie opened the conversation.

"Well, I promised I would turn up!"

"An' ya sure did Son an' I'm thankin' ya. I wasn't sure if ya would but I'm real glad ya did. Look diff'rent, don't I?" Ben smiled hugely at the boy. "Feel better too. Ya ain't ashamed of me now are ya?"

Charlie appeared preoccupied and nervous. He kept looking over his shoulder at the car as he answered.

"Yes, I–er–I did not recognize you at first. Not until you spoke, then I knew."

Ben nodded.

"Yair, I don't talk too good. Never did have a good edycation, tha's why if we gonna be friends I don't want no more waggin' it from ya. You go an' get all th' learnin' ya can. We don't want ya t' be endin' up like me–do we boy. You'll do that fer me won't ya?"

He studied the blue eyes as he spoke, almost demanding the boy's obedience.

Charlie nodded as Ben continued.

"You do th' right thing an' I'll do th' right thing, then neither of us'll get inta trouble. I better wait 'til termorra night ter see yer dad, give us both time ter think it out proper. What d'ya think a' me boy, looks a bit like you, don't he?"

Charlie agreed, then with a serious face, asked bluntly.

"Ben."

"Yair?"

"What are we going to do—I mean—what do you want me to do?"

He frowned as he struggled for words.

"Are we just going to meet here all the time?"

His worried frown touched Ben.

"No boy, no, far from it. It ain't good fer either of us t' be seein' each other like this. No, like I said, we is gunna get th' okay fr'm your dad so I c'n come an' see ya. It ain't no good ter do nothing sneaky. I'm goin' t' get a job—yeah—that s'prises ya don't it? But I sure am, I wanta be able ter come an' take ya out like you was me own kid. Sorta an uncle—yeah, that's it—I'll be jus' like an uncle to ya. Don't get me wrong Charlie boy, I don't intend t' try an' take y' love away from y' mum an' dad. I jus' want a little bit ter rub off on me, an' I'll love ya jus' like ya was me own son. You don't min' that do ya boy?"

He peered at Charlie for his reaction. The boy was silent. Ben pushed his cause.

"When I got some money an' self respec' I c'n take you t' th' zoo an' the movies an' even Luna Park. What do ya reckon?"

The car door slammed and the motorist came over.

"I think it can be arranged Ben" he said, startling the hobo to his feet "I am Charlie's father, he told me all about it; everything. Wagging school, the tunnel, your problem; my boy has faith in you Ben, he thinks you are sincere; he is giving you a chance. For his sake I had to test you out, don't spoil it and break his confidence in you Ben. Keep your end of the bargain and I will see that he keeps his, it could

19

do both of you a lot of good. Charlie needs an interest at the moment and you could provide that, a good friend is an asset to anyone!"

He reached out a hand, Ben accepted warmly, tears glistening.

"Thank you Mister, an' thank you too little mate—Charlie.

THE END

H. R-P.

3   Bryan   30/6/78

Part One   (A true Story)

Tim finished his act with a double single twist somersault over Shirley, his five year old sister and moved behind the side drapes. He returned holding his seven year old sister Faye by the hand and between them they lifted Shirley high, and then marched off stage together. Three times they had to bow, smiling happily to the strong applause. Harry Spencer, their father-manager who taught them all their tricks, gave the signal for an encore. The children swung into it with the gusto of the veterans they were. After the performance, in the dressing rooms, Tim stamped his foot in annoyance as he argued with Bryan, the family friend and attendant–come driver–come floor manager–come costumer. You name it–it fell to Bryan to do. The only thing he did not do, was attend to the receipts. Missus Delilah Spencer, affectionately known as 'Del', did that. Young Tim, the nine year old head of the 'Famous Spencer Trio' was adamant that the rubber mat, upon which they performed, had to be replaced since it was getting dangerous. The stamping of his foot emphasised the point.

"But Bryan, I slipped twice, once on the Pyramid and again at the Swirl. You know if I fall on the Swirl someone will break a leg. We have to have a new rubber mat!"

"We can not afford a new mat Tim!" Bryan told him. "You know what your mum said; we get a new mat after Easter, not before. We still have to pay those striped costumes off, now get into the shower–quickly!"

He divested the boy of his soiled outfit and the lad scampered off to the showers in his briefs, still rebellious.

"I won't perform at 'The Club', that's all!"

The shower door closed as Harry entered the room.

"What was all that about?"

Bryan shook his head as he answered.

"Little bugger is rebelling, he reckons that he will not play at 'The Club' tonight. He says the mat is too slippery."

Tim's dad was old to be the father of such a young family. He had married a woman twenty years his junior but that did not matter; they had a great love of each other and their children.

"Ah! He will be all right. Just kid to him, can you manage the kids for a bit? Del wants me to go over a contract with her. I think we have booked 'The Tiv'!"

"Sure," Bryan answered as Harry left, smiling at the startled expression of his friend.

The two girls emerged in clean undies, their hair dripping wet from their showers.

"Good grief girls, why didn't you wrap the towels around your heads? You will catch a chill." Bryan used the towels they carried to dry their hair, and then got the hand dryer working on them.

"We have not got much time, only half an hour to dress and be at 'The Club'. Start putting on your costumes; they are on the hangers there. I will hurry Tim along."

There were still five minutes left as Bryan pulled the van in near the stage door. Just enough time to 'warm up' the children and get the mat ready. Tim was not at all happy and still insisted that he would not go on, despite the sharp tongue of his mother and the threats of his father. The arguments were beginning to affect his young sisters too, as they studied the mat apprehensively. In the wings, Bryan took young Tim aside. They were great friends, he and the children and Harry did tell him to kid to the boy.

"Look Tim, we can't let all these people down, they look forwards to seeing 'The Famous Spencer Trio'. You know that the show must go on!"

Tim pulled away.

"But it is dangerous, I'm frightened of a slip, it is embarringsing if I fall!"

"Hey! Where is that sure-footed Timmy you have been telling me about?" Bryan thought for a moment. "Tell you what" he eagerly said "do a good job tonight and I will let you come with me to the workshop tomorrow. Between us, we may be able to roughen it up on the sander. How does that sound?"

He had the boy's interest.

"What will that do?"

"Make it like new. You will not be able to slip if you try, the sander will tear it up like suede!" Tim was not sure what suede was but his mentor made it sound good and the boy had new hope.

"Thirty seconds to curtain!" The stage manager yelled. Bryan had a last word to Tim.

"Now a good show mate, pretend it is a new mat, do it for me. We will have a good day tomorrow."

Tim nodded happily as he took his sisters under his wing and gave them the customary instructions.

"Now remember your counts. Don't start your run Faye until I have done my last flip, an' Shirley, you wait until Fay's last flip. You came on too quick last time; dad says you make an impact or something; so you must wait!"

The performer's light glowed, it was their cue. Toby took off–the show was on the road. The parents and Bryan had their fingers crossed; they knew the mat was not good enough now!

The children's act had a duration of ten minutes. It was all fast somersaults, swirls, balancing and acrobatics. The children practised daily in the passageway of their home, mornings and evenings, much to the annoyance of the neighbours. The continual thumping must have been hard to cope with. Occasionally, on a fine day and if the rain had not fallen for a week or so, they had the added thrill of practice in the park. However this was not often as there were too many distractions. Usually a curious crowd gathered and got in the way or yelled obscenities, taking the children's mind off their work. This could be dangerous especially on the foot somersault. This manoeuvre was where Faye would lie on her back with legs sticking up and knees slightly bent. Arms out upon the ground for support and Tim in a similar position behind her, Shirley would sit on Fay's feet and then, on cue, Faye would kick up and Shirley would do a back somersault to land in a sitting position upon Tim's feet. He in turn would somersault Shirley back once more and she would land on her feet behind Tim. It was a difficult feat and if Shirley missed, she could land on Tim's face or chest; however they were well practised and usually accomplished this trying part of their act to perfection. There was a time when they used to do this somersault with Shirley standing on Faye's feet. When she did the back somersault, Shirley was expected to land in a standing position upon Tim's feet. A miscue one time almost destroyed Tim's future and so this extremely difficult move was abandoned. But even in a sitting position, this manoeuvre was fraught with danger; therefore they were seldom allowed to practise in the park.

The audience at 'The Club' were far removed from the critical gatherings at the local park and were quite spellbound at the amazing agility of these three talented tiny tots, and indeed, they looked little more than babes on the large stage. As each feat was completed the applause rang out, giving heart to the performers but not one of the patrons was aware of the suspense on the stage and in the wings. When the slip came the audience were not aware of it, so well did the youngsters cover it up; however the hawk eyes of the three dependant adults did not miss it and Del gave a slight gasp while the two men winced. It was as Tim said it would be, on the swirl. This manoeuvre entailed Tim swinging the two girls around with Faye having her legs locked around Tim's neck, while leaning backwards and down; arms outstretched. Shirley holding Faye's feet while her own swung freely as Tim spun around. He would pirouette three or four times but because of the uneven weight distribution due to Shirley being so small–if his feet were not gripping–Tim would be pulled off balance. His foot inevitably did slip at the height of the spin and only for the fact that he was fit and strong for his age; there would have been a disaster! The watchers in the wings knew there was something amiss when Tim did not do his last trick, the double, single twist somersault. The children took their bows but did not reappear for their encores. To Tim's credit he did not limp until he was off stage and in the wings. There were tears in his eyes as he limped to his father who picked him up and rushed him to the dressing rooms, followed by his mother and sisters. Bryan hurriedly rolled the mat behind the curtain, mindful of the cries from the audience for more and made his way to the stricken lad.

"How bad?" He queried.

"Sprain!" Harry frowned. "You had better take over and work on it."

"Not yet, they are screaming for an encore!" Bryan stated.

"He can't go on like this!" Harry snapped.

"No, but he better put in an appearance, stand him by the wing drapes; the girls can do their handstands. Carry him up—quickly!"

Bryan had taken over and when he did that, everyone took notice. He was not one to mince words, it had to be done. So it was that Tim stood by the curtains near the wings hands outstretched, introducing his sisters while they performed their handstands and minor acrobatics. The audience was satisfied. Once again in the dressing room Harry got the girls showered and dressed in their pyjamas, leaving Bryan to attend to Tim. After the costume was removed and a cold towel applied to check any swelling, Bryan massaged the leg thoroughly—showered the boy—then massaged the leg again. Then ten minutes of exercise walking the boy around and around the room in his dressing gown. The poor little fellow did not once complain but was leaning heavily on Bryan's arm. Bryan wrapped him in his own greatcoat and carried Tim out to the van. The boy was sound asleep before they got there. Gathering the gear quickly and after settling the girls in comfortably, they called it a day and made for home.

"But you promised, Bryan!" Tim sat in bed, his leg quite stiff and sore. "I can get up and walk all right—true I can, please—you promised."

His handsome little face was now screwed up and frowning. Bryan shook his head as he answered.

"No young man. I am the doctor and I say you must rest the leg today. We will have you up a couple of times for a massage and to walk the stiffness out but otherwise you stay put, young Tim. Do you hear me?" He gave his stern, threatening look.

"Aw gee! It is not fair, you promised."

"Look mate" Bryan got serious "you are lucky it happened on the last performance of the week. You rest today and as tomorrow is Monday, we will have a whole free day together;

we can do the mat then. We are lucky that we do not have to work on Monday night, now be a good lad and mind what I say. I will come in later and we will have a game of chess, all right?"

"Okay." Tim drawled as he reached for one of his music sheets. 'One thing' he thought 'I will not have to do my piano lessons.'

When Bryan sat in the kitchen with Del and Harry over a cup of tea, the matter of the 'Tiv' contract came up for discussion.

"Only a week" Harry mused "have to use the same routine, won't have time to practice up a new one!"

"What about Tim's leg?" Del put in. They both turned to Bryan.

"What do you think?" Harry asked.

"New routine's out, going to be hard to practice the old one. We can not take a chance of aggravating Tim's sprained leg. He may not be ready, you know!"

Bryan's statement gave them cause to worry.

"God! Two weeks at the Tiv and we may have to knock it back!" Del moaned. Harry cut in.

"The kids come first Del, the other is only money."

"Yes Dear, I know. I would not risk the children you know that; it is just so disappointing. Right when they are at their peak too. What about Tim's leg Bryan, how long?"

"Couple of days I reckon. He should be all right for Tuesdays performance but we had best cut out the Swirl and all of the twists, let the girls do the brunt of it for a change. They will lap it up and they can handle it!"

The parents nodded their assent. Bryan was very perceptive and usually knew what he was talking about. They knew he loved their children almost as much as they did themselves and the children loved and respected him. They took notice when he spoke. Everyone took notice when he spoke for that matter. Bryan continued.

"I will take Monday off, we are pretty slack at work and I have been working long hours until lately; I could do with a break. I promised Tim a day so I will make it Monday and do the mat. He could probably do with a day off school too!"

Harry agreed.

"What ever you think Bryan. How will he go Tuesday night do you reckon?"

Bryan considered before he answered.

"Well, with the girls in the fore and steady attention, he should loosen up. I will start him on light training Monday after lunch, then when you give him his regular lot when the girls come home from school Harry, just take him easy. If we ease him through the week's commitments and make the mat safe, I am sure we will be able to honour the two weeks at the Tiv."

He turned to Del.

"How did you manage to swing it, Del?"

Her eyes lit up as she allowed herself a smug smile.

"Luck, just plain luck, a support act cancelled out and one of the talent scouts was in the audience looking for talent!"

Harry sat back, the proud father.

"No doubt about it, the nippers have got talent." He bragged.

Bryan rose, stating.

"Well I promised Tim a game of chess; I will give his legs a going over and walk him a bit first though, thanks for the cuppa!"

True to his words, the following day found Bryan with Tim at the work shop. The girls kicked up a mild fuss because they had to go to school but as Bryan said.

"If you get ever sick Tim will probably want to stay home too but he will not be allowed, so off you go. Fair's fair, 'bye now."

The girls saw the logic of the situation and departed. Tim had seen Bryan's workshop before but had never seen the sander in operation, so he was all excitement and questions. Bryan answered most of them but found it hard to keep up with the flow and was glad when the sander was set up and with the weight attached to hold the mat in place. When machinery is operating, children are not allowed in the work area, so Tim was placed in the office behind the glass panelling. This effectively cut off the continuous flow of questions. When he had securely fastened one end of the mat to the winding drum, the motor was started and then the sanding process was begun. Bryan wore earmuffs but Tim, in the office, had to content himself with placing hands over his ears. The noise was deafening. The mat resurfaced, Tim studied it in awe.

"Wow! Look at that. Let us lay it out and I will give it a try out, eh Bryan?"

Under Bryan's constant attention and the watchful eyes of his parents, Tim soon regained full use of his leg. At the first few practice sessions the limb was favoured a little but with plenty of work and constant massaging, it came good. The 'new' mat had much to do with it too and even the girls noticeably improved, if that were possible. Tim was positive the mat now had spring which was missing before and he also insisted that his landings were softer. The girls agreed, as they always did when Tim led them. Bryan said they were Tim's little 'rubber stamps'. The girls were not sure what that meant but if Bryan said it, it must be right so they agreed to that too!

A week of successful shows followed. Two nights they had three shows, one night two and on Thursday evening they only had one. However that was arranged on purpose, as there was some distance to travel and on no account could they let the youngsters become over-tired, as that would be courting disaster. Came Saturday night, the opening night at the Tivoli. This was to be their big event. Gone for two weeks the local Cabarets, Clubs, Football Club Nights and Town Halls. Their big chance had arrived; they were now on at the 'Tiv'. Such prestige, the whole 'entourage' had marvelled at the fine 'write ups' in the press of their club tours and they had good billing on the 'boards'. Why, the star of the 'Tiv' for the fortnight was that world famous comedian from England, Tommy Trinder and they were billed directly beneath him on the programme in the first half. Of course on the bill-boards outside their name was in quite small print as there were many, much more well-known acts to appear than the 'Famous Spencer Trio'; but that did not dampen their enthusiasm. The whisper was around the stage hands and performers, that Tommy Trinder had purposely put himself before the child act because children notoriously steal the show. He was an old stager and had heard reports of them.

Behind the scenes the children were all agog with the hurley-burley of the big-time. Everything was hustle and bustle with people of various callings running to and fro. Stage hands, performers, floor managers and costumers all scurrying this way and that. It was nothing like their small club acts where, more often than not, they were the only performers. Bryan had insisted that they be early so that the children could become a little accustomed to the tempo of the 'big-time'. There was so much to see and he did not want their opening show to be full of nasty distractions. On one occasion the youngsters had to be rescued because some aspiring Prima Donna shooed them away, not realizing they were one of the acts. Faye and Shirley were spellbound by the vast array of beautifully dressed people running hither and yon.

"Mummy! They are just like the people in my fairy tale book. Look, there is the Queen and the beautiful Princess!"

Del smiled.

"Yes Love, it is all a big act. They probably think you are fairy tale people too, when you have your costumes on. Come children, Bryan will be waiting to dress you; he will worry that you may get lost. Off we go!"

Once dressed, the trio were allowed in the wings to study the procedure and get an occasional glimpse of the vast audience.

"Gee Bryan!" Tim exclaimed. "There are millions of them. Look, there are three or four landings full up. Did they all come just to see us?"

Bryan laughed.

"No Tim, they have come to see everyone. There are a lot of famous people performing tonight!"

He gathered them all about him for their warm-up and final instructions.

"Now you must remember, do not look at the audience until you take your bows. Just think you are doing one of the ordinary town halls and keep your timing in order.

29

The tall comedian came running off, the curtains fell and Bryan rolled out the mat as the comedian returned in front of the curtains for his 'encore. The big moment was here, the curtains rose again, the cue light was on–go! Bryan patted Tim's back and the boy raced on, straight into his multi-somersault opening like the veteran he was. A perfect performance by all three brought the huge audience to its feet and not one but two 'encores were demanded. As the 'encores looked like continuing overlong, the floor-manager waved them off to one side for the next performer. The three rosy-cheeked children bubbled over with their own enthusiasm to be congratulated by their three managers. A good majority of the other acts also gave praise but it was all capped off when the great man himself, Tommy Trinder, came over in person and said. "Very, very good performance children, can you do that every time?"

"Yes Sir!" They cried in unison.

"Well now" he smiled "where is your manager? We will have to see about taking you on a tour of England with my show–won't we?"

Tim looked at his friend and mentor, Bryan; and said. "Wow!"

THE END.

H.R-P.

4   Tim   (A True Story)   3/7/78

We were eight metres down; the undertow had a ten metre wash. I distinctly remembered the tall twisted kelp tree spiral up from where it was attached to a rock and towering above to the surface, as I passed it again; this time from the left. I realized it was not the kelp moving but me being washed back and forth as the waves battered against the high basalt and sandstone cliffs down which we had climbed but an hour since. My air was dwindling, I had to surface. A glance let me know that Tim had gone off on his own again; I could see him past the rock ledge to my right. At the surface, I blew my snorkel clear and took in the welcome air. I waited for Tim to surface and as he did, I raised my mask, spitting out my mouthpiece at the same time.

"For Christ's sake, keep close!" I shouted at him. "A bloody shark will come and it will take one of us!"

Tim grinned. He was very large man now, deep set chest, broad shoulders and muscles just fighting to break through his skin.

"She's apples" he shouted back "if a shark comes I will save you from it!"

He replaced his gear again and dived before I could reply.

'Bloody fool' I thought to myself 'who is going to save him if I do not see a shark attack, because he is around a corner somewhere?' I replaced my own gear and attempted to follow him. I was fuming because I only came down for safety's sake but he was so sure nothing could hurt him that he forgot he had a partner he was supposed to watch. It was the first rule of diving—watch each other! Tim often went diving with his mates who were all about his own age and of course, being nineteen, he thought he knew it all. Today his mates were all out shooting but independent Tim wanted a shark, telling his mates that rabbits were child's play and he would only go with them if they would hunt for pigs or deer. The haunts of these animals were too far away, so his friends pooh-poohed the idea and then went their merry way.

As a young child Tim was part of a children's acrobatic troupe, playing the local town halls and night clubs and even had a two week's stint at the Tivoli Theatre, a vaudeville outlet of years gone by. That is when I had more control over the young man as I was very closely associated with the family and was a part of the team. Since the boy had grown up, his independence was pulling us apart, which was fair enough as he has to live his life the way he wants it; providing a shark does not rob him of it first. I endeavoured to get closer to him but as he was twenty years my junior, twice my size and in his prime; it was a difficult task. I swam the surface looking down, he could not get far away as he had a habit of diving deep all the time, looking for the big ones. I spotted him under the ledge where he disappeared a few minutes earlier. As he had returned to it he must have seen something on his previous dive. I took a breath and went down. When Tim saw, he motioned with his spear for me to go around the other side of a large rock lying on the bottom. It apparently had fallen from the cliff decades ago, for large beds of various shells and seaweeds, mingled with coral almost covered it. I did as he indicated, not knowing for what I was supposed to be looking. Just in case, I checked my spear gun and held it ready. Tim's head and shoulders were visible past the rock and he was frantically probing and Jabbing at something. Suddenly I saw it, a large groper. A good metre in length with a belly reminiscent of those Eastern Buddha's, it lazed in my direction as Tim flipped around the rock. I could have speared it as it was moving slowly but after all, it was Tim's fish. I let him have it.

The spear he released shot straight and true. The groper well impaled, we made for the surface with the fish trailing on the end of his line. I had more need of air than Tim, for he could stay under water a good thirty seconds longer than I could. So it was that I had taken another breath then looked back to see him rising. He had stopped halfway up and was reeling the fish in; perhaps its huge weight was too much of a drag for him. As I went to assist, he sensed me coming and shook his head, waving me back but I kept coming. I had seen past him and my heart froze. Tim had his back to it and was too engrossed with his fish but I had seen the two metre shark flashing up towards him! I had to do five minutes thinking in two seconds. Should I risk a barb past Tim—he could easily move into it—or should I keep swimming and try to distract the shark? There was a slight possibility that the boy might see the monster in time, should I take the risk, sure; but which one? Almost involuntarily I sighted the shark and released the spear. As it narrowly surged past Tim, he became aware of it, possibly feeling the vibrations as it passed. He jerked, watching its flight as the shaft penetrated the big fish. It was not a good shot of course, hitting two thirds down the body. The shark shuddered, veering away. Tim quickly fitted a loose spear to his gun and reset it. With amazing speed the shark spun around and came in to attack, but it was the struggling groper that it honed in upon. The stricken bleeding fish made feeble efforts to escape its predicament. The front half of the unfortunate groper plus Tim's spear disappeared into the awesome maw of the ferocious scavenger. The tail end of the groper dropped to the bottom as did the last few centimetres of the broken shaft as it slipped from its retaining thread. My spear gun was wrenched from my grasp as the shark lunged past. Tim however, possibly because of his great strength, managed to retain his. With its prey in those large jaws the shark had stopped the mad rush and was slowly circling as it wolfed down its meal. Tim swam to it and discharged his weapon. As we saw the shaft strike directly behind the gills, the shark shuddered, turned over and slowly spiralled to the bottom.

Tim released his grip on the gun and shot to the surface, his lungs bursting. As the youth was 'getting his wind' I kept surveillance underwater in the event of other sharks being about. My theory was, if you see one, there could be others. Tim had regained his breath and ignored my shout to return to shore. He began to dive again. I grabbed his flipper and tugged at him signalling a return to the surface, he came.

"Whatsamatter?"

"There could be other sharks down there" I warned "better get back to shore!"

"Not bloody likely" he laughed "do you think I am going to leave that set of jaws down there? 'Sides, the guns are worth dough, we can't leave them!"

Tim disappeared again, I immediately followed. As I have already expressed, he was a more powerful swimmer than I now and it took an almost superhuman effort on my part to catch him; but catch him I did. It was a move of desperation as I realized the danger involved in returning to the bloodied depths, not so Tim; either that or he did not care. Once again I grabbed his flipper as he was half way down. He kicked his legs loose. I lunged again and managed to grab an ankle, then wrapped both arms around his legs and kicked with all my strength for the surface. His legs pinned and useless for swimming, I still marvelled at the strength of the young fellow. I was not making a great deal of headway and thought maybe I would have to let go or run out of air and drown myself.

Suddenly the resistance vanished and I saw that he was voluntarily surfacing; no doubt his own exertions had sapped his air supply. As we broke the swells and threw up our face masks, he shouted.

"Swim like hell, there are dozens of them fighting down there!"

"No!" I urgently shouted back. "Take it easy; swim slowly and with as little movement as possible. Otherwise you will precipitate an attack; they are most likely aroused to blood and will go for anything that moves, slowly Tim!" I warned. "And keep your eyes on them—snorkel in!"

It was the same tone of voice I used years ago when he was a young acrobat under my care and he responded accordingly. Once again my wish was his command. The emergency had triggered his memory and he recalled that I usually knew what I was about. No matter what, it worked and we began the slow watchful swim shorewards. For once, Tim was beside me, moving at my pace and carefully probing the depths. I felt him tap my shoulder and looked in the direction he indicated. Travelling just behind us and about seven metres below, a blue pointer of about two and two-thirds of a metre was trailing us. Tim had taken his knife from its scabbard on his lower leg and held it in readiness, I did likewise. They were flimsy weapons in comparison to the spear guns, but they were all we had. The next move was up to the shark! The shark dogging us swung away and returned to the depths from whence it came. The reason, we suddenly found, was that we were upon the reef that lay just out from and along to, the shore. Gratefully we hauled ourselves onto it and removed our headgear and fins.

"Gosh, I am glad that is over!" I sighed. Tim was all excitement.

"He was a big 'un Bryan. Did you see him shudder when I sank my shaft?"

I was annoyed with him and could not help retorting.

"I told you sharking was dangerous, once there is blood about they seem to come from miles."

"Kilometres!" Tim corrected me.

"All right, damn kilometres then. You are a bugger to skin dive with, you must practice the 'buddy system'. If I had not come after you that shark could have taken you instead of the groper!"

There was an uneasy silence for a bit as we sat there, then Tim spoke.

"Bryan!"

"Yeah?"

"Sorry mate, I know you are right. I would have been able to get him on the first charge if my gun wasn't spent!"

I shook my head.

"But it WAS spent wasn't it and you never saw the thing until my spear passed you, you were playing with the bloody groper!"

Tim tried to change the subject.

"I wonder when it will be safe to go back for the guns."

"Bugger the guns!" I snapped as I gathered my gear and stepped into the shallow ripples on the shore side of the reef.

Tim followed, albeit a little reluctantly. The young fool still had ideas of swimming back; I was sure.

As we reached the warm sand and began taking our wet-suits off, Tim's girl friend walked across to us. She had climbed down the cliff when she saw us returning.

"Any luck?" Lindy cheerily asked.

"I reckon!" Tim proudly boasted. "Got ourselves a large groper and a three metres shark!"

"Ha har!" She cocked her head and with hand on hip, said. "Very funny. Throw them over and I will put them in my purse for you."

Tim kissed her and solemnly stated.

"True, love. I had the groper and a shark took it, so we killed the shark!"

"Sure, sure, a likely story. Like all fishermen, the one that got away."

"Listen Lindy." He picked her up and took her to the water. "Are you going to believe me or do I drop you in?"

"Bryan, save me!" She shouted in mock alarm.

"Kids!" I muttered as I grabbed my towel.

We had returned to the cliff top parking bay and had the barbeque cooking chops and sausages in the quiet, sunny little corner between the car and the twisted ti-tree that acted as a wind-break. It was a beautiful warm and sunny day and the sea breeze was minimal. Looking out over the ocean I could not help but admire the beauty of it all. Sea birds in many varieties were gracefully wafting on the light currents as they sought their various fish meals from on high. As I idly gazed along the ragged rocky shoreline, dotted with occasional sandy bays like the one from which we were just delivered, I marvelled at the myriad shades of green and blue waters with snow-capped crests of foam that welled, then raced and finally surged to shatter themselves in a frenzy of froth and spray; as they battered their hopes against the unyielding solidity of the timeless frowning cliffs.

"Come and get it!" Lindy called.

After our swim I can assure you there were no stragglers. Tim and I wolfed into the sausage sandwiches as if Lindy had already begun throwing the scraps to the birds. The edge off our appetites, we ate the chops more leisurely and thoroughly enjoyed them. As we each indulged in a slice of Lindy's lovely sponge—made especially for the occasion—we gazed down at the angry eddies below.

"It is a cruel and savage place isn't it? I would hate to have to live in it!" Lindy said.

"Be a damned cold place to spend a life-time." Tim put in, then. "Look at that!"

We were just in time to see a large section of the earthy lime-stone atop the cliff around the other side of the little bay, break away to slowly slither and crumble as it picked up speed and careered off the granite foundations and fall with a staccato of splashes like machine-gun fire; as it was enveloped into the bosom of the surf. Surf? The tide must be coming in and the breeze was strengthening a little. The ocean was beginning to gather momentum. I could feel the anger growing within it.

"Looks like it is going to get a bit rough out there soon!" I surmised.

"Well, we had best hurry up then–quick Bryan–grab your gear!" Tim said.

I looked at him in amazement.

"Whaffor?"

"You just said the water is getting rough, so we had better hurry up and get down there quickly!"

"What the hell are you talking about?" I queried.

"The shark, the spear guns, I want to get what is left of my shark; I don't want to lose those jaws."

Lindy gasped.

"Oh no!"

I said.

"You must be mad!"

But it was too late; he was already on his way down.

We were on the beach arguing. Tim was half in his gear.

"I don't want to belt you one Tim, its madness."

I was standing between him and the water. He stood erect.

"Think you can?"

"I know I can't mate, but I will have to try. Those sharks will still be around and it is your life you are gambling with–besides–you have only just had your lunch" I stepped closer. "If the sharks don't get you, you will cramp and drown!"

"Be reasonable Tim" Lindy pleaded "I know you are brave, you do not have to prove it!"

Tim gave her a cuddle.

"It's not that sweet. I just always wanted a set of jaws to hang up, I have one now, I only have to pick it up; it will only take five minutes!"

"It is too soon after eating son, it is utter stupidity!" I repeated.

Our pleas had some effect at last.

"Okay" he snapped "I'll wait half an hour but I am still going, even if it is only to get the jaws!" He sat on the sand.

"There's another thing" I told him "you have not got the guns, they are out there" I pointed seawards "you have no protection when the sharks come for you!"

He drew his knife.

"I have this that is enough!"

"Bullshit. A shark will take that and your arm!"

"I will manage."

"Well you will bloody well go on your own. If you want to risk your fool neck—bugger off and do it. I have more respect for mine!"

I wandered off looking in the odd sand and rock pools but keeping a wary eye on Tim. He was nestled close to Lindy. I imagine he was allaying her fears by necking to take her mind off the subject.

Almost three-quarters of an hour had elapsed since the stand-off and Tim was still embracing Lindy in the warm afternoon sun. We were sheltered from the wind in this little cove but the sea was rising, there was quite an appreciable swell now in comparison to the morning calm.

"Bryan, come quickly!"

It was Lindy. I glanced up. Tim had gone but as I searched the surf I saw his white tipped snorkel just off the reef.

"Damn, just when the fish are on the feed!"

I hurried into my wet-suit, adjusted the accoutrements and splashed through the shallows after him. I was exceedingly apprehensive as I glided out after Tim, searching the sea-bed with furtive eyes. Yes, I was scared. I could feel my skin tingle as if a shark was already breathing down my neck. I was almost at the spot where our earlier adventure took place. There was no sign of Tim but that was natural under the circumstances, for the incoming tide was stirring up the sandy bottom making visibility difficult. Algae, seaweed and kelp were floating around everywhere. Sure I was in the right spot I took a deep breath, made sure I was holding my blade in the most secure manner, and then dived to search for Tim. Every second I expected to see the gaping maw of a ferocious man-eater or feel the clamp of those jagged teeth take a hold of my leg. So far, there was no sign of a shark; thank goodness. Suddenly I spied him. Tim shot past me to the surface, I raced after him.

"I found it!" He shouted. "It's caught in some kelp."

He replaced his snorkel and dived, I followed close to his flippers. At the bottom, there was the grisly thing. At least part of the head of it, the rest had been eaten away by the other sharks and many little fishes. A section of the gills was snagged on a spiral of kelp and Tim was hacking it with his knife. I helped and between the two of us it came away, we thankfully made for the surface; dragging our ugly burden with us. We did not mince matters but headed straight back for the shore; I was amazed that we did not see any sharks at all. May be they were there and we just did not see them. It seemed an eternally long way back to the reef. The swell had risen greatly and with the burden of our load (the prize was a handicap) as the rough sea tugged at it. We did get a little help from the rising surf until almost upon the reef, and then we were worried that we might be smashed against it! Tim reached it first but waited for me to climb up so that I could take his cherished prize. We threw it up and over into the shallows that were now getting deeper and more violent.

"There!" Tim exclaimed. "Not a bloody shark, I told you that you were worrying about nothing!"

Next he passed the two guns that he had attached to his belt. I took them and reached down to assist him. He felt he had won a point over me.

"You reckoned it would be alive with sh–oops!"

Tim faltered a bit as I pulled him out.

"What's up?" I asked.

"Think I got caught on something—?"

He lifted the foot that had got snagged. There was only the sole left. The fin of the flipper was gone showing a great jagged half-moon bite, barely missing his foot.

THE END.

H. R-P.

5   Jamie   24/6/78

The happy chuckles of a joyous child used to echo around the spacious lawns surrounding the caretaker's cottage. That time was only a week ago, as young Jamie romped merrily with his small pet, Tim-Tim. Tim-Tim was the same age as Jamie, he was bought as a house-hold pet for the new-born baby to grow up with; they became inseparable as the years passed by. When Jamie was a little down in the dumps, Tim-Tim seemed to feel it and would playfully yelp as he dropped his soft play-ball at Jamie's feet, daring the boy to take it from him and would wag his tail furiously as he pretended to leave the ball alone. If the boy made to grab at the ball, Tim-Tim would quickly seize the frothy thing and scamper off; Jamie in pursuit. This tactic always seemed to work and the boy would once more be out of the doldrums and happy laughter once again echoed throughout the grounds. It was during one of these romps that Tim-Tim ran excitedly through the open gates of the gardens and headlong under the wheels of a passing automobile. That his demise was quick and merciful did not placate the shocked child. It was so sudden—one moment Tim-Tim was there happily running about—the next he was a twisted lifeless bundle on the nature strip; the distraught motorist apologising profusely upon a matter over which he had no control. Jamie stood immobile, disbelieving the evidence before his eyes. His mother gently led the boy away, explaining that Tim-Tim did not watch where he was going—it was most unfortunate—Tim-Tim should have been more careful. No one should suddenly run onto the road like that, the poor motorist could not be held responsible.

"He is just knocked out Mummy, isn't he? He will be all right tomorrow!" A tearful Jamie stated hopefully.

"No Darling! Tim-Tim has gone to heaven. He will be up there running around with all the other little doggies that have been good to their masters. Come inside dear, Mummy will make you a nice cup of hot chocolate!"

Jamie was sobbing softly as mother took him inside.

"He will come back Mummy—I know he will!"

Laura Doran cuddled her son to her.

"Jamie Dear, once a thing dies it does not come back but you will always have the memories of your happy times together to think of, you can remember as much as you like; the happiness and fun you shared with Tim-Tim. No one can take that from you!"

Jamie drank of his hot chocolate in small sips, interspersed with tears. He left more than half of the drink in the glass and climbed the stairway up which he used to race Tim-Tim, as he sadly made his way to the window over-looking the road. Many a time he nursed Tim-Tim as they both looked down at the busy roadway beneath and watched the cars speeding past. Jamie could see the area where Tim-Tim met his end quite clearly from this vantage point. He stood up suddenly, Tim-Tim was gone! So was the motorist, the street was deserted. Maybe—maybe it was just a dream—he only imagined there was an accident. Tim-Tim would be waiting for him downstairs! Jamie raced downstairs, frantically calling.

"Tim-Tim, here boy—come on—Tim-Tim!"

Laura grabbed the boy as he hurried towards the door.

"Jamie darling, Jamie!"

She ushered him to a chair and when settled, sat him on her lap.

"Tim-Tim's gone, he is dead Love. Tim-Tim won't come back, I am sorry love but you will have to face it!"

"No! He is not dead, I won't let him die!"

The boy struggled violently to be free. Tim-Tim would come at his call, he always did! Laura spent the next fifteen minutes comforting and trying to console her son. The boy eventually quietened and was lulled into a restless sleep in which his eyelids flickered and the small body twitched. Laura quietly laid him upon the settee and covered the young lad with a rug. Jamie slept.

Through a haze of shimmering sunbeams enveloped by gently floating autumn leaves as they idly wafted to the ground after being flung high into the air by the energetic passing of his small master, Tim-Tim came racing at full gallop to Jamie. The boy rolled upon his back as Tim-Tim jumped joyously upon him, and then began worrying the cascading hair as it fell about the boy's eyes. Tim-Tim stuck his small snout into the boy's face and licked his cheeks. Jamie gurgled with pleasurable excitement as he tried unsuccessfully to grab his playmate. Tim-Tim ran off into the billowing haze, Jamie hot on his heels, but Tim-Tim had disappeared!

Jamie suddenly sprang from the settee.

"Tim-Tim, where are you? Come back!"

Laura dropped the pot she was holding heavily upon the cooking range as she ran to her stricken son.

"Oh, Jamie darling, did you have a bad dream love? There, there–it is all right love–it is all right!"

Wide eyed, Jamie clutched at his mother.

"Mummy, Tim-Tim was there, I played with him!"

"Of course darling but it was only a dream, you have been on the settee all the time; having a sleep. You dreamed it love!"

"No! It was so real–he licked my face–see? It is still wet!"

Jamie showed wet fingers to his sympathetic mother.

"Darling, they are your own tears, you have been crying. Oh pet, Tim-Tim is really gone!"

Laura changed the subject, it would do no good to have her son brood at length over his pet, and she must find other interests to take his mind off his sad loss.

"It is nearly tea time Jamie, now be a good lad and wash your hands and face. Daddy will be home soon and he will not want to find his big boy crying, will he?"

Earlier, while Jamie slept, Laura had 'phoned the office and told Darren of the demise of Tim-Tim. To try and ease the boy's loss, Darren bought a toy train that had flashing lights and an engine which flickered sparks as the motor groaned and chugged. Perhaps a noisy distraction might give the youngster's mind a little peace. The exercise was a dismal failure. Although Jamie accepted the toy, his 'thank you' was just a polite gesture. A toy, no matter how noisy or new, would not take the place of a boy's best pal; a lively cuddly licking playmate. After a cursory glance, Jamie sat on the mat in front of the heater where Tim-Tim always sprawled. It was a lonely mat now, the whole room seemed empty and bare to the grieving boy. His father extolled the virtues of the toy and set the lights flickering as he caused the train to chug towards Jamie. It touched his leg. Jamie violently brushed it away and turned reproachful eyes to his father. They glistened with unshed tears. No! He did not want a toy, he wanted Tim-Tim! Darren ignored the incident and sat on the rug beside his son.

"Hey Son, I know it is tough losing a pal but lots of things and people and pets die—it is all part of life—part of growing up. Mum and I loved Tim-Tim, we both lost a good friend too you know!"

Jamie was staring vacantly past his father, at the door. He thought he heard a faint scratching. Of a sudden, in the deepening shadows by the doorstep; a well-known whiskery face peeped. The ball it was holding dropped from the panting mouth, a tail wagged expectantly. Jamie jumped to his feet, shouting.

"Tim-Tim, he is back; I knew he would come back—Daddy! Tim-Tim is back!"

As Jamie gleefully ran to the door and disappeared outside, Laura and Darren exchanged concerned glances.

"You had better keep an eye on him dear!" Laura worried. "I don't want the dinner spoiled!" She watched through the window as Jamie searched frantically into each nook and cranny where Tim-Tim was wont to hide. Her mind was not on the job at hand, her thoughts were directed at the possible disorientation the shock of losing his pet may have had on her son's mind. Darren came across the bewildered Jamie as he knelt by Tim-Tim's rarely used kennel. The pet had been so pampered by his young master that more often than not, it would be allowed to sneak back into the boy's room at night and sleep on the end of his bed or on a rug by the heater. If the youngster's parents noticed the pet indoors they would put it out onto the back porch, where Tim-Tim would spend the night on the door-mat awaiting his master's early rising. Tim-Tim only used his kennel in which to hide from Jamie when they were playing, or if he happened to acquire a choice bone and needed privacy to enjoy gnawing it in peace.

"Here boy, here Tim-Tim—oh—stop hiding Tim-Tim, where are you?"

Jamie stood as Darren, sympathetically, placed a hand on his son's shoulder.

"He was at the door Daddy, he raced away—I saw him—he did Daddy! Where did he go?" Jamie lifted glistening eyes towards his father. Darren led his distraught son to a garden seat and sat beside him, the reassuring hand still about the young shoulders.

"Pal, you will have to understand, Tim-Tim really is no more! He was run over and killed. He died Son; you will not be able to play with him again!"

"But I saw him twice Daddy. Once at the park and just then at the back door—he ran out here!"

Darren sadly shook his head.

"Son" he explained, detailing as best he could "you loved Tim-Tim so much that you do not want to believe he died and you just can not bring yourself to believe it, but that will not change the fact that he truly is dead. You remember all the fun times you had with Tim-Tim and they become day-dreams. You really believe you actually see him, but you don't, what you think you see; is really only a dream. Believe me, if Tim-Tim was there Mum and I would see him too, but we don't."

Darren paused for a while to let his words sink in a little. Jamie opened his mouth to argue his cause again but was stilled as his father held a finger aloft and continued.

"Mum said the man who accidentally ran over Tim-Tim, took the body away and buried it. The man is going to make a nice cross with Tim-Tim's name on it and he said he will take you there one day when you get over losing your pet; when it won't hurt you so much to think about Tim-Tim!"

Resignedly, Jamie walked hand-in-hand back to the house with his father. During the evening meal, both parents attempted to console and convince the boy that his sightings of Tim-Tim were only figments of his imagination. Jamie would not believe it was imagination; the visions were so real—so true to life. Each sleepless night thereafter was a reflection of that preceding. Always Tim-Tim would come to him and they would merrily romp in fits and starts throughout the night. The boy often awakening to find his mother caressing his forehead and cooing.

"It's all right Love; you have just had another bad dream. Settle down honey!"

Now a week had passed since he lost his pet and Jamie was becoming frail and very ill through pining for his lost playmate. Laura and Jim Doran knew something would have to be done before the incidence of Tim-Tim's demise had an irreparable affect upon their son. They consulted the family doctor who recommended a specialist in child behaviour; this man gave them a possibility which may snap Jamie out of his hallucinations.

Darren went on a secret mission and left Laura to care for their listless son. It was one of those beautiful still, sunlit days when under normal circumstances, Jamie would have been romping with Tim-Tim in the spacious gardens. This day however, Jamie was bedded down on the settee where he finally lapsed into another fitful sleep. Once more, as in countless dreams before, a familiar canine friend came bounding out of the haze and dropped his play-ball at Jamie's feet. Eagerly the youngster picked it up and threw it far; Tim-Tim immediately took off after the ball with Jamie in hot pursuit. A hectic time was spent in which the two rolled over and over on the downy-soft cloud of lush green grass bedecked with a myriad autumn leaves, that cascaded about the romping pair as Jamie threw hands full high into this nether-world and watched them settle gently on the heaving back of that bundle of joy—Tim-Tim—his little playmate. Under the warming rays of sunshine that filtered through the high outflung branches of the huge trees beautifying this idyllic playground, the two good friends rested; gathering strength and catching their wind before once again embarking upon another carefree and happy frolic. It was during this passage of their play that an Angel materialized and with arms opened wide, called to Tim-Tim. Tim-Tim was bewildered; he knew not which way to turn.

"Tim-Tim!" The Angel called. "You must come to me; it is time for you to go to Heaven. Say goodbye to your master and thank him for the fun you have had together!"

Eagerly the little dog bounded over to Jamie and enthusiastically licked the boy's face. Jamie held his pet firmly, tears streaming as he shouted defiantly.

"No! Tim-Tim does not want to go to Heaven—he is mine—he wants to stay here!"

The Angel smiled understandingly.

"Tim-Tim has been good to you Jamie, there are many children up in Heaven, and it will be nice for you to know Tim-Tim is having a good time making all the boys and girls in Heaven happy too. You will always have happy memories of Tim-Tim to dream about—come Tim-Tim—come with me!"

As Jamie watched his friend happily float away with the Angel and fade into a gossamer mist of nothingness, he could still feel the wet tongue slopping his face.

"Tim-Tim!"

He murmured, as he put his hand to the wet spot. The hand was licked! Jamie awoke to find a real live puppy like Tim-Tim, licking his hand.

"Tim-Tim!" Jamie exclaimed, as he sat bolt upright on the settee.

The puppy continued its playful rallies.

"Not Tim-Tim, Jamie." Laura explained. "But it is another puppy exactly like him. I know he will never replace Tim-Tim, but you can have just as much fun with him and he will love you the same as Tim-Tim did!"

Jamie studied the replica of his best pal, silently.

"Do you like him Son?" Darren queried, anxiously.

Jamie reached out and stroked a velvet ear; his hand was still taking a licking.

"I had a dream!" The boy paused, and then smiled at his parents. "Tim-Tim went to Heaven. An Angel took him so he could play with all the children in Heaven, 'cause he is such a good dog! Did an Angel leave this puppy for me?"

"I am sure the Angel did Son!" Darren sighed.

Jamie cuddled the puppy; a happy chuckle escaped his lips.

THE END.

6   John   (A True Story)   21/7/78

The year was nineteen forty one. Australia was at war with Germany, the Americans had not yet entered the hostilities. The North coast of Australia was heavily at risk of attack by the enemies. Shortages on the home front were common. There was rationing of food, clothing, fuels–you name it–there was a shortage of it. The troops had to be maintained and every person had to pull in their belt, as it were. The street lighting was virtually non-existent. Vehicles travelled at night only if it was urgent business and then they had to have their headlights heavily masked. Many vehicles were equipped with charcoal burners as an alternative to petrol. In an outer suburban Children's Home, a group of seven small boys aged from nine to thirteen, were stealthily quitting the premises via the storm water drain, which abuts the Northern Boundary fence and is well hidden by a line of tall poplars; whispering gently in the mild evening breeze. The children were tired of being unwanted, unloved, undernourished, underclad and in constant fear of being given 'three of the best' on the bare backside by the principal, for such trivial things as telling fibs or breaking shoelaces. They were running away. Somewhere, someone out there would have them and love them. Their parents did not and there was no compassion in the Boys Home. Thirteen year old John, the eldest and instigator of the break-out, shushed his followers as they neared the fence by the front gate. All they had to do now was make sure the way was clear of interfering busybodies who may be walking the dark streets, then run like the devil to get so far away as their small legs would carry them. Having successfully negotiated the first few streets away from the Boys Home, the seven little fugitives entered the forbidding black abyss of the local unlit park. Ten year old Danny quivered as he faltered by the first tree.

"We can't go in there, it is too dark!" He turned wide, frightened eyes towards his leader.

"Good, no one will see us!" John said.

"But Mum used to say the bogey-man will get you in there if kids go in at night–I'm scared!"

"Yair!" Echoed Jerry, the other ten year old.

"Ah! Don't be a sissy!" The baby of the group, Maurice, jeered.

"There is no bogey-man, stupid. Your mum only said that to keep you home at night. Maurie's only nine and he is not scared. Come on."

John urged his team forwards. Alan and Ken were eleven year old twins and they pushed Danny between them. Alan murmured.

"Stick with us, we will look after you!"

Peter, the second eldest and John's shadow, asked.

"Where are we going to stay tonight?"

"Under the bridge." John answered. "It is only small but we can cuddle up together and keep warm, it's not a cold night anyway!"

They found the small footbridge they were seeking; it was large enough to cater for the seven youngsters and would keep any dew off them. Luckily, being summertime the small gully under the bridge was quite dry and the area was well sheltered by bushes, so very little draught could be expected. They settled themselves as comfortably as they could. All was quiet for a few minutes, and then Danny piped up.

"I want to go back, I am scared. We will get killed when we go back to the home!"

"Idiot." John flung at him. "We are not going back, we have run away. We are going to find a new home that is why we left!"

"Yeah, dummy!" Maurice echoed.

"Hey! Move over Ken, you are sitting on my leg."

Danny pushed him off; he fell against Peter who thumped Ken, saying.

"Shove off, you are pushing me out!"

John shushed them, frantically telling them that if they made too much noise, a policeman would come to investigate and they would all go to jail! The seven runaways lapsed into silence and one by one, fell asleep. All except Danny, he was sure his mum was right. He was still in between the twins and should have been warm, but he shivered. Some of the others were snoring quietly, they were sound asleep. Danny knew he should have stayed back at the Boys Home; they would all get the cuts when they were caught. He knew the police would be after them in the morning when they were not there for roll-call. He would go home now and sneak back into the dormitory then he would not be missed but he was frightened to go alone through the park. Perhaps he should kid one of the others to go with him? Heavy footsteps sounded on the bridge overhead. Danny shook violently, he knew it, and the bogey-man was here!

The heavy footsteps were accompanied by unseemly language, and then a bottle dropped and smashed upon the bridge. A voice thick with the effects of strong drink cursed.

"Bloody thing–thing–think you can get away do you? Take that!"

He was heard to kick the broken remnants away as the released liquid spilled over the edge of the bridge upon John's outflung arm. Ken awoke with a start.

"What's up Dad?"

"It's not your dad, someone has wet all over my arm!" John expostulated.

Danny began to cry.

"It is the bogey-man!"

"Wha's that?" The drunken voice slurred. "Talk back t'me will ya?"

He gave the remains of the wasted bottle another kick, and then wandered off mumbling about ungrateful bottles running away from him. The other twin, Alan, woke.

"What is going on?"

"Shush! You will wake everyone up; it is only an old drunk." John cautioned.

"Every one is already awake. I want to go back to Saint Martin's, I'm scared!" Danny put in.

"Don't be a baby." John chided. "Who else is awake?"

Ken made a quick check.

"Peter, Jerry and Maurice are still asleep. Do you think the old drunk heard us?"

"Does not matter, he is gone. Go back to sleep!"

John rolled over as Danny pushed in beside him. They resumed their slumber.

The sun was not yet peeping over the horizon but a slight glow in the East, attested its coming. The morning air was crisp and John was already running on the spot to warm himself.

"Crikey I'm hungry!" Ken said.

"Me too." Echoed his brother. "What are we going to have for breakfast?" Jerry demanded.

"Dunno–we will find something–let us run around the park to warm up!" John changed the subject.

Little Maurice, the last to awaken, frantically yelled.

"Hey, wait for me!"

Seven youngsters jogging around a park before sun-up was most unusual, however this thought did not occur to the children, they were more interested in warming up. Their jaunt took them to the far extremes of the park and it was there that they came upon the drunk of the previous night, sleeping it off under a tree; bottle laying empty by his side.

"See Danny, there is your bogey-man, just an old drunk!" John informed.

"I still think we should go back. I was scared last night an' I am hungry now. When is breakfast?"

"We will find something. Come on; let's go up to the shops." John led the way.

As the horde walked the shopping centre, they passed a fruiterer's with the wares proudly displayed out front in boxes. John casually grabbed an apple as he passed an action that was copied by Peter and Ken. Alan was not so lucky, the fruiterer saw him.

"Hey! You thieving little brats, put them back!"

The man surged forwards as the boys broke into a run. Jerry, who happened to be the last in line, was grabbed by an arm. The man held on grimly.

"Leggo! Help–rape–stop him John!" Jerry screamed for his leader who was off around the corner.

Jerry kicked the fruiterer in the shins. The man released him with an oath and as he rubbed the affected leg, the boy ran helter skelter after his mates. As the boys hid in a lane a few blocks away, resting from their exertions, Ken gave half of his apple to his twin brother. John did likewise with Maurice and Danny scrounged half of Peter's. Unfortunately there were seven of them and only three apples. Jerry had to be content with a small bite of each half. The septet strolled to the end of the lane. Danny and Jerry were in earnest conversation. Lunch time came and went; the seven had travelled through Canterbury to Surrey Hills. It was noticeable that Danny and Jerry were lagging. As John urged them on they responded but next time he looked, they were lagging again. A military jeep went past and when it stopped and then turned around, the boys all ran to a nearby churchyard, went out the back gate which luckily was unlocked and sped down the back lane. It ended in a storm water drain; they climbed over the fence and followed it. After about a half mile the drain emptied into a tunnel. They climbed the fence again and found there was a park on the other side.

"Ah gee!" John moaned. "It is the same damn park we slept in last night; we have come in a damn circle!"

"Let us get some more apples." Ken suggested.

"Yair, let's!" Maurice agreed.

"Don't be silly!" John snapped. "The bloke has prob'ly called the police. Let's go the other way this time!"

As the dejected band made their way in the new direction, Jerry and Danny were again in deep consultation with each other. After ten minutes of wandering along back streets, John checked on his team. The two ten year olds were missing. At Camberwell the five boys were lucky, they came across a Salvation Army Collector standing outside a hotel seeking donations for his cause. He stopped the boys.

"Hello children, where are you off to—should you not be at school?"

"No Sir. We are just returning from sports!" John spoke up.

"Oh! Did you have a good game?"

"Yes Sir, thank you" John had an inspiration "we have lost our lunches though—I think a dog must have got them!"

The good man was most sympathetic.

"Oh dear, oh dear! You poor lads—here, I think I may have something to help you—yes, there you are, take that and may God bless you children!"

He handed John a five shillings piece, it sparkled in the sunlight.

"Oh gee! Thank you Sir!"

He beamed his pleasure as the other four all smiled their thanks. They hurried off lest he change his mind and want it back. Perhaps he understood more than the youngsters thought, however the man believed he was serving his cause well. The children certainly agreed. Five serves of hot potato chips and they still had a half a crown left. The happy boys wolfed down their belated meal as they walked towards Carlton, just outside the City of Melbourne limits. This was a heavily industrialized area and the lads were attracting many curious stares. John became worried.

"I think we had better find somewhere to settle down for the night." Peter pointed to an old empty house. "What about there?"

They investigated and found entry easy through the broken down back door. The house was a mess, no furniture but odd pieces of bagging and broken glass littered the floors in every room. The boys decided to settle themselves in the middle room, when two derelicts tramped around the side of the house and barged in the back door. The children stood petrified as the ragged men became aware of their presence.

"Here—what're you sneakin' little kids doin' in here? Out, all of you, hoppit—lively now!"

The five hurried out as the other man pushed the last one—little Maurice—saying.

"An' don't ever come back or we'll boot you in the pants!"

Dejected, the youngsters trudged along. They were very tired as they had been walking quite incessantly and a much needed rest was due.

"Damn!" John cursed. "That would have been a good place to spend the night.

"Yeah!" Came the customary agreement from little Maurice.

Ken suggested that maybe they could find another old house. His twin agreed and they all studied every house they passed, in amongst the factories. The daylight was beginning to fade when a policeman on a bicycle saw the five ragged urchins. He rode across to them.

"Hey you lot, I want a word with you!"

The boys stood in fright at this unexpected occurrence. John was thinking fast as the man left his bicycle and approached.

"Run!" Yelled John, pushing Maurice ahead of him.

Peter moved instantly but Ken and Alan were each held firmly by an arm.

"Come back here you boys, by George you'll cop it!"

The three paid no heed but kept running. The twins were taken away, crying in fear of their punishment. It was almost full night by the time the weary trio climbed under the huge span of a bridge over the Yarra River. They were exhausted and very frightened. Little Maurice had wrenched his ankle in the hurry to get out of sight under the bridge, he was quietly sobbing in pain. John and Peter were sympathetic but could do little more than rub it hoping that would help. The three spent a restless night, worried about the poor unfortunate twins. It brought home strongly to them the fact, that if and when they were caught, their punishment would be severe. Maurice's sobbing burst into wails of agony.

"Come on Maurie—don't cry—try and sleep then you won't feel it."

He put a comforting arm about the little chap as Peter tried to rub the sore ankle better.

"Don't Pete that hurts!" Came from between sobs.

"Sorry Maurie."

Peter sat on the other side of Maurice and between them they soothed the boy to sleep. The bigger boys were also tired and they too, nodded off. Morning found the foot quite swollen and very sore. Maurice again was crying with the pain of it and wishing he had a mother to fuss over him. It was found to be too hard for the little bloke to walk on and they decided their cobber would have to have medical attention. He would have to give himself up!

"Now remember Maurie, you have been on your own and you don't know where we are—got that?"

Maurice nodded as he got last minute instructions from John. The two older boys had virtually carried the little fellow almost to the police station and were now hiding around the corner of an alley way.

"See you pal—we will wait until you get to the door."

The boys shook hands all round. Maurice with his tear-streaked cheeks made his painful way to the awesome door of the police station. The brave lad waved at the door, then entered.

"Gee! Five gone, only two of us left Pete!"

John was chewing on a piece of grass as they rested beneath a gnarled old gum tree on the boulevard at Kew. It was three miles and two hours after they had farewelled the unfortunate Maurice. Both boys were starving. They had spent the last two and sixpence on more chips the night before when they were thrown out of the old house by the derelicts. So with nothing to purchase food with they knew the only way to survive was to steal it.

"We will have to get something to eat, I am dying." Peter grimaced.

"Tell you what" John eagerly said "when it is dark we will find a house with some fruit trees and we will pinch some!"

Peter shook his head.

"You won't find them in the dark and I'm hungry now!"

"C'mon then, let's start looking." John got to his feet.

The boys trudged the weary miles and saw only a lemon tree, they snatched a couple of lemons each but after sucking at one apiece, they threw the others away.

"What we need is apples. We will have to climb a back fence; most people have fruit trees in the back yard." Peter informed.

The two had found an apple tree and were stuffing their shirts in the back yard of a house, when John noticed the rear door was ajar. He crept up and peered in, the house seemed deserted in the growing dusk. He could see the blacked out windows but no lights were on as yet within. He motioned for Peter to follow; they stealthily crept into the house. John was cutting slices of bread in the kitchen and Peter was peering into the ice-box when the news broadcast on a wireless set could be heard as a door opened and a woman came down the passageway. She switched the kitchen light on and gasped.

"Mercy be! What on earth are you boys doing here?"

She approached the better to see them. John was cornered, he raised the knife threateningly.

"We're starving lady–let us go–please!"

The terrified woman just nodded and moved aside, hand to her mouth stifling a scream. She watched the two back out. John dropped the knife at the doorway and they ran for their lives out of the back gate.

"Gee whiz, that was close." Gasped Peter as he fought for breath.

It was a few minutes before the errant pair were able to eat without fear of choking. They were well away from the house they had entered and felt safe sitting in the back seat of the old wrecked car they had come across on a vacant allotment in Bulleen. Having sated their appetites they settled down for the night. A grey dismal day found John all alone. Peter had left him, possibly as soon as he had woken. Both knew the area fairly well, it was only a couple of miles to the Boys Home from where they began their adventure. Their wanderings had taken them in a large circle to the city and back. No doubt the fright of the night's events had sent Peter back to Saint Martins. John thought over the past few days. Originally they were seven hopefuls looking for a home and love–now only one remained. John was determined he would not go back. He would find a home somewhere. He was idly wandering past some tall pines in a large paddock in North Balwyn, when a police van stopped by the fence and a police officer called him over. John ran towards the other fence, the policeman after him. The second policeman drove the van around to cut him off; so John made for the pine trees and began climbing. The two policemen were now at the bottom of the pine tree and calling for John to come down. He took his shoes off and threw them at the officers. One of the men began to climb up after John, he climbed higher, then out on a limb as his position became desperate. The branch bent touching the one directly beneath it, the boy grabbed the lower branch releasing the top one. He followed this procedure until almost to the bottom of the tree, when the branch he was gripping broke away and fell, landing the boy in his bare feet onto the broken glass at the base of the tree. His feet were badly cut. He lay in agony as the policemen attended him, the tears flowing freely as one of the officers supported and comforted him.

"It is all right, Son. Things will be better at Saint Martins now, there is a full inquiry going on. The authorities will be dividing the place into cottages. You will have a Mother figure and a Father figure now."

THE END

H, R-P.

REEDE THESE

7   Rory   30/7/78

Based On a true story.

Holiday time! Ah, the glory of a drive through nature's realm has to be experienced to be really appreciated! Bryan and his two small charges were doing just that and the children gazed in awe at the towering gums reaching high as they sought the warmth of the friendly December sun. Stuart's round happy face was aglow with excitement as he peered upwards through the windscreen, in an effort to see the topmost peaks of the eucalypts.

"Gosh Bryan, they grow for miles, do they reach the clouds?"

"Yes!" Bryan informed. "These trees often poke out above the clouds, especially in the spring time. That is when one has to drive through the fog as one crosses this mountain range. It is called 'The Black Spur'. Lots of people died in years gone by when there were only horses and carts in which to travel. Many people and horses fell over the steep side of the track, as it was then, some never to be seen again. The road is much better nowadays, however there are still fatalities; mainly due to bad driving!"

John, the quieter of the two boys, peered out from under his straight, dark hair as he casually asked.

"Is that a kangaroo?"

Bryan had seen the animal even as John spoke but Stuart had been studying trees and when he looked in the direction indicated, said.

"Wow!" As Bryan answered.

"No Pal that is a wallaby. It is a small cousin to the kangaroo. There are quite a few up here in the hills, they are all 'protected' here because this is a 'National Park'."

Eventually the ranges were crossed and the long journey over the flat lands beyond was gradually being shortened. The destination of the trio and their packed van, was a cold trout river South-West of the popular holiday resort of Eildon, in Victoria; Australia. The two boys would camp for ten days and then change places with another two, whom

58

Bryan's Son, Don, would bring up when he came to stay for a week-end; before taking the first two back home. The four boys were having a camping holiday as their reward for being the most dedicated, well behaved and obedient of their class of thirty or so swimmers, over the past year in Bryan's swimming school. It was a coveted prize as only a few could be accommodated in the short three weeks available. Of course there were some who were unable to attend the camp anyway, because of family commitments. Bryan tried to make it as fair as possible and things always seemed to work out well. Even if at times he had to stretch a point and take an extra one. They arrived at their camp site at noon and it took only an hour to obtain the key to the gate of the paddock, which gave access to the river and set up the tent. As this was usually done in the heat of the summer, Bryan inevitably got a headache from his exertions and was not long in getting the billy boiled for a relieving cuppa. There were set rules in Bryan's camps. The first one was 'obedience' followed by strict instructions not to wander around camp on the first day. The main two dangers being the freezing, swiftly flowing river and the threat of snakes. This was the habitat of the 'tiger' snake and to a lesser extent, of the 'brown' snake. Before anyone walked freely about the camp, snake sticks had to be fashioned and on the morrow, a snake hunt would be organized to rid the area of the danger to the children; who were not 'bush' trained as yet. Having enjoyed a relaxing tea break, the three campers set to and put their camp in order. Tables set up, the beds made ready, a storm water drain dug around the tent with run offs and inconspicuously behind a clump of scrub; a bush toilet was erected. Their home was now complete.

"Let's go fishing." Bryan declared.

"Yay!" Chorused two hopeful anglers.

They fished directly in front of the tent because the area was not checked for dangers and it was, as yet, undisturbed water. Bryan had brought a tin of worms as bait for the boys to practice their fishing skills with, the salt-water mussels he would save until tomorrow when the children had a little experience and would not waste them. There was no response from the fish as the hopefuls eyed the three corks nonchalantly bobbing in the swirling water and frothy eddies.

"You sure there are fish in here?" His curly fair haired head tilted as Stuart asked the question.

"Of course, be patient! We will catch plenty of fish here, they will bite soon, you will see!"

As Bryan answered, a frenzied snorting was heard. The two boys jumped erect as they beheld the farmer's very large bull thundering down upon them, bucking and shaking its head. As the bull charged, Stuart fearfully asked.

"Will we jump into the river?"

Although the boy could swim like a fish and Bryan jokingly maintained that John could beat one, he said.

"No! Just stand behind that willow there, I think he is only frisky."

Bryan broke a few fine willow twigs and waved them at the animal, as it slithered to a stop amid a cloud of dust and eyed them enquiringly; still shaking its head. Bryan calmly told the boys to stay put as he offered the willow leaves. The bull sniffed, and then snatched a mouthful. Bryan walked upstream away from the camp, breaking more twigs as he went. The bull followed. When he had the animal happily munching the greenery in a clearing well away from camp, he went back and got the boys. They had an enjoyable ten minutes hand feeding this quiet giant that a few minutes ago they thought would eat them; the fishing forgotten in the light of this new experience. Bryan kept a watchful eye on the boys as he got his axe from under the table and went about the business of cutting green willow snake sticks. The boys left the bull to see what Bryan was up to, he explained as he worked.

"You see boys, we have to find slightly curved thin branches about three or four feet long roughly one and a quarter metres. Being a branch, it tapers well with a straight thin end for a handle and a thick curved end for a waddy. Now I trim all the little twigs off and you may feed them to the bull, then there is no waste and the area is not left untidy."

Bryan demonstrated how the snake stick should be used if a snake happened to be in their way.

"See! Feet slightly apart, both hands gripping the thin end of the stick, bend your knees as you swing down with a quick thump hitting just a third of a metre behind the snake's head, then jump back out of the way; just in case you missed. Always keep a snake at arm's length even when it is dead, if it swings and the fangs puncture your skin you can still suffer a bite."

After a little practice, Bryan was satisfied they knew how to go about it if ever the need arose. They fed the rest of the greens to the bull and it wandered away. Bryan suggested they had better have tea and pack the fishing gear away as the day had slipped on and it would soon be dark and bed time.

The happy days passed with each catching a share of fish and spending the sunny daytime in the warm waters of the lagoon that backed off from the little creek which emptied into the river near their camp. They had searched the area immediately around their camp on the second day and only found one snake for which Bryan was thankful. The less snakes around the better and safer for all. Stuart and John had many carefree happy hours floating upon their air-beds and splashing in the lagoon, heated by the hot sun and its reflection from the high stony walls of outcropping that rose some fifteen metres above on the opposite bank. All too soon for the boys, the weekend came and they were to leave. It was heralded by a car tooting its horn at the gate. Stuart and John eagerly raced up with the key and returned in the car, babbling of their exploits to their mates who came up from Melbourne with Don; Bryan's Son who was just eighteen. Bryan had taught his son to drive when the lad was but fourteen and most of the youth's experience was on bush tracks; until recently when he became eligible for a motor driving license. He was quite proficient and a sensible driver, otherwise Bryan would not have risked the children with him. After lunch, Don decided to fish at the rapids some five kilometres away, the four eager lads pleaded to accompany him. As Don did not mind and Bryan had the fullest of confidence in his boy's ability to tend their welfare, he relished the break from his charges and relaxed in the quiet tent with a book; then dozed.

Came the day of departure for Stuart and John. They were loath to leave the happy camp but were eager to get back home to see their parents and relate the new experiences that had come their way. Don waved goodbye as the two new lads and Bryan saw them off from the paddock gate. Stuart and John making ridiculous faces at their two pals through the rear window. As the car disappeared from sight, the two new youngsters keenly raced each other back to the campsite. Bryan, jogging in the rear, was hard pressed to keep up with them. Michael, the curly-topped redhead and taller of the excited pair, was first to reach the tent. He was standing quite still as Rory and Bryan reached him, staring at the tent flap.

"What is the matter Michael?" Bryan asked.

"I saw something go into the tent–I–I–think it was a snake!"

All three stood outside discussing the situation.

"Think you would know a snake if you saw one?" Bryan asked the boy.

"Yes, I have seen them at the zoo."

"You are not playing tricks Michael, I hope?" Sternly from Bryan.

"No Sir, honestly!"

"Very well. I believe you. Now, let us not panic."

Bryan handed one of the snake sticks to each boy from the pile beside the tent and the same drill was given to each of them, as was taught to the other two.

"Now you boys stay outside one on each alternate corner of the tent, so that the four sides can be watched at once. I will carefully check under everything inside and remember, if the snake comes out let me know as you hit it–yell so that I will know where it is!"

The search began, Bryan lifting bedding with the stick and any item on the floor that may harbour the reptile. There it was, under an air-bed. Bryan flicked the air-bed away and in the fluid return stroke, whacked the interloper smartly across the back as he had taught the children–calling as he did so.

"I have it!"

The boys rushed to the doorway and then timidly gaped as Bryan carried the metre and a bit tiger snake out on the stick. It was still wriggling and squirming.

"It's still alive!" Rory shouted, jumping back.

"No!" Bryan informed them. "That is only the nerves reacting, making the muscles contract. It is quite dead but it will wriggle and writhe for some time yet!"

Bryan cut off the head and dug a deep hole in which to bury the dangerous thing.

"Now that the head and poison sacs are gone, the rest is quite harmless. Have a good look at it to get rid of your curiosity. Feel the scales and study the colour of the snake, then we will skin it and have a taste of the meat!"

"Oooh, yuk!" Came from a disgusted Rory.

"Isn't it dangerous to eat?" Michael queried.

"No! It is just ordinary meat the same as an eel or a rabbit, in fact it does taste a lot like an eel only a little less oily."

Bryan hung the carcase on a sharpened twig set in a tree and slit the snake from the top of the tail to where the head was with his small, sharp skinning knife. Then peeling the skin back with an even, steady pull, it came away in one piece. He wrapped the skin around the dry branch of a tree that had many ants crawling its length, and then tied the skin firmly with some twine from his fishing tackle.

"There! Now the ants will clean any remaining flesh from it and the sun will dry the skin out for us. Later I will show you how to tan it by using wattle bark and cow dung, then it can be fashioned into a belt for one of you!"

"Ooh me!" The boys chorused together.

"You know the rules." Bryan said. "The best behaved or the one who earns it through camp duties!"

The two were keen to be the proud owner of a snakeskin belt and their good behaviour appeared assured. Bryan mentally noted he must try to get another snake in fairness.

The meat gutted and prepared, two curious boys eyed the cooking pieces dubiously. Bryan placed the finished product on a plate and dipping a piece in vinegar, popped it in his mouth. Two wide-eyed youngsters watched his obvious enjoyment with mouths agape.

"There you are–try a piece–it is delicious. You know, the Aborigines have lived on this meat and goanna's, for many centuries!" Bryan said, nodding.

Each of the two selected a piece, eyed it apprehensively, and then took a small nibble.

"Yuk!" Rory spat his away.

Michael kept nibbling, then popped the piece in and chewed it well.

"Hey! I like it–can I have some more?"

"Not can–may–may I have some more." Bryan corrected. He smiled at Rory. "No good to you Rory old son?"

"No, I am scared of snakes, I don't like it!"

"Fair enough, we will eat the lot, won't we Michael?"

"Yes, I reckon." The boy took another piece.

That evening, Bryan set a cod line well away from the camp proper in a deep hole well suited to the fish. Tea was eaten, the dishes washed and they were cooking potatoes in foil in the embers of their camp fire.

"When we have eaten the spuds it is bed time boys. I will just check that hemp rope around the tent–we do not want another snake in–then I will settle you boys into bed and then I have to check my cod line."

"Gee Bryan! Can't we come with you; you may have a big fish on?" Michael asked.

"It will be dark soon and I won't have you running around at night. That is when the snakes come down to the water to feed on frogs and take in moisture!"

"Please, we will be careful!"

"Well, obedience, remember!"

Brian checked the rope as the boys finished their potatoes.

"Right! Put your gumboots on and grab torches–I will get the snake sticks."

The boys disappeared into the tent as Bryan began making his way to the hidden cod line.

"Hurry boys." He called back as he waited by a gum tree on the river path.

"Coming!" The two rushed out.

"We could find only one torch; I think Rory's fell down behind the table!" Michael explained.

It was quite dark when they checked the line. It was snagged. Bryan tried to pull it in.

"Ah! I will have to leave it until the morning. Let us get back; it is not safe near the river at night."

Michael ran ahead with his torch Rory in hot pursuit.

"Wait boys, not so fast!" Bryan called. It was too late.

Rory sprang into the air.

"Snake I've been bitten!"

Bryan reached Rory as Michael came back. They quickly shined the torches around near the vicinity, there was no sign of a snake but there was a scotch thistle weed right where Rory was standing.

"Are you sure you were bitten, Rory?" Bryan demanded.

"Yes, on the heel!" Rory raised the member for Bryan to study.

"Where are your gum-boots? I distinctly told you to wear gum-boots!"

Rory's lip trembled.

"I couldn't find them in the dark–will I die?"

Bryan had the lad's runners and socks off and was studying the filthy heel as he answered.

"No, of course not, we will get you to the doctor very quickly. Don't panic!"

There were two puncture marks about three centimetres apart and another lesser one on the hard skin of the heel, just below. They were not deep and very little discoloured. Bryan wished that he had got his cavities attended earlier as he sucked deeply of the boy's dirty heel, spitting out two or three times. He took his small snake kit from his pocket and applied a tourniquet above the knee. Bryan lifted the boy and carried him, saying.

"Now just relax mate and try to stay awake, if you feel sleepy just start talking instead. Michael, you lead the way to the van and look ahead carefully–shine both torches. Off we go, quickly!"

Sitting Rory on the front seat with Michael on the edge of it, they negotiated the gate and were speeding along the gravel road, when Rory began to feel ill. Bryan slewed the van to a stop outside the only farm house in the vicinity and stood by as Rory emptied his stomach. The farmhouse door opened and a male voice enquired.

"Who is it!"

Bryan shouted.

"A child has been snake bitten. Ring the hospital and tell them we are coming in!"

Back in the van Bryan set it sideways around the corners and roared up the main streets of the township, horn blaring, demanding right of way. At the hospital a nurse was just coming to the door as they stopped by it. Bryan carried Rory into the room to which he was led by the Nursing Sister. Only ten minutes had elapsed since the boy was bitten. The sister was checking the boy as the doctor arrived.

"Where is the patient?"

He studied the leg, then the youngster's eyes and pulse.

"Are you sure it was a snake?" The doctor asked Bryan.

"I did not see one but the boy is sure!"

"It is not dark enough, looks more like a thistle prick" the doctor said "better keep him in for observation Sister!"

"It was a snake. It was heavy, I felt it!" Rory cried.

Bryan believed the boy but the doctor was not convinced.

"Come back for him in the morning, we have the antivenene at hand but I think he is suffering fright more than anything. What sort of a snake would it be do you think?"

"Definitely a tiger" Bryan informed "it was right beside the river!"

The next morning found Bryan and Michael at the hospital. Rory pleaded to go back to camp saying the needles were blunt and he was quite well enough. Bryan asked the doctor and he said yes, it is only the shock the boy was suffering from. As Bryan stood by the boy to help him to dress, Rory stumbled and clutched at Bryan; who looked into Rory's eyes. They were facing outwards, one to the left and the other to the right; quivering.

"Can you see double, Rory?"

"Yes, and I am giddy. Please take me to camp."

"No! You better lay back a minute while I talk to the doctor!"

The medical man returned and studied the patient closely.

"Yes! Looks like he was bitten after all—but only a small dose—he must have flicked the snake off as he ran and did not get the full issue."

"The lad is fearful of the hospital Doctor, can I nurse him back at camp. He will be more relaxed there?" Bryan asked.

"Well now, I don't know. Better leave it until this afternoon, if he is stable then, I do not see why not. But you must keep him cool and feed him only raw eggs and a little milk. No excitement whatsoever!"

So it was that three quiet days were spent with Rory sleeping peacefully on an air-bed, enclosed under a canopy of mosquito netting in the shade of a weeping willow. The quiet river rippling by with Bryan and Michael keeping a constant watch over him; as they fished. On the fourth day Rory came out of his drowsiness and demanded solid food. All at camp were exalted. Then, belatedly, the reaction hit Bryan and the little touch of venom in his cavities put him down, feeling quite ill for a day. The boys stayed near and managed the camp for him until the next day, when he recovered and the holiday began in earnest. In the last five days they had a feast of activities to make up for lost time. Horse riding, scenic trips, tanning the snake skin plus another that Bryan killed on the road one evening as they were returning. There were canoe rides and sheep mustering at a nearby farm, offered by the kindly farmer. When Rory was bitten, Bryan telephoned the lad's father who said.

"I know nothing of snakes; I will leave it in your capable hands to pull him through. You have my confidence and it does not appear too serious—is it?"

Upon their return home, Rory's father put out a welcoming hand.

"Thank you!" He simply said.

Rory did likewise, saying.

"It was a great holiday!"

THE END.

Harvey

Harvey and Bryan were seventeen, born a month apart in different suburbs of bustling Melbourne, in Victoria, Australia. They came from entirely different life-styles and at first would appear to have nothing in common. Harvey was born of well-to-do parents in the posh inner suburb of South Yarra–the 'elite' side of South Yarra–and was educated at a private boarding school. His father, a successful businessman come politician. Harvey's parents fawned upon him. Bryan was a victim of the 'working class' suburb of Middle Park. His father had died in a mill accident when Bryan was but seven years of age and his mother had to work in a processing factory, to make ends meet. Bryan went through the 'State School' system and had a couple of years in 'Tech', until he was forced to go to work to supplement the family income. That was his total education. However, he loved the bush and a new vista opened for the boy when his uncle took him camping when he was but a ten year old. He so enjoyed the bush life that he incessantly hounded his uncle to take a camping holiday at every opportunity. Uncle Albert had been good to Bryan and his education took on a new lease of life as he learned of bush lore. For seven years Bryan had accompanied his uncle on an average of at least once and sometimes twice a month. He became quite a proficient bushman himself. Then Uncle Albert took ill. Bronchial pneumonia set in accentuated by his heavy smoking and he became bedridden. At seventeen Bryan already felt he was man enough to tackle the bush on his own. He spoke of this to his team-mate at the local football park. Both he and Harvey prided themselves on their ability on the football field and had become great mates. Harvey had not had the pleasure of a camping holiday. Sure, he had been on bush picnics with his folks but never on an actual sleep-out camp. Bryan was pleased to have a companion on his first camp attempt without his uncle. There was no great effort needed to convince Harvey's parents to let him accompany Bryan, as they were well aware of his frequent trips through the media of their son. Harvey often returned from his sporting activities and spoke of the conversations he had with Bryan.

The pair set out by train, having put their bicycles in the luggage compartment and were eager to reach their destination seventy kilometres away. The journey by train seemed to drag out and when the two youths alighted and gathered their gear, they were already feeling tired. After consulting a map of the area, they harnessed on their equipment and set forth. It would be noon by the time they reached the tiny township of Toolangi, where they intended to camp. Having worked out in advance their destination and intending to buy some lunch when they got there, it was a great disappointment after a gruelling uphill fifteen kilometres ride with heavy packs; to find that the 'township' of Toolangi was in reality only a timber mill with a collection of some ten houses. Not a single sign of a store even. The locals all drove to nearby Healesville for their weekly supplies. The boys were tired and hungry, so all that was left to them was to make a temporary camp by the roadside and prepare some of their tinned camp food. They managed to scrounge a billyfull of water from the foreman of the mill, out of the huge concrete tank set in the ground by the office. It was actually a reservoir for the use of fire-fighters but was quite good drinking water.

The two made fun of their first camp meal and were not too eager to push on as the uphill ride had tired them considerably. Bryan and Harvey tidied up and began the search for a suitable camp site. It was two or three kilometres past the logging camp that the duo found a small side track leading down to a valley some half a kilometre off the main road. A rippling creek danced merrily over the quartz pebbles and a picnic area with a hewn table and chairs was available.

"Wow!" Bryan gasped. "This is just fine. We can set our tent up over there between those two gums. We will only need a ridge pole!"

Harvey waited quietly, noticeably ill at ease in these unfamiliar surroundings and not knowing how to go about anything. Bryan knew what he was doing and instructed his mate. They soon had their small two-man tent erected and comfortably set up for the night. The bicycles under the over flap of the tent on the scrub side, comparatively under cover and their carry packs and foodstuffs safely under the table hidden beneath some large boulders they arranged around their 'cache', to keep any bush animals or stray dogs at bay.

"Well Harvey—what do you think—cosy?" Bryan asked.

"Yes, I suppose." Came dubiously from the city boy. "It is going to be cold though, isn't it?"

"No! Not in our sleeping bags and under a blanket."

Suddenly a thunderclap heralded the start of a solid downpour. It started to rain. Bryan's Uncle Albert had always taken great pains to instruct his nephew in the finer arts of camping and this instruction had paid off. Through the flap of the tent, the youths watched the rain water stream from the guttering they had dug with a tomahawk around their tent. At least they would remain dry. The storm built up in intensity and Bryan was moved to comment.

"Damn it! We have left the food under the table and we are going to get very wet yanking the rocks off to get something to eat for tea, couldn't cook it anyhow. Damn the rain!"

"I hope it stops soon." Harvey sighed. "It's not much fun if we have to stay in here too long!"

"Yes, we are pretty high in the mountains here—it could rain for days."

"True?" Incredulously from Harvey.

"That's right. Uncle Albert reckons the high country gets the most rain 'cause it is higher and colder—ah! She will probably blow over!"

Bryan peered at the heavens through the flap but got little consolation by the dark thickening clouds. It rained all night! They went without food rather than get the inside of the tent wet upon their return to it with the tinned food, at least there was tinned fruit they could have eaten. That did not need to be cooked. The pair slipped into the sleeping bags and tried to sleep through the incessant storm that grew ever more in intensity. Morning grey tinted the horizon and Harvey whispered.

"Bryan! Are you awake?"

"I am now—what's the matter?"

"The rain won't stop and I am starving!"

Bryan opened the flap and peered out.

"Ah! It is not properly light yet—go back to sleep for an hour!"

Bryan climbed back into his sleeping bag as he continued.

"If it is still raining, one of us can nick over and grab some tucker. No need for both of us to get wet."

Harvey cocked an ear.

"Listen! Can't you hear that rustling and creaking? I think the trees will all come down!"

"Hmmpf." Came from Bryan. Harvey shook his shoulders.

"Dammit! Don't go to sleep—I am worried!"

"What about?" Muffled, from Bryan.

"The noises."

"Don't be dopey! Trees always do that in the wind, the branches rub together. They grate and groan in the wind!"

Harvey was still very dubious.

"I heard one heck of a crash last night. It sounded as if it was just over the creek—I think a tree fell!"

"Prob'ly, our two are solid, they won't fall. Go to sleep."

Bryan snuggled himself more comfortably, and then suddenly sat erect as a sharp rending sound came from directly overhead.

"What is that?" Harvey trembled.

"I'll have a look." Bryan said, as he poked his head through the flap.

The rain had eased a little but the droplets stung his face as he strained his eyes upwards. Harvey poked his head out too, just in time to witness a tree some twenty metres away, topple in their direction; it was falling directly at them!

"My God!" Harvey screamed as he tried to push out past Bryan.

They both became firmly wedged in the partly tied opening, tearing the tent but not releasing them. The falling tree struck heavily against one that supported their tent, a shower of heavy droplets, leaves and broken branches bespattered them as the monolith crashed heavily across the picnic table; shattering it to the ground. The tent collapsed upon the youths and they were flung to the floor of their tent by an outflung branch. The bicycles twisted and bent on top of them. After the crashing had ceased and the little clearing became settled, quiet reigned. The birds were silent, even the rain had stopped. Bryan was pinned by one leg. It was still in his sleeping bag but a part of a bicycle that was forced through the tent, was firmly wedged across the leg and held there by a branch. He was not sure if the leg was broken or not—he did not think so—he could wriggle his toes. He called to Harvey.

"Hey! Are you all right?" There was no answer. He called more frantically. "Harvey, are you okay?"

Harvey was face down in the mud, his head and shoulders still outside what was left of the tent, his muffled reply nearly made Bryan choke himself under the tent which covered him.

"Dunno—I think I am dead!"

Well tangled in the tent, Bryan could not see what was happening but he was aware of Harvey extricating himself from his predicament.

"Help me Harvey, I'm suffocating under here; rip the tent open!"

It was quite an easy matter to tear the tent, it was already in ribbons. Harvey located Bryan's head and made an opening large enough to have his head and shoulders exposed. Bryan gasped at the welcome moist air.

"Well, come on, get out!" Harvey demanded.

"Can't, I'm caught under a bike; see if you can drag it off, Harvey!"

Harvey sighed as he checked the machines.

"They are absolutely ruined. My bike cost Dad a hundred and seventy dollars—look at it now!" "Damn the bikes Harvey get me out!"

Harvey tugged and strained, then stood back.

"Can't do it—you're stuck—I will have to get help!"

Although the rain had passed and the morning sun was attempting to break through the dismal grey curtain, the monotony of the falling droplets off the overhead trees, were beginning to annoy and literally dampen Bryan's spirits. Caught face down and by the leg, he was only able to turn slightly and observe the extent of their catastrophe. Neither of them had eaten since the belated lunch of the previous day but the pangs of hunger were momentarily forgotten as their dire circumstances struck home. Nearly three kilometres from the nearest settlement and another fifteen to the closest shopping centre, also, they now had no means of transport. To add to their problems, the food supply was hopelessly locked in under the weight of a huge tree which also imprisoned Bryan. He could see that the bulk of the eucalypt had missed them by a mere four metres as it fell. Luckily it had been diverted by one of the trees that supported their tent; else they would have been crushed for sure. It was fortunate also, that only the far extremes of the outflung branch hit their tent. The branch was held off them by an elbow bend in the branch that took the weight, but the ground clearance was only half a metre. It was under here that Bryan was entangled with the bicycle. His leg was not sore, so Bryan imagined that he had been spared a break and it was miraculous that the metal of the machine had been so horribly twisted, yet his leg was not noticeably affected. Harvey looked about hopefully. Perhaps if he found a strong stick he could lever the branch enough so that his mate could wriggle free. He suggested it to Bryan.

"I don't think so Harvey, the stick could snap and the branch might settle lower and really break my leg. Hey! I know. Get the tomahawk and chop through the branch!"

Harvey quickly crawled beneath the foliage where the goods were stashed under the table. He foraged about for awhile before returning dejectedly.

"No good Bryan, it is hopelessly jammed under the rocks. I better walk back to the timber mill; it is only a couple of kilometres."

"Okay mate, but hurry won't you? I am getting cramped and I am all wet and cold. Just follow the track and turn left at the road—don't wander through the bush—you will get lost!"

"Right, hang in there Pal; I will be back in a tick!"

Harvey raced off, pleased to be doing something constructive. He would show Bryan he was not a dill altogether and even carried a stick as he remembered reading about the country folk doing. He was not sure why they did it but imagined it was to kill snakes with. That thought worried him. Harvey was not aware that snakes were hibernating at this time of the year. He came upon a wide track that appeared to be heavily used. Was that the road they had ridden along yesterday? Yes it must be it was a lot wider than the one he was travelling upon. Harvey turned left as instructed and hurriedly made his way deeper into the lonely bush. The road he was seeking was yet another two hundred metres past that turning. Bryan began to sneeze. He had on countless occasions, attempted to extricate himself but only succeeded in making his ankle sore. The whole leg was being affected by the lack of proper circulation and numbness was beginning to travel up his leg. Time passed, he dozed. A motor could be heard, it sounded like a four wheel drive by the chugging and whining. The vehicle slowly came into view and a small boy's voice could be heard chirping above the motor.

"Gee, look Dad, there's a tree down, hey! I see a bike. Stop Dad, I want to look at it, maybe it works!"

As the vehicle stopped, Bryan opened his mouth to yell but only croaked. He did not realize how dry his throat had become. An awkward gangling boy of about nine years was almost upon Bryan before he realized anything but the bicycle was there.

"Hey Dad, there's a dead body!"

The boy jumped back as his father came to investigate. It did not take the man long to see that the 'dead' body was alive and to take in the story of what had come to pass. Having assessed the situation, he bid his son get the water-bag off the land rover while he carried his chain saw from it and started the motor. The lad poured some water into a tin pannikin and assisted Bryan to drink. The man cut the end of the limb to relieve the weight a little, and then used part of it as a chuck to stop any accidental sagging of the tree. He sliced another section which released the bicycles. Once they were off, Bryan was free. He was helped erect but could not stand on the leg; it was too numb. He massaged it. As the man helped Bryan into the land rover, he got the story from the youth.

"The tree fell early this morning and we were lucky we were not killed!" The man agreed, adding. "It was a vicious storm there for a few minutes, often happens up here; 'though I think more trees fell this time than I have seen come down before!"

They checked Bryan's leg as he sat on the seat of the vehicle. The leg was slightly swollen and some skin was missing in places but otherwise it seemed to be in working order. No serious damage. The man introduced himself.

"I am Peter Gatterick and this is my boy Jamie—say 'howdy' Jamie."

"Hello." Shyly from the youngster.

Bryan introduced himself and said.

"Gee! I hope it did not inconvenience you having to drop what you were doing and come to rescue me—sorry if I caused you any trouble. It must have taken my mate a bit of time to find someone willing to come!" Peter looked at him in amazement.

"What on earth are you talking about? I just came to gather some river pebbles for the garden!"

"But—didn't you see my mate. Didn't he tell you I was stuck here?"

"No, we just came from the logging camp and we did not pass a soul on the road. Your mate must have wandered off down O'Brien's Lane—that's bad!"

Harvey had walked about two kilometres before he began to suspect he was on the wrong road. Not at all sure, he carefully studied his surroundings; it was all so unfamiliar. He recalled that he never took a great deal of notice when they cycled from the small settlement, just what terrain they were traversing at the time. Now he wished that he had taken more care. His suspicions grew as he realized the gravel had petered out and now in the distance he could see a gaping hole in the path ahead. 'Landslide', he thought. Indeed that certainly appeared the case for he was now standing on the edge of a sheer drop that should have been the middle of the road. He clambered down the metre and a half deep water wash and made his way across the sticky morass that had a small watercourse traversing it from side to side. By the time that Harvey had negotiated the fifty metre miniature chasm, his shoes and lower legs were caked with mud. He clambered out upon the other side and was pleased to note that the road continued. The youth had actually crossed a gravel quarry but was not aware of the fact, believing instead that the severe storm of the night before had really washed away the road. Around the next bend and the ugly truth dawned with stark finality, the road was no longer there; just a barely discernable path. What to do now? By the time he walked back and then found the right road, he would have travelled at least five more kilometres and it would be time consuming. Then what of poor Bryan trapped under a tree? He would be suffering terribly by now. Harvey's stomach was gurgling but he did not have Bryan's troubles. Surely the road he was seeking must be parallel to this one? He would strike through the bush and see. Harvey could always retrace his steps and he may save time and distance by continuing. Besides, he could not face that horrible mud bath again. It was rough going through the scrub and Harvey was beginning to wish he had kept to the track, he should have gone back! It was not too late; he turned to retrace his steps then realized he was unable to pick the way. Harvey was lost! He sat on a log to ponder his situation. If the main road was near, he should hear the traffic; then recalled how deep into the country they were. There would not be a great deal of traffic on these lonely bush roads. Why on earth did he come on this useless camp anyway? No use crying about it now, more pressing was to get out of it; Harvey pushed on. The teenager was very worried about himself being lost but was more concerned about Bryan, who was lying in danger and his only hope was a city boy who had gone and got himself lost. Maybe they would both die out here—what a rotten thought! Harvey was wet, dirty, tired, hungry and extremely worried when a voice said.

"'Ullo, whatcha doin'?"

Harvey jumped in fright, searching frantically for the owner of the voice.

"Up in the tree, dummy!"

Harvey searched above and beheld a straw-colour haired boy of twelve perched on a branch, tying bits of wood and old sheets of tin together. He was building a cubby-house. Relieved to see someone, Harvey implored of the boy.

"Do you live handy? Please take me there, it is an emergency!"

The boy continued his tying.

"What's a 'mergency?"

"Oh dammit! It's like an S.O.S. Take me to your home immediately; my mate is in trouble—hurry boy!"

The lad just sat looking down.

"I'm not s'posed to take strangers home—Dad said!"

"Oh! For God's sake, don't argue boy—we need help!"

"Why didn't you say you needed help? We always help people; Dad says we might need help ourselves one day."

The lad dropped from the tree and waved an arm calling the teenager to follow. The path the young fellow led Harvey along was well worn as if the boy had spent many hours travelling it. Perhaps a child of his tender years had little else to do in the bush than to climb trees and build cubby houses, Harvey thought. They came to a fence that was supposed to protect the vegetable garden but it was of little use, for the chickens were scratching all over it. As Harvey beheld the lad's home, he urgently rushed up to notify the people of Bryan's predicament and enlist their help. Just as Harvey neared the outer shed, a stringy little lad noticed him and yelled.

"Hey Dad! There's another stranger here!"

A man appeared, closely followed by Bryan hobbling on a make-shift crutch.

"Hi Harvey!" He greeted. "What kept you?"

THE END.

Howard Reede-Pelling.

77

9   Peter   11/8/78

Moira Davey's mind was in turmoil as she pondered the extent of Peter's injury. The hospital gave few details when they rang to notify her and to check his medical history. All she knew was that he had been laid low by an over zealous football tackle. The team manager told her that much as he hustled her into the taxi, he was elaborating.

"It was just one of those things Moira." John Canders raised his hands in a gesture of despair. "As a winger he was fast, you know that. It was purely accidental; Travers is a typical full back and had to put Pete down to stop the try. It was just unfortunate he landed heavily on top of Peter. We are not sure but Travers seems to think it is a broken neck, he said he heard a distinct snap!"

Moira covered her face in her cupped hands and sniffed.

"Poor Peter–poor Peter, oh God! How I tried to talk him out of football–he kept saying, next year–!" She burst into sobbing.

John gently patted her on the shoulder.

"Come now Moira, it may not be that bad–no one knows for sure yet–he has to be X-rayed. All we know is he is unconscious and there was a snap, it may not have been Pete at all–could have been a stick in the grass; we do not know–don't go overboard until we are sure!" He attempted to cheer her. "If he is conscious when we arrive, you will be wanting to look your best to brighten him up you know!"

Moira nodded as she patted her eyes and cheeks with her handkerchief.

"Please God that is all it is, he is such an active man. Oh, can't you go any faster driver, please?" The taxi driver shook his head.

"Sorry Ma'am, regulations you know!"

However he set the vehicle along at an increased rate. 'Just keep your eyes out for blue lights!' He muttered.

At the hospital, Moira and John were kept waiting. The doctors were unavailable as they were attending Peter but the Sister got them both a hot cuppa to try and settle the distraught wife. Meanwhile, in the operating room, Doctors

Schneider and Phelwhumple were discussing the X-ray shots of the patient's neck. Doctor Schneider tapped an area of the spine within the skull housing on the illuminated picture.

"There." He said. "Third vertebra could be compound!"

"Mmm" mused his colleague "appears slightly misaligned—slight dislocation perhaps?"

They both studied again, minutely.

"That left side shot there; do you think there is a rupture of the spinal cord?"

Doctor Felwhumple asked.

"Possibly—of course a vesicle may be responsible for that—especially if there is a compound and an odd chip is floating."

"It would have to be affecting the cord, there is no suggestion of a concussion; he is comatose!"

Doctor Schneider turned to the attendant Nursing Sister.

"What is the response Sister?"

"Quite normal Doctor" she reported "breathing, pulse, temperature—heart rate is a little fast though—not enough to cause concern."

"Thank you Sister."

He lifted the eyelids of the patient and studied the eyeballs intently. Was that a flicker then? No, imagination! He took his fingers away and felt the pulse himself as he addressed Doctor Felwhumple.

"There is no attenuation and he is not concussed so far as I am able to ascertain, if in fact as the shots infer, he is suffering a compound, the possibility of a rupture to the cord is the cause of the patient not responding."

"Sister" Doctor Felwhumple ordered "place the patient in the 'collar'. I think forty eight hours should tell us something if we adjust it correctly!"

Doctor Schneider nodded his agreement.

After continual scrutiny of the X-rays, both medical men were sure the most positive action they could take, was to put the upper torso of the victim in a state of inertia and adjust the unit the few millimetres that would take the fracture to it's correct position; then re-Xray in two days to ascertain the response. Failing this, a delicate operation upon the nervous system was inevitable. John and Moira were in a corner of the waiting room, impatiently looking up as each person came or went, expecting at every entrance of the medical staff, word of Peter's condition. Moira would have been more frantic had she known the real truth of her man's desperate situation, but ignorance is bliss. Fortunately for Moira. The staff was preparing the inert body of Peter for the cradle in which he would be a prisoner for the next few weeks. As the doctors were setting the final adjustments and working out the exact millimetres of pressure to be exerted, the sister called.

"Doctor! The heart rate is increasing and there is a definite temperature rise!"

Doctor Schneider had only just turned the handle a fraction but stopped at Sister's call. How could Peter tell them he was not in a coma–that he was in fact conscious of everything that was happening? He was absolutely immobile, not even an eyelid could he flicker–and the bastards were going to wrench his neck out! Quick checks and further tests failed to change the opinions of the doctors, so it was that the traction was completed to their satisfaction. At the resumption–when Doctor Schneider began the alignment–the pain was so severe that Peter would have screamed. Oblivion relieved his torture.

"Your husband is stable Missus Davey" Doctor Felwhumple informed "we must bide a while; however we will constantly monitor his progress and most certainly will keep you informed!"

"But his neck Doctor is it broken?" Moira clutched his arm.

The doctor placed a reassuring hand upon hers.

"There is a slight fracture–it appears to be affecting his control system. We will not know precisely until we X-ray him in a day or so, there er, there is a possibility that he may be permanently incapacitated–we don't know!"

Moira gasped.

"A quadriplegic?" She sat down, shaking her head. "Oh God, no!" The tears welled.

Doctor Felwhumple beckoned the nurse to bring tea as he sat beside Moira.

"Let us not be hasty, the tests are barely begun. I am just pointing out the possibility—we are of the opinion that he is comatose—he could just as quickly snap out of it. Give the patient time!"

"Then there is still hope?" Moira was suddenly alert. "It is not permanent?"

"It is in the balance, we just do not know. I must prepare you for the worst but as I said—time—we must be patient!"

Moira stood up.

"I want to see him—please—take me to him!"

"Of course, follow me."

He led the two down the corridor and into the intensive care ward.

"No hysterics now, his sub-conscious could be active!" The doctor warned.

Moira nodded as she beheld the prone form of her loved one. So still, so deathly pale. To think that tornado of activity had been thus stilled. She gently clasped his limp hand to her breast, kissed it, then again held it to her bosom.

"Oh Peter, Dear Peter, why you; why my man?"

The doctor quietly left, leaving the attendant nurse as John Canders placed a chair for Moira. They sat in silence.

Two days had passed; Moira was in hourly contact with the hospital when she was not sitting at Peter's side. She would have slept in the ward next to him but for her domestic duties—the children had to be looked to—those days seemed to be interminably long. The children, being so young were unable to understand why Daddy did not come home. Had it not been for Missus Canders offering to mind the babies, Moira was sure she would have had a breakdown. On the third day as she made towards the reception desk at the hospital, Doctor Schneider saw her and called.

"Oh! Missus Davey, I have some encouraging news for you!"

"Yes?" Moira urgently questioned.

"Just a moment since we have ruled your husband has full sensual perception—there is a good response to his reflexes—I think we may rule out quadriplegia!"

"Oh, thank God! Is he conscious?"

Doctor Schneider became serious.

"No, he could be weeks or months in a coma—even years. But now we have strong hopes for him, you see, today's X-rays have shown the traction to have been successful. The pressure has been released from the spinal cord and he is accepting the intravenous feeding quite well. Doctor Felwhumple said time—I second that—time will tell!"

Moira could visibly notice an improvement in Peter, his colour had returned. Although she stroked his head constantly and softly kissed his forehead—even whispered encouragement into his ear, Peter lay dormant, unresponsive, and utterly frustratingly immobile. On her way out, Moira sought Doctor Schneider; she had to wait until he finished in surgery. He came out drying his hands.

"Yes Missus Davey, how may I help you?"

"Is there any hope for my husband Doctor? I mean, is it going to be years of waiting—hoping—just watching him lay there. He may as well be dead!" Her lip trembled.

"Come now, do not give up hope. Things are most encouraging, he could snap out of it just like that!" He snapped his fingers.

A week had passed and Moira could no longer keep the eldest child quiet. She was becoming more and more unmanageable with the absence of her father. Moira thought that perhaps if she saw her father sleeping, she would know Daddy was still about and may be satisfied. She took Glenda with her as she was of the opinion that at three and a half, the tiny one would not really be affected by Peter's trauma. Glenda was in awe at the strange surroundings and did not notice her father until Moira put Glenda's hand on him, and said.

"Shh! Daddy is asleep!"

Glenda responded.

"Shh."

As Glenda looked from her father to mother and then back at her father, fascinated by his strange 'hat'. She whispered.

"Dad" then screamed "Daddy!"

Moira cuddled her close, hushing.

"It is all right Dear, Daddy is asleep."

Peter's eyelids flickered and a groan escaped his lips. It was the best he could manage in response to his daughter's frantic cry. He was beginning to regain consciousness. Moira was in tears—her man was going to be all right!

THE END.

Howard Reede-Pelling.

The convoy was fifteen cars long as it wound its happy way through the undulating countryside of Corinella, and then negotiated the main intersection past Dandenong that gave way to Hastings on the left and Dromana–Portsea on the right. The convoy safely over the crossing, the lead vehicle returned to the regulation speed of seventy five kilometres an hour, as it made for the destination of Flinders; another half hour away. Part of the enjoyment of these club outings is the drive through the picturesque countryside. Sometimes hilly timber country and sometimes flat country, but always interesting. At the local rest area of the small township of Flinders, at the Southern tip of Victoria, Australia; the vehicles stopped as prearranged so as to allow any stragglers to catch up and also to let everyone stretch their legs. It would be a half hour stop, so many a camp stove was lit and a warming cup of beverage enjoyed. The many children present attacked the play area as their parents gathered together for a chin-wag. Flinders in the early days was a Mecca for fishermen, now however, as one looks from the high rocky cliffs overlooking the ocean, the fishing boats to be seen were few. Only the odd local and an odd visitor dared to brave the rocky shores and turbulent sea. The area was more a resort away from the bustling metropolis of Melbourne for the wealthy. At the time of departure, the trip leader, Barney Rede called the members of the Table Gem Club together for the first count; noting that two more cars were now in the convoy. They only had another five kilometres to go and it was not long before Barney left his eldest son, Phillip, to open the gate and the seventeen vehicles made their ways over the cow paddock; to the old quarry overlooking the high dangerous cliffs. As the last car was flagged into place and young Phillip alighted, the final instructions were dictated as to the do's and don'ts. They had permission from the farmer to use his property and they also had the blessing of the Shire to fossick on the foreshore, both must be honoured by the club. No shenanigans and all children to be kept in close tow by the respective guardians.

Right, get to it and good hunting! All moved off, taking hammers, chisels, crowbars, buckets, gumboots and shovels. The Gem Club members were seeking zeolites. They had timed their arrival to coincide with the ebb-tide and all were warned in advance at previous meetings, that three o'clock was the dead-line to return, as High tide was at four fifty two precisely. All members were to quit the shore line by three. A happy day was had as the club members dug and gouged at the various venues, depending upon what they were seeking. The shore was strewn with igneous granite and basalt that had fallen from the heights or was embedded in the base of the cliff. Previous fossickers had broken many apart looking for the elusive grand specimen of Chabazite, Gmelinite, Analcite, Natrolite, Chalcedony and even the occasional Clear Quartz Crystal. At the lunch break get-together on the shore, the various finds were shown around and often given to those who were not fortunate to find their own, if perchance one person came across a bonanza and had a surplus. The children were mostly interested in gem seeking but as the adults were invariably using the tools, the children found it awkward to become involved too deeply and were crab hunting under rocks or were playing in the sand. Barney noted that his daughter, Kerry, was usually close by her mum, Phyllis, and young Phillip had his little brother, eight year old Damien and another lad, with him by the sandy inlet some hundred and fifty metres away.

Barney checked his watch—it was time to leave. He went the rounds, notifying all that it was time to go and brought up the rear, struggling under the weight of his tools and the added stress of his loaded bucket of rocky specimens. The climb up the steep hill was bad enough at any time but with the buckets of rocks every one carried, it was a very tiring strenuous affair. All were glad to set the weights down for a breather and refreshments when the parking area was reached. Eunice Linwood approached Barney as he was trying to take a count of the members. "Is my Graeme with your boys Barney?" She asked.

"I don't know Eunice, I will check." He spied his son looking at John Tambart's treasure.

"Phillip, is young Graeme still with you?"

"No Dad, he went with Mister Dooley."

A quick search failed to find either person in the car park area.

"Must be still coming up the cliff Eunice, I will look!"

Barney clambered over the fence and went down the cliff path to get a better view of the track up and the beach. Not a soul in sight, they must still be around the rocky bend past the small inlet.

"Throw the rope over Sonny!" Barney called to her husband. "Just in case—I'll go and chase them up!"

Barney knew they would be in sight by now if they were coming. Much later and the full tide will be in—most likely they have got stranded—cut off by the rising waters! Barney found indeed, the pair had been stranded by the incoming tide. Old Chris Dooley had young Graeme in front of him and was laden with a bucket of tools and samples in hand, which was making their climb over and around the bluff; most difficult. Barney, some seven metres above them, saw they were having trouble surmounting a parapet too high for comfort. He called down.

"Hey Chris, tie the bucket on this rope and slip the tools in the loop!"

Chris acknowledged with a wave, he was too puffed to talk. Barney looped his end of the knotted rope around a projection and held firm, as first the boy, then the old man made the ascent; no trouble with the aid of the rope; then pulled the bucket and tools up.

"What kept you Chris?" Barney asked.

Chris had regained his breath a little and pointed to a beautiful cluster of Chabazite Crystals.

"That there specimen—could not risk rushing to get it out in case it shattered—it was worth the delay, then the water. I could have waded through but young Graeme would have got washed away. If I carried him I would have had to leave my gear, so we had to go by way of the cliff; she's pretty mean!"

Graeme walked back with his parents who had followed, then came the final get-together and showing off of prizes as the social gathering happily recounted their separate exploits. Being trip leader, Barney was last to leave as it was the duty of the Field Trip Officer to see that the area was left neat and tidy and to make sure the gate was properly shut. Seeing that the club had left early because of tidal conditions, there was plenty of time for a leisurely drive home. A good opportunity to browse at the wayside fruit and vegetable stores for fresh fruit and greens, also the odd nursery where Barney had to use a lot of persuasion; to get Phyllis and Kerry away from the gorgeous array of blooms and ferns without it costing him to much. The highly successful field trip came to a happy conclusion as they motored into the driveway of their home, tired but happy. Phillip was first out and as he got the keys to unlock the rear door of his father's panel van to help sort out their goodies, so as to try and commandeer one or two of the better specimens for his own collection, he chirped.

"Hey Dad, where is the next field trip to?"

"Coonawarra Son, down Leongatha way!"

"What's there Dad?"

"Fossils Son—fish!"

"Ooh!" Little Damien gasped. "Are we going fishing?"

His father laughed.

"You could say that Son. Help Phillip with the gear please!"

Inclement weather all but caused the postponement of the trip to Coonwarra when next The Table Gem Club set forth. There was a much smaller turn-up Barney noted as they left the meeting point at the Leongatha Post Office. Only nine vehicles in all braved the rain as they left Melbourne, these were rewarded with the clouds clearing and the sun poking through as they neared their fossicking spot. Coonawarra was a limestone area, at one time, millions of years ago, it was under the sea and there were some spots that had some very nice specimens of Leptolepis Coonwarriensis; a fossil fish. This was the goal of each member of the club, to obtain one or two nice specimens for their collections. A limit was to be placed upon the acquisition of these valuable fossils. The club had obtained permission from the authorities concerned for the day's fossicking; strict guidelines were to be enforced. Warning triangles had to be placed on the roadway either side of their operations, as the deposit was just off the roadway in a cutting. The strata of fossils traversed this road and continued down the hillside and across the railway cutting some hundred metres below. The railway line was halfway up this hill. Down lower in the valley, a small creek trickled merrily through the flat dairy pastures. It was just as well there were so few in attendance on this particular trip, as parking space was scarce. The vehicles all managed to pack into the small flat just off the road but not a great deal of space was available for spreading picnic tables. Those fortunate ones who owned panel vans were lucky, as they could use the open rear flap as a table. Members who owned sedans had to make do in the cabins of those vehicles. A little cramped, but they were used to it; their travels often called for these slight inconveniences.

As each pair of club members took turns at the cramped excavations, Barney took the small fry with him to the railway line. He knew there were only two trains a week on this line, but did not find out just what day and time they could be expected along. The odds were in their favour but he warned the children to all stay close, so he could keep an eye upon them and they would be well within call in case of an emergency. The object of this excursion was to try and locate the other end of the strata, where it crossed the railway line and also to keep the youngsters away from the reasonably busy highway. In all, he had eight children with him, three of which were his own. They successfully negotiated the rocky hillside and made their ways along the deserted railway line, to the spot that Barney imagined the layers of fossils should have passed. However, though he sought diligently and the children scratched about a little, there was no sign of the strata. Possibly it was deeper into the earth; volcanic pressure causing queer disturbances to the Earth's crust millions of years gone by, most likely being the cause. When Barney decided to give up his quest and gather the nippers for a return to the roadway, he found that they had strayed in all directions. His own two boys and young Graeme were already at the creek lower down with two others making their way there. His daughter Kerry was some fifty metres back along the track, still picking at the embankment and the two other girls had continued along the line for a walk. Feeling the girls were safe enough on the railway tracks, Barney walked to the fence and shouted to the boys to return immediately. The two on their way down heard and began to retrace their steps, but the three in the creek were oblivious to his call, evidently the rippling of the creek drowned it out. Then—horror of horrors—in the distance came the shrill whistle of a steam train!

Realizing the boys were safer in the paddock now, Barney hurried back to the line. Kerry greeted him as he got there, she was sent to await the boys at the fence and tell them to stay there. He hastened along the railway line, the girls were not in sight when he rounded the corner to the cutting—but the train was—it was chugging along five hundred metres away.

"Hello Mister Rede!"

It was Kirsty, she and her sister Janine were sitting atop a mound by the end of the cutting—each holding a bunch of wild flowers they had picked—awaiting the train. Barney joined them then bid them climb to the top of the cutting with him so that he could watch the other children around the bend on the other side of the cutting. They were all at the fence eagerly awaiting the coming train; with the exception of young Damien who was still coming. The children had heard the shrill whistle and were racing to witness the rare wonder of a locomotive. As the large iron monster passed, the engine-man noticed the three on the cutting and gave a cheery wave as he set the steam screeching from the whistle, just for the children's benefit. The girls waved back happily. Again the whistle screeched as the fire-man joined his work mate to wave at the other youngsters who were gleefully jumping about and waving back. Phillip tried to race it but fell flat on his face over a tussock. Barney laughed when he saw the boy rise, evidently none-the-worse for his tumble. He gathered the excited children together and they made their ways back to the other members at the excavation. Only one or two very good specimens of the fossil fish were unearthed, however most of the members at least got part of a fish. The difficulty being the very soft lime-stone in which they were to be found, it broke very easily. Every member did get a fine sample of Graptolites, including Grasses, Ferns and Molluscs. The day was still far from over when the excavation was refilled, so it was decided to take the children back through Leongatha and on to Korumburra, to visit the old mine diggings at the small and historic township of Coal Creek. It was a usual feature of the club's activities when on Field Trips, to have an alternative venue in mind just on the off-chance that the original site may be unworkable due to closure or bad weather. Barney normally did his homework well and made sure the day's venue was open and available. But, it was better to be sure.

The small Coal Creek settlement covered only about eight hectares and encompassed a railway station, police station, courthouse, school, coach yard and a 'smithy'. This last was a great attraction to all and most braved the heavy choking smoke of the open 'bellow-operated' forge at which the 'Smithy' toiled; fashioning small souvenir horseshoes for the visitors to keep as mementos. Another attraction was the long winding mine that entered the hillside, travelled under the main road, then circled back to come out at the huge overhead derrick up which all visitors climbed. This was in effect, a look-out tower. A lovely view of the entire historic settlement could be enjoyed, including the lake at the far extremity of the area.

Wild flowers and water lilies were in abundance and the children were not to be restrained when they realized there was a lake to be enjoyed.

"Let's catch a duck!" Phillip said to his brother.

"Yeah, an' a frog!" Damien concurred.

They eagerly set forth followed by the other children. Parents hastened in pursuit, fearing the place may be demolished by over-zealous youngsters. Of course the bird-life on the small lake were quite used to vociferous children and sedately kept just out of reach of grasping fingers, then scurried to safety when small objects were cast at them. The adults soon brought order and serenity to the scene when they arrived belatedly and after a quick look around, it was announced they head for home

One of those crisp mornings that usually herald a fine windless day, found the Rede Family at the meeting point for the next field trip, awaiting the other members of their club. The family had left at eight that morning and a leisurely drive found them at the appointed area by ten. Usually fifteen minutes to half an hour was allowed for stragglers to arrive, because if they were not in convoy, the late comers more often than not were left without the faintest idea where the rest of the club had gone. Some of the fossicking areas were new to the majority of the members and it was club policy to arrive and leave these areas together. Any late-comers would have to fend for themselves and just make an ordinary picnic day of it–missing out on the gem chase. When ample time had elapsed and it was expected all who were coming had turned up, Barney led the convoy away. Club ribbons fluttered from most of the vehicles giving a happy atmosphere as if they were celebrating a football win or some such. In reality, the functions of these ribbons were to identify each vehicle as a fellow member of the club in the event of separation during convoy. There were times, especially when crossing busy highways, that the convoy was broken. On these occasions in normal circumstances, the leaders would wait over the crossing until all had joined them. Of course now and again, an odd car got left and through the agency of the ribbons, was able to recognise the club vehicles when they joined up in the stream of motorists again. The ribbons were especially beneficial in heavy traffic. This day's trip was to a secret rendezvous to add a little excitement to the outing. Barney had deliberately not disclosed the destination, telling members only what tools and equipment they would need. Speculation was rife among the members as normally the meeting gives an indication of the eventual destination, as there are only so many places known to fossickers. This particular meeting place was in the midst of half-a-dozen known areas; so the direction of travel was the only clue to go on. As one known fossicking area after another was by-passed, the club members were becoming more and more excited. Anticipation was high of a new unworked area, and such was the case. Barney had done his homework well on this occasion and as the vehicles were led down a narrow hilly lane with the trees overhead forming an archway, most of his following were agog with wonder. What would they find down this winding path leading deeper into the valley? Finally parking in a small clearing just before a shallow ford, the cars spewed forth their eager occupants, children rushing to the water's edge to skip stones and hunt whatever wild life they could find; watch out frogs and tadpoles! Today was to be a shovel and sieve day—gold panning! Besides gold there were garnets, zircons, occasional quartz crystals and sapphires. These last were very elusive and usually the most sought after but it would not be for the want of trying if none were found.

"Gold Barney?" Betty Mc Kinnon, the club secretary asked.

"Right, the lot and sapphires like you have never seen before!"

Barney had been there months before on a normal family picnic and had—out of curiosity—tested the area on the assumption that gold may be there. He was overjoyed when he saw the spoils in the residue in his pan. A special delight was the three carat uncut sapphire in the top sieve. Two or three more family picnics were enjoyed by the Rede Family before he let the club in on it. Today was the day! As this was a new spot, every member was making the most of it, even the children; a good find now and again would ensure that they would not stray. Strict rules were enforced when all were so far into the dense scrub. No risks would be taken of children becoming lost.

"Yabba-dabba-blankey-doo!" Called a stentorian voice.

All eyes turned to behold the jubilant young president of the club, John Tambert, waving a gold-pan for all to see.

"At least twenty specks of gold and look there—a sapphire; small, but good quality!"

The enthusiastic diggers rushed to look then eagerly returned to their chosen spot to delve in earnest.

"Hey! I have a nugget!"

It was one of the junior members, Cameron Tracy. He was a fourteen year old whose voice was breaking and the deep, then falsetto chirp brought heads around once more. As he lifted, then dropped the nugget, a clear tinkle could be heard from his gold-pan. His excited and flushed face, the epitome of the mood that was rampant in the group. Barney lay back with Phyllis, watching their children and all of the members enjoying themselves; happily grubbing in the gravel creek bed.

"Can't beat a gem club for getting out and about, honey; can you?"

Phyllis squeezed his arm, content to watch and enjoy Barney's company in the lovely atmosphere. Little Damien stood up.

"Come on Dad! Find me some nuggets–come on–please Dad!"

As he dragged his father by the hand, Damien called back. "C'mon Mum!"

Barney shrugged hopelessly at Phyllis. She laughed as she followed them to the creek.

THE END.

H. Reede-Pelling.

WHY?   20/9/78.

Innocent the young
    who roam and run,
laughter rings thru' sunlit days
    and life is bliss,
for Master and Miss
    when youth and beauty plays.

A life to live
    and joys to give,
no fears no worries nor dreads
    should laughter stop,
those young lives drop
    what good are children—dead?

Howard Reede-Pelling.

Part One

Tall and slim, Trenton Lawry smiled at his son Cawley as the youngster peered out the side window of the single engined Cessna. He could see the resemblance to his wife, for the boy took after his mother's side of the family. Leonie was only a pixie compared to the man she vowed to love, honour and obey; as were all her kin and young Cawley had her looks as well as stature. He was not a handsome lad by any means as his Aunt Jacqueline often said, 'Cawley's plain but loveable'. That summed the boy up fairly well. The two months since Leonie quietly passed away in the intensive care unit of the local hospital, with terminal cancer, had been a horrific blow to both of them. As an adult, Trenton could understand, he had been prepared for it–but Cawley–poor little Cawley, such a thing as mother going to sleep never to awake again, not to be there when he needed her; was inconceivable to the six year old. There were many tears, they had both cried, the wife and mother was still gone; their tears could not bring her back! Cawley needed a mother-image desperately now, so Trenton knew Aunt Jacqueline was the only logical choice. They were flying there in the Cessna Trenton almost lived in–his business plane. As a broker of some note, he was in constant demand and preferred personally to check the stocks and holdings with which he dealt, so it was good business and more, a necessity; to have a quite independent means of transport. His office was in Brisbane but Leonie's sister Jacqueline lived in Perth, three thousand six hundred kilometres away; they were halfway there. Trenton had re-fuelled at Coober-Pedy and now they were well out over the Great Victoria Desert near the Lake Maurice area. Next stop would be Kalgoorlie some one thousand two hundred kilometres away. Cawley took his gaze from the window and said.

"Not much trees down there Daddy, why not?"

The blonde curls bounced and his pale blue eyes sparkled as the boy awaited an answer.

"That is a desert down there Love, very little rain falls so the trees all die of thirst; only the strong ones can live there because it is so hot."

The snub nose was pressed to the window again for a minute then.

"Daddy."

"Yes Love?"

"Can people live down there with no water to drink?"

Cawley was wide-eyed with wonder as his father explained.

"Oh yes, people can live there, but not without water. They have to take cans of water with them, the white people anyway!"

As he digested this information Cawley was again silent, peering down at the desolate unending landscape.

"Is there other sorts of people down there Daddy?"

He mumbled into the window, still watching below.

"Yes, dark people, they have black skin and are natives of Australia; they are called Aborigines. They know where to find water where white folk like you and Dad would never think to look!"

"I would not like to live down there, there are no shops."

"No Son, no shops and very few houses. The houses that are there are called 'Stations', not like railway stations, they are called cattle stations and there are lots and lots of cattle. Those stations are usually nearer to the mountains though, where there is more water and grass–

??"

Trenton's conversation was cut short as the shock of a large bird tearing through the airscrew stalled the engine and the blood-splattered carcase of an eagle bounced off the windscreen, leaving a blood-smeared feathery mess to be quickly wind washed across the front and side of the cockpit making visibility most difficult.

"What happened Daddy?"

"It is all right Love, just a bird hit us, are your straps done up tight?"

Trenton wrestled with the controls trying to restart the motor. As it sluggishly revved, the whole aircraft shuddered. Through the fuzzy screen, Trenton saw that one blade of the airscrew was severely bent, he would have to land; try to glide in to a firm spot and hope the blade could be straightened. He cursed the bird. It must have been huge to stall the engine like that; most likely it came from Mount Woodruffe about two hundred kilometres north. That was a mountain some eighteen hundred metres high, the bird must have been an eagle from there. Trenton was not unduly worried, there were emergency rations as per regulations aboard and it would take only a short while to straighten the prop', he could make proper repairs and check the aircraft when they got to Kalgoorlie. The trouble was, to be able to judge a hard landing surface through the fuzzy windscreen! Trenton was engaged in the operation of his radio as he thought these things and at the same time pored over his flight programme.

"Mayday–mayday–mayday. Victor–hotel–foxtrot–tango lira, do you read me, come in–over?"

Only crackling static was heard. Trenton continued to try and raise someone, surely there would be at least a pedal-operated two-way out here somewhere? He tried again.

"Mayday–mayday–mayday. Latitude twenty eight degrees fifteen minutes South by one-thirty zero–do you read–over?"

Still just static, the urgent need now was to land safely, he would continue the broadcast when they were down. Trenton peered out of the small clear section of a side window, was that a good enough clearing there? It seemed sound enough even though there were scrubby salt bushes and occasional boulders, he was sure the gravely looking ground was solid enough to take them. Trenton circled the selected area gauging the proposed runway as best he could in the difficult circumstances. If he came in from the West into the slight northerly that was blowing (he could tell by the waving leaves of the saltbush) and aimed at that cluster of scrubby trees to guide him; they should be right. There was no second chance, the small plane had by this time lost too much height; it was do or die–this was it! The aircraft made a perfect touchdown and Trenton was surprised at how solid the surface was, it must be a salt-pan they were on but that clump of trees was coming up too quickly. Cawley was too small to see past the engine even if the windscreen was clear. The boy had made similar landings many times with his father, he had no worries. Trenton saw the danger too late to try to avoid it; the boulder struck the aircraft directly below the cabin, forcing the steering column up into the pilot's chin. The vicious snap as his neck broke was lost in the grating rumble as the small plane slewed around backwards and spun over sideways to plough, upside down amid the copse of scrub. The grind of twisted metal and shattering of glass a holocaust of noise as the salty sand spewed up in a choking billowing cloud that gently settled on the wreckage as the piercing shrieks of a terrified six year old echoed across the desert.

The screams were still raging as the last vestige of dust found a resting place. Luckily for the child, the wreckage did not catch fire. The static could no longer be heard but the transmit light was glowing on the set—Cawley's screams were being broadcast. Intermittently the screams ceased and became snivelling sobs; the youngster was upside-down in his harness. He managed to take his weight by holding the straps and unclipped himself. The outflung hands of his father caught his attention, the eyes were staring vacantly.

"Daddy!" Frantically screamed the bewildered orphan.

An hour of agony had passed for the child. Repeated efforts to wake Dad had failed, outside the sun beat mercilessly down upon the arid, parched desert. The breeze that had been, was no more. Quiet reigned as the youngster fell into a frustrated, exhausted sleep over the body of his father; arms encircled the waist as far as they could. Cawley had tried to unhook Daddy so he could sleep more comfortably—Daddy should not sleep upside-down like that—but Dad weighed too heavily into the straps, so Cawley fell asleep. The boy woke with a start, was that Daddy waking? Flies were crawling on Daddy's face where the blood was congealed about his mouth—BLOOD?

"Daddy, Daddy!"

The screams came again as Cawley savagely beat his little fists at the flies. Daddy did not move. Cawley would get some water and wash Daddy's face, which would wake him! No, he knew it would not, something was wrong with Daddy, Cawley would wash him anyway; he stepped out of the wreckage—then froze! Ten paces away, peering at him out of eyeless masks, were four huge black giants with long pointed sticks and another half a dozen smaller ones peeping from behind them. All were making funny noises with their mouths. Cawley screamed and turned back to hide behind the body of his father, shouting.

"Daddy—Daddy, oh ple-e-ease Daddy!"

A black face peered into the cabin. Cawley stopped screaming and just whimpered—shivering in fright. The blonde curls and wide pale eyes stood out starkly in the shaded corner as the long black arm reached over towards the boy. Cawley stared at the frowning sunken eyes hardly discernable in the dark features, he cringed into the corner. Suddenly—like a ray of sunshine—the large lips parted to show gleaming white teeth as the aborigine gave an encouraging friendly smile and beckoned with a limp hand.

"Come boy—gibbit han'." He beckoned again.

The blonde curls flickered as Cawley slowly shook his head. The aborigine reached over and firmly grasped the small arm, easing Cawley out; the youngster shrieked and dug his fingers into the blood-stained jacket of his father, hanging on grimly. The fingers were gently pried loose and the lad carried screaming out and passed to a black lady who wore a grubby blue and white polka dot dress. She sat and cuddled him into her bosom as she crooned an eerie song. The sobbing and struggling ceased, Cawley slept.

All was quiet when Cawley woke, he could see the curved roof above but it was not at all familiar. His own room had a high pale blue ceiling with a glittering chandelier of prisms that let rainbow colours dance merrily upon the walls when the sun shone in each morning. This was a very low dark ceiling. It was not the roof of Daddy's Cessna.

"Daddy!" The boy screamed as he sat upright, looking around.

He was in a bark humpy but he did not know what it was, the lady in the spotted dress rushed in to him; a plastic cup in her hand. She knelt beside him stroking his curls.

"Drink!" She put the cup to his lips.

Cawley turned away, struggling to get up.

"I want my Daddy!" He demanded.

The woman set the cup down and pulled the boy onto her lap.

"Daddy he die—go walkabout in dreamtime—no more here!"

'Daddy die' the words brought back memories of his mother. Daddy said to him when he asked why he could not go and visit Mummy. 'Mummy died Love, she went to sleep and she will not wake up any more'. They both cried a lot when Cawley finally comprehended what it meant—no more Mummy! Now this big black lady said 'Daddy he die'! Cawley knew it—deep down he knew it—when Daddy just hung there upside down and he would not wake up. Then there was the blood and that odd look on Daddy's face. Cawley whimpered again as the black lady nursed him and offered the plastic cup once more. He took a few sips, and then gulped as he realized how thirsty he was. As he drank he became more aware of the cup—Daddy's cup! All around him were Daddy's things, even his jacket. The boxes of supplies that he saw Daddy put into the luggage compartment of the Cessna was there and his own little case; now open and half empty. Even bits of Daddy's Cessna were strewn about. Cawley wanted to cry but he was sick of crying, it did not bring Mummy back and he knew it would not bring Daddy back. He struggled out of the woman's clutch—she smelt funny—not nice or perfumy like Auntie Jacquie. Cawley stood at the entrance of the humpy, taking in his surroundings. It was all strange, the Cessna nowhere about even though bits of it were everywhere. There was a long skid mark leading across the ground from a long way out and stopping by the engine cowling beside the humpy. Cawley did not know he was dragged there asleep in it with a lot of the paraphernalia from the wreck.

Three children shyly watched him from the shadow of a tree under which they were sitting. They looked familiar somehow but they were black, he knew he never met black people before. How could he know them, yet he was sure he had seen that shirt before. Cawley used to have a tee-shirt like that, exactly the same in fact—it was the same—that was HIS shirt! Cawley remembered the open case, he walked over to the three; they stood up as he neared. One was a boy of about eight, another was a girl of his own age and the one wearing his shirt was a ten year old girl. She was too big for it but that did not seem to worry her, Cawley realized that they all had his clothing on one way or another. He grabbed the shirt and tried to pull it off.

"It's my shirt!" He glowered.

The girl pushed him to the ground. Cawley got up and punched at her, again trying to get the shirt; she slapped his face. Tears welled but he did not cry out. The lady in the blue dress rescued him, jabbering at the girl, who turned away sulkily. The angry boy was made to sit by the humpy and the lady rummaged in his case, extracting a golliwog that his mother had sent him for a present. She threw it at him. Cawley hugged it and just sat brooding, the lady sat beside him. All seemed to be waiting for something.

"I'm hungry." Cawley demanded.

"Eat soon!" The woman rose and began stirring some ashes into a fire.

The raised excited voices of the children caused young Cawley to look up. An aircraft that had excited them was droning in from low on the horizon to the east. Instantly the woman sprang into action, jabbering at the children; she beckoned Cawley.

"Come!"

All of the wreckage from his father's Cessna were hurriedly pushed under the scrub and the sandy soil thrown over, then bits of bark, scrub, grass—whatever was at hand put on top to hide all traces of the salvage. Cawley was unceremoniously bundled into the humpy and a woman sat guard at one end while the ten year old girl secured the other. Cawley must be kept out of sight; his blonde curls would be a beacon to an aircraft. The dark people had much to hide; they would not risk losing the wealth they had suddenly acquired.

The twin engined Avro was passing at four hundred metres, two kilometres away it made a tight circle and re-checked the humpy, then disappeared in the west. The aboriginal children pointed to the south and then ran off excitedly in that direction. Cawley poked his face out to see what held their interest and cringed back into the humpy as he beheld three ferocious-looking black men carrying a wallaby and some bits of tree roots. They were horrible giants to the small white boy, even the three teenagers appeared ferocious. One was a girl of eighteen, it was she who had the roots and some leaves. The other teenagers were boys, one about thirteen and the other sixteen. Both were dragging dead tree branches. When the party set their various burdens down, the womenfolk began preparing the meat and roots while the children broke branches and piled the pieces near the fire. Cawley noted that each of the men wore some part of Daddy's clothing, the big man with the black beard took Trenton's corduroy trousers off and disgustedly flung them into the humpy—they were too hot. Cawley whimpered as he stared at them, Daddy never left his clothing like that, he would fold them and put them away. As the boy eyed the things that belonged to the Lawry Family, a tear trickled down his cheek. No Mummy and now no Daddy—what was to become of him? Cawley felt very alone—lonely and lost. His whimpering was ignored as the butchering went on, it was only women and children doing the work, the menfolk had provided, the women prepared. Cawley was aware of the men walking towards him—laughing at some hidden joke—he cringed back into the shadows of the humpy. The men sat outside the humpy and spoke in their own tongue, one produced a pipe and they took turns in puffing at it; the acrid smoke caused Cawley to sneeze. Bulgowra, the same man who took him from the Cessna, flashed his great toothy grin as he reached back and dragged the boy out into the late afternoon sunshine. Bulgowra let his fingers brush through the soft fair curls that scintillated as the golden rays caressed them. Cawley's head was unceremoniously jerked around as the great black hand firmly gripped his chin and turned the face so Bulgowra could study his eyes. Two pale blue orbs fearfully watched the black blood-shot ones inquisitively studying him. The raw sun and dry desert winds were turning the tender light skin pink and Cawley's eyes appeared switched on to the aborigines, who possibly had never before seen such a combination. The boy was the subject of much talk and as the men laughed amongst themselves, Cawley was pushed out towards the cook fires and the women and the children. Great sections of the butchered wallaby were set on the red embers, constantly being turned. Another fire had an old pot that Cawley thought may have come from his Aunt Jacquie's house, although how they got it from there; he did not know. At a word from the lady in the blue dress, all sat around the fire to eat. The menfolk ate great juicy hunks of the meat hacked off with a flint knife, the small children were given pieces of bark into which was scraped an evil-looking stew from the pot. Cawley eyed the sticky mess dubiously and looked about as if expecting the dog to come up and eat it; this family had no dogs. The other children were scooping the stew into their mouths with great relish, Cawley sat wide-eyed watching them.

"Eat!" The lady pushed the bark receptacle closer as she spoke.

Fear prompted the boy to dip his fingers in and lick them.

"Yuk!" His face screwed up at the unfamiliar taste, he dribbled and spat it out.

Bulgowra jabbered at his lubra, gesticulating at the meat and then at Cawley. A bone with burned meat was stuck into his mouth, it tasted good so the boy took it out and began nibbling; then ate with enjoyment—he was starving. The bark plate was taken and emptied into the pot.

For two days the family stayed at the same spot until all the meat was disposed of, at times the men went away taking the teenagers with them. They always returned at the same time of day and each with something—be it water bearing roots or lizards—but always with leaves and some wood for the fires. The nights were very cold in the desert. During this time many aircraft passed overhead and as each approached, all visible evidence of Trenton and his belongings (including Cawley) were hidden. On the third day they broke camp and all the goods were stacked on anything that could be dragged along, then the party set forth. The men at the head carried only their armaments and the women and children dragging or carrying stores and equipment. Cawley was given a woman's bonnet to wear (goodness only knows where it came from) as they became aware his light skin was in danger of breaking out, it had already started and the boy was plagued by the evil-smelling mess they rubbed into his face, hands and feet. His shoes had been taken from him but returned when it became obvious that he would have to be carried, if his feet suffered any more from the sun and the hot sand. A further burden given him was the bundle of sticks he was made to carry. Twice they gave him the bundle and twice he threw it down, each time he was given a smart whack. The third time the bundle was offered, he carried it; albeit sulkily. Cawley was a handful to them, a real set-back. The majority of nomadic aborigines are a skinny long-legged people and they do tend to walk with long strides, Cawley was only six and small at that. He had great difficulty keeping up with the family unladen but with his bundle of sticks, the boy constantly lagged. His existence had been a torment and invariably nightmares disturbed his sleep with agonising visions of his parents fading away. The diet he was forced to nibble was not like the dinners Daddy's house-keeper Maudie set for him and the lack of his daily milk, in fact any great amount of liquid for that matter; was dehydrating him. The boy was ailing, becoming weaker and the torture of his sunburn; unbearable. As far as the eye could see in any direction, was a flat desolate country with occasional billabongs, remnants of the flood-times and very dry now. The party were moving south-east and it was in this direction that the only alteration to the skyline was discernable. A low lying range of hills that undulated at first, then peaked at two hundred metres was gradually getting bigger as they headed for it. They were just a purple haze in the distance. All except Cawley were atop a small dune awaiting him.

"Come." Demanded the Lubra, waving him on. Cawley stopped, exhausted.

"Come!" She again demanded, this time shouting angrily.

The child dropped his bundle and screamed.

"Daddy–Daddy–Daddy!" Then fell in a sobbing heap.

The Lubra went to him, roughly jerked him erect, and then pushed the bundle at him again. He dropped it and sat down; she slapped his face leaving a white mark on the burned surface. Still the boy sat there, eyes glistening up at her reproachfully; he lay on his arms on the hot ground. It became obvious to the woman that she had a very sick child on her hands; she ignored the bundle and carried the youngster up to the others who were waiting. After many words were exchanged, the loads were rearranged and a travois made from whatever was at hand, including the bundle of sticks that were dropped. The eighteen year old and her mother secured their combined load to the travois and between them, dragged it along with the sick boy covered from the merciless sun by a bag 'Howdah'. It was the fifth day since Trenton and Cawley Lawry had crashed and the youngster was dying of dehydration, malnutrition and exposure, when the party came in sight of their destination. All day they had travelled through thickening areas of saltbush and mulga where wild-eyed cattle roamed. The low hills were clearly visible now and the homestead for which they were heading but a matter of three or four kilometres away. A conference was held and it was decided to just leave the child at the door for fear of having the white man know they had looted the Cessna.

Part Two

The sun had barely set in the west as the wall clock in the lounge room at 'Jenkarrie' chimed nine. Summer evenings were always long in this flat arid land. Jack Kandriffe turned from his paper-strewn desk and peered over the top of his reading glasses at Marjorie, his plump energetic wife.

"Them kids all bedded down Love?"

Marjorie continued darning as she answered.

"All except Steve, he is in the bunkhouse with Jeff and Doughboy!"

They sat in silence a while, she studiously darning the never-ending holed socks her menfolk continually piled into the mending basket and he shuffling through papers. A heavy object rattled across the tin roof.

"Goodness Jack! What was that?" Marjorie stopped darning.

"Prob'ly them damned Abo's again—I'll see!"

Marjorie was peering through the curtains of the darkened back room, when Jack slammed the front door shut and entered the lounge, carrying a bundle.

"Strewth Love, where are ya? You'll never guess what I've got!!"

Marjorie hurried in behind him, he turned and she beheld the pitiful limp armful, eyes sunken; face festered and smelling of a pigsty.

"What on earth—oh Jack—is it dead?"

"No! I can feel it breathing—hurry woman—lay a blanket down somewhere!"

"In the back room, the spare bed!"

She ran ahead switching on lights as she went and had a clean sheet across the bedcover by the time he reached her. Marjorie was left attending the patient and Jack shouted from the back door.

"Jeff—Doughboy—Steve, come here—on the double!"

The bunkhouse door opened and spewed forth three figures, two tall and slim, and the other dumpy. The queries on their faces went unanswered.

"Mount up quickly, take spotlights and scour the vicinity for visitors. Someone called without coming in–get to it–go!"

As Jack went to assist where possible with the sick child, he could hear the riders start out on the night's quest.

"What's wrong with her Love, is she bad?"

Marjorie had taken the filthy clothes off and was gently dabbing and bathing the still form in tepid water reinforced with disinfectant.

"I don't know dear. Looks like exposure and dehydration– and–she is a boy. I think you had better radio Kalgoorlie and get the doctor to fly out, Jack!" He hurried to the transmitter.

'Jenkarrie' boasted its own power supply and generated enough voltage to dispense with the old pedal-radio, which had served them so well in the past. A pair of sleepy-eyed children dressed in pyjamas and dressing gowns appeared at the doorway. Colin, a wiry haired boy of twelve, pushed past his ten year old sister, Madge to make his statement.

"I heard horses Ma, what's going on?"

"And someone threw a stone on the roof, it woke us!" Madge added her rosy freckled cheeks pushed between Colin and the door jamb.

Their mother did not look up and snapped.

"Back to bed both of you, immediately. You will find out all about it in the morning. Go on–scoot!"

The children grumbled but obeyed. Her full attention was needed by this unfortunate little lad–his life may depend upon it and Marjorie had no mind to be distracted by inquisitive youngsters. Her husband returned from the transmitter in the den.

"Doctor Johnstone was not available Dear, he has not returned from his last call but the operator said he will leave at first light tomorrow–how is the boy?"

Marjorie shook her head as she frowned a reply.

"He is not good Jack, terrible sun and wind burns. I've bathed him all over but I will have to get a dab of antiseptic on these sores dear, will you get it for me?"

Jack returned quickly with the first-aid kit.

"Gently turn him over while I do the back of his neck and behind his knees."

107

As they worked on the boy, he feebly croaked.

"Daddy—please Daddy!"

"It's all right son, Daddy will be here soon."

Jack laid the boy's head back on the pillow and the pale blue eyes flickered open—squinted—then shut again.

"The lights too bright, put the lamp on Jack!"

When it was done and the boy again opened his eyes, they were astounded at the level unflinching gaze, almost accusing.

"Keep a damp cloth on his forehead Jack, he looks a bit feverish. I'll make some broth!" Marjorie hurried out and the portagas stove was lit and pots and pans began rattling. The blue eyes were moving about, taking in the details before them; then returned and stared at Jack. He smiled reassuringly.

"What is your name son; can you say your name?"

"I want my Daddy!" Jack gently dabbed at the glistening forehead.

"Daddy will be along soon—soon as we can find him."

Tears ran down the now blotched face.

"That's it son, you have a good cry, everything will be fine now; we will get you back to Daddy. Will you tell me your name?"

A very imperceptible nod was followed by a croak of "Cawley."

Marjorie came back with a bowl and spoon.

"Let me sit there Jack and I will feed him!"

"Gee, that was quick Marge, how did you manage it?"

"Drained the stew that was left for the pigs tomorrow and mixed some beef extract into it, didn't want it too hot!"

Jack gently lifted the boy into a sitting position and braced him with a couple of pillows, as Marjorie softly placed her apron over the boy in case the broth dripped. It was slow feeding, Cawley had difficulty in swallowing but his eagerness proved how hungry the lad was; Marjory only gave him half.

"That's enough for now Love, feeling better?"

The eyes keenly followed the bowl as it was placed upon the bedside table; again a slight nod was evident.

"More in a minute Love let that settle first."

Marjorie fluffed the pillows and settled Cawley down again, then folded the sheet back to cover him, making sure it was loose enough not to weigh too heavily on the tender sun burns. It was a warm night but as his body was slightly damp due to the sponging, she did not wish the sick child to catch a chill. The horses came cantering back to the house and the three men crowded into the kitchen. Jack shushed them with a finger to his lips and explained about the boy. They looked through the door at the dozing lad, and then Jack closed it so they could talk without disturbing Marjorie and her patient. He then fastened his attention on the three hands to hear what they had found–if at all there was anything to be found.

Jeff Clarkson, the tall stringy young jackeroo was explaining how he finally caught up with the family of aborigines and extracted the details from them.

"–and it appears–" he continued "–that they saw the 'plane crash when they were on a 'walkabout'. Said they are headed for Maralinga where a brother lives, an' they tried to help but th' kid's Dad was dead. They reckon they buried him under a cairn beside th' wreck. Won't know if they did 'til someone gets out there to check. They were worried we might think they were responsible for th' boy dyin', that's why they nicked off without knockin'; knew we could tend the boy better!"

"It's the boy from the Cessna that went missing, isn't it Dad?" Jack's eighteen year old son queried.

"Yes Steve, I reckon it's him all right–poor kid. Only six and lost both parents. He is a sick boy–Doc' is coming tomorrow–so you lot better keep the noise down for a bit; okay?"

"Won't die will he Jack?" The normally happy plump features of Johnny Duffy (affectionately nick-named 'doughboy') were now wrinkled with concern as he made the query.

"Don't know Doughboy, he is badly burned, suffering from malnutrition and exposure. Marge reckons he is dehydrated and I think he is a little feverish too. Going to be touch and go if the fever hits him properly. I hope the doctor gets here early tomorrow!"

The three young men left to unsaddle and tend their horses before they settled themselves with a hot drink and retired for the night. Marjorie was reheating the broth when her husband returned and explained the circumstances that led to Cawley being left with them.

"Jeff got a rough idea where the plane crashed, so I better get on the set again and tell the authorities; how is the boy Love?"

"Just dozing, I don't think he really knows what is happening. I think he has been through too much and he is far too young to cope with it—poor mite—I'll give him another go at the broth then see if I can woo him to sleep. I will have to sleep with him tonight Jack, think you can manage without me dear?" Marge gave him a worried smile.

"Well, it is going to be damned hard" he smiled and kissed her "but it is a worthy cause Love; I will manage!"

Jack gave her a gentle squeeze and kissed her again before going back to his den and the transmitter. He had some important news for many people and was keen to get the burden over and done.

It was an eager household that awaited the prognosis from the doctor who had flown in just after nine the next morning. He had been in with the patient for twenty minutes and that time was used by Detective Inspector Vance Hoolihan, who came with the doctor, to make inquiries. His back-up helicopter would arrive later to take on the search for the body of Trenton Lawry and the wreckage. Satisfied that he had gleaned all the information he needed from the adults, he decided to question the child at a later date. The doctor said it would be detrimental to the sick child to be reminded of his father and the trauma through which he had miraculously survived. So far at least. The Station owner came from the house and addressed the gathering.

"The boy should be all right—" happy mumblings and light cheers greeted the opening remark "—but he is a very sick lad. Doctor Johnstone said he should be hospitalised but the trip could be too exacting, so we will nurse him here. Nothing so serious he can't be tended here but if the fever gets any worse, the doctor will send a Nursing Sister to live-in. He is going to leave the anti-biotics we will need and assures me the boy will live. Now off your rumps, there is work to be done!"

Jeff, Steve and Doughboy wandered off to the stables. Jack Kandriffe fastened a stern eye on his children.

"Come on, off to the classroom, you have studying to do!"

"Aw gee Dad! Can't we wait for the helicopter to come?" Colin whined. "Do we have to study this morning?"

"No you can't wait and yes you have to study this morning. Get to your books, you can come out when it arrives; off you go. Madge, Clare, hurry along!"

"All right Daddy, I'm coming."

Little eight years old Clare haughtily cocked her head at her father and hurried past as he pretended to smack her tail. Shortly after the doctor flew out, the police helicopter arrived. When refreshments were enjoyed, Inspector Hoolihan climbed aboard with the pilot and two passengers. One was the inspector's assistant and the other man represented the Aircraft Safety Board and would be looking for possible causes of the mishap. When peace and quiet reigned at 'Jenkarrie Station' again, Jack sat on the end of Cawley's bed and softly spoke with Marjorie.

"Well Love, you've certainly got a handful with him and all of us think you will manage?"

She squeezed his hand, taking her gaze off the resting child to look at her husband.

"Of course Jack Dear, with the mob I've got do you think one more will make any difference—I am going to love it?"

Jacqueline Prentiss collapsed into deep shock at the news that Trenton and Cawley Lawry were missing, presumed dead in the vast wilderness of the Victoria Desert; only two months after her sister in law had passed away with terminal cancer. They were a marvellous family unit, loving, hard working; everything ahead of them augured well for a rosy future. Then dear Leonie began getting pains, only a year after Cawley was born. Dear little Cawly, how she loved her nephew. Jacqueline made frequent trips to Brisbane when Leonie had become stricken with cancer but could not stay for very long periods; she had a family of her own to attend. Soon, when Leonie was permanently hospitalised, Trenton had to engage a housekeeper–nanny for little Cawley, as business pressure kept the young father away overnight quite often. Maudie was like manna from heaven to the worried father and his load was eased so he could spend more time with Leonie in her last agonising months. Jacqueline was thrilled and eagerly looking forwards to their arrival after Trenton had asked if she could mind young Cawley for a spell. Trenton needed a break to rethink his future and Cawley needed a mother-image. Then this horrific news that they were missing enroute, presumed dead. DEAD! Poor little Cawley–dead! Jacqueline had collapsed and was slowly recovering in the Perth General Hospital. Being aware of family circumstances, it was with relief that Inspector Hoolihan welcomed the doctor's decision and the Kandriffe's enthusiasm, to have the youngster attended at 'Jenkarrie'.

Three days had passed since Cawley was found a limp, lifeless looking bundle; however constant care and the medication administered by Marjorie Kandriffe under Doctor Johnstone's daily supervision via the transmitter, had wrought wonders. Cawley was able to sit easily and often friskily jumped about. The fever beaten and the effects of his exposure fading fast. The boy was still fairly weak as a result of the dehydration but that too, was becoming a thing of the past. All at 'Jenkarrie' were quite intrigued by the sparkling pale blue eyes and the shock of almost white curls. Cawley was the favourite of all–especially the children. They spent all of their available time with him and upon many occasions had to be forcibly removed for fear of over-exciting the recuperating youngster. It was a great day when Marjorie announced the boy was ready to go out and play on the wide veranda encircling the house. The children were released from their studies to act as nurse-maids and make sure that Cawley did not wander out into the fierce sun again; he was not yet ready to tackle that. Came the day when Cawley was to get out and about in earnest and the eldest son of 'Jenkarrie' Station was given the responsibility. Steve was taking the lad on short rides around the home paddocks on one of Jack's thoroughbreds. Cawley, dressed in some of Colin's hand-me-downs and wearing a wide brimmed felt hat stuffed with wads of paper to make it fit, was all agog with excitement as he sat in front of Steve; held there by the strong arms and with a firm grip on the loose ends of the split reins.

"Giddyup!" He giggled. "Giddyup horsey!"

Steve heeled the stallion ahead gently. Jack put his arm around the waist of his plump wife and squeezed her to him.

"You did a marvellous job Love—just look at him. Fit as a desert lizard and full of life, we're going to miss him Love!"

"Oh!" Marjorie turned a distraught face to her man. "I was hoping the day would never come—I—I—know it is sinful but I do hope his Aunt hasn't got over her illness yet. No! I didn't mean that, do you—do you think she might like to stay here for a week or two; you know—to recuperate?"

Jack smiled as he kissed his Marge.

"We will try awful hard to convince her—eh?"

Word came all too soon that indeed Aunt Jacqueline Prentiss was on her way, she was expected with Doctor Johnstone for the noon meal the next day. The doctor would make the final check on the lad and then the boy would be free to go back to Perth with his Aunt—or whatever. Cawly was so happy these past few days. He had friends to play with, nice food to eat, and a beautiful big horse to ride with 'his Stevie' and very soon Aunt Jacquie would be coming for him. It was almost time for lunch and everyone was excited. They could hear the doctor's plane in the distance, the throng were gathering to greet it as Cawley thought of his nice 'horsey'. He would have one more pat of it before Aunty took him away. Cawley escaped unnoticed and made his way to the stall where he knew the stallion was kept in readiness for the afternoon's work. Cawley could barely reach the latch but by standing on an upturned bucket, managed to slip the catch. The flighty thoroughbred snorted fearfully at the unfamiliar fumbling and swung around to retreat to the far extreme of the box.

Cawley had the door half open when the stallion's rump hit it, slamming the hard wood against the tender head. The small body sprawled across the bucket as bright red rivulets stained through those near-white curls. The sparkle no longer shone from his pale blue eyes. Cawley was dead!

THE END

Howard Reede-Pelling.

Alternate ending
Cawley

Continued . . . .

Cawley had the door half open when the stallion's rump hit it, slamming the door shut which in turn threw the youngster to the floor. Cawley was unhurt and struggled to his feet as Steve entered the stables, seeking the boy. Steve lifted Cawley aloft and coaxed the stallion across so that the lad could pat him goodbye.

Cawley was reunited with his Aunt Jacqueline amid promises of returning to visit their new-found friends. The pale blue eyes beneath that mop of unruly near-white curls, smiled a 'thank you' to the Kandriffe Family as the happy, healthy child waved farewell!

THE END.

Howard Reede-Pelling.

There were eight of them; bare to the waist except for the floppy wide-brimmed hats they wore to protect those hard grim faces from the fierce blaze of the merciless noonday sun. Sweat streaked bodies burned brown, almost black by exposure to the elements glistened at each movement, attesting the rigors of an outdoor life on the fencing line. Bradley eyed the gang cautiously, gauging his reception as he allowed his magnificent sorrel to pick its way at a slow walk through the paraphernalia, untidily scattered around the camp. Each ganger watched the slow approach but it was the tall Ramrod with the pugilistic face, who stood and gave an almost imperceptible nod as he drawled.

"G'day."

"'Afternoon." Bradley returned the greeting with a nod of his own and taking in the gathering with appraising eyes.

"How's the chances of a cuppa?"

The Ramrod tilted his head in the general direction of the cooking utensils. Bradley ground hitched Chester as he dismounted and selected a cup from the rack by the lean-to.

"Name's Miles. Bradley Miles, been ridin' most of the morning since sun-up!"

The Ramrod nodded as if he knew all along.

"We're about to have lunch—rabbit stoo—'nough for ya, grab a plate!"

"Thanks mate, that's big of you." Bradley gulped his drink. "I will unsaddle Chester and join you!"

He led his mount to the shade of a clump of eucalypts near the water-hole by which the men were camped, unsaddled and gave the animal a quick curry-combing as it drank, then washed and returned to the gang. It was evident he had been the subject of conversation while he tended Chester, for the talking stilled as he returned.

"I'm Steve." The Ramrod stated and introduced the others.

"Ben, Jack, Gino, Wally, Grubber, Pete an' that overfed hog there is Graham Purdin but he prefers you call him 'pudden'; he's our cook! What brings you out this way Brad?"

"Mission of mercy actually, I'm Jackaroo for old 'Whitey' Allison of 'Bendenning Station' over Kantangurra way. I'm going to Binnalonga to bring his Grandchildren back for the school holidays. I'll stay overnight and return tomorrow."

Pudden slopped a ladle-full of stew onto a plate and shoved it under Bradley's nose.

"Stinks pretty, eh? Grab a fork."

Conversation lagged as the men wolfed into their meal. It was good and stemmed the gnawing in Bradley's stomach. He had been thinking seriously of stopping at the next water to rest his horse and open a tin of beans, when he came upon the camp. Pudden's stew sure was a lot better than the beans and he brought a smug smile to the cook's face when he told Pudden so.

Grubber was a nuggetty man, by far the smallest of the fencing gang but as they would agree, had enough brass to make up for them all.

"Fine animal you got there Friend!" He addressed Bradley as he wiped a hairy forearm across his mouth. "Breed him yourself?"

Bradley was justly proud of Chester and enjoyed showing him off.

"No, but I did break him, got plenty of spirit that one, if a stranger gets too near he may nibble a leg off; so watch him!"

The cook began to clean up and the men set about their fencing again, leaving Bradley to finish the plate of stew at his leisure.

"Might see you on the way back Brad." Steve shouted as he hefted a coil of fencing wire onto his broad shoulder.

"Sure, thanks for the cuppa!"

Bradley handed the plate he was using to the cook and saddled his mount. As he sat the saddle before moving out, Pudden ambled over.

"Say Brad."

"Yeah?"

"That Grubber—if you're coming back—be careful of him!"

"Why?"

"Well, he's—er—he's itching to get away and reckons he ain't gonna wait for the supply truck. Just watch he don't nick

117

off with your sorrel when you return. He is a rough joker an' been causin' blues, just thought I'd warn ya!"

"Thanks Pudden, I'll keep it in mind. Need anything I can bring back?"

Pudden stroked his chin thoughtfully.

"Well, a bit a' baccy wouldn't go astray!"

"You're on. See you tomorrow!"

Bradley gave Grubber a close scrutiny as he acknowledged their goodbyes, better to know possible enemies well so as to thwart them. Perhaps nothing would come of it but he would keep a close watch on the nuggetty little man just in case, presuming of course, that he passed this way. After all, he would have the safety of the children to consider on the return journey.

Wendy and Tom Corby welcomed Bradley at the milking sheds; for it was there that he came across them after finding the house deserted. The school bus had not yet arrived with the children and Bradley made good progress after leaving the fencing gang.

"Just in time to give us a hand with the milking Bradley!" Tom grinned.

"No worries, I've done nothing all day!"

Wendy said.

"Tell you what Bradley. You help Tom and I will stable Chester and prepare a scrumptious dinner for us; how's that?"

She nimbly sprung into the saddle and trotted up to the stables.

"You know Tom." Bradley mused. "Wendy is the only one who can ride Chester besides me. She has a spell on that sorrel, I am sure of it."

The milking was halfway over when the school bus arrived and two noisy youngsters raced each other to the milking sheds. Country bred, they knew better than to storm in on the milking, so their last fifty metres was traversed with respect for the cattle.

"Uncle Bradley, you are here already?" Freddie exclaimed, clapping his hands. "Where's Chester?"

"Typical." Tom stated. "Not–'how are you Uncle Bradley'–all he is interested in is your horse."

"Aw gee Dad!" Freddie kicked his toes in the dirt. "Uncle Brad's got the best horse in the world, I wasn't really being disrespectful!"

"Well you are now. It is Uncle Bradley–not Brad!"

"Sorry Uncle Bradley."

"Not to worry young fellow. Chester is in the stables but you had better wait until I am with you before you go and visit him. Okay?"

"Yes Sir."

"May I visit too?" Justine eagerly asked.

"After you help Mum with the dinner Justine, you both had better put your work clothes on–now scoot!" Tom demanded, and then added. "Come back and help with the milking Freddie!"

The children raced off, excited about the coming holidays with their grandparents but equally excited about being allowed to ride all the way there on horseback. True to her words, Wendy put on a marvellous spread and no one was in a hurry to move after dinner.

"What time do we leave in the morning Uncle Bradley?" Justine asked.

"At sun-up Justine, we have a lo-ong way to go; don't we Uncle Bradley?"

Freddie's eager face beamed across the table as he answered her question.

"Wrong you know!" His mother stated. "You will have a good breakfast before you leave and a solid one at that isn't that so Bradley?"

"That is for sure and with a bit of luck we will even have a cut lunch for the noon meal?"

He looked inquiringly at Wendy.

"All under control." She said. "The meat is already sliced; I only have to put the things together in the morning. I made a cake this afternoon too, so you won't starve."

"Are we going to camp overnight Uncle Bradley?"

Freddie knew the answer but thought he would ask anyway, one never knows and it does not hurt to ask.

"You are not." His father sternly answered. "There will be ample time to get to Grandpa's place before dark. Grandpa is expecting you for the evening meal, so no shenanigans!"

"Yes Dad." Freddie turned to Bradley again. "Will you take us to see Chester now please?"

"Goodness!" Wendy exclaimed. "You will be with Chester all day tomorrow!"

"But we want to see him now; we haven't seen him for ages Mummy." Justine argued.

Bradley arose from the table.

"Come on then, I'll introduce you again so he will remember you tomorrow."

Bradley complimented Wendy on the lovely dinner as he and Tom left the room, amid the noisy clamour of two energetic youngsters. Chester whinnied a welcome as he watched his master enter the stall to pat his neck.

"Come on old son, there are a couple of admirers for you to renew a friendship with; now you be gentle!"

Bradley beckoned the children over, they came with wide grins.

"Do you think we could ride Chester Uncle Bradley?"

Her bright eyes sparkled as Justine asked the question.

"Maybe tomorrow just after we saddle up you may have a short ride around the saddling paddock. I don't want him too upset as we have a long ride ahead of us and we mustn't waste time playing."

Chester snorted and tossed his head sedately as Freddie ran his fingers through the deep honey-coloured mane.

"What a terrific colour he is Uncle Bradley!" Freddie breathed wistfully. "Gee! I wish he was mine, bet you wouldn't sell him to Dad, would you?"

Bradley ruffled the boy's hair.

"Money would not buy him, mate. A man gets attached to a good horse, they become pals, you would not expect to sell a pal; would you?"

"No, I suppose not. I bet if he was mine, we would be good pals!"

Bradley ushered the two out and all three returned to the house.

"I am going to have a sorrel like Chester when I begin to earn money Dad!"

Freddie stated as he ran to tell his parents all the finer points of the stallion. "Me too!" Justine chipped in.

"You are already earning money Son, when you help Mum and me around the farm; you are earning part of it. When we get on in years all this will belong to you and Justine, then you will be able to get whatever animals you need to run the farm properly. Everyone has to earn their place in the world, so it depends how much effort you put in to it, to determine what gains you make for yourself!"

Justine was all agog with interest.

"Does that mean we could each have a horse like Chester Daddy?"

"Exactly Love, the more you help the more you gain."

"Gee! I am going to work real hard around the farm now, well, after the holidays anyhow." Freddie's last statement caused the adults to grin understandingly.

"That is enough gas-bagging for now you two." Wendy interposed. "Off to your rooms and gather your gear for tomorrow. Don't pack more than you need, you have to travel light remember, only one pack-horse. We need the other for ploughing and don't forget to shower!" She called as they raced each other to their rooms.

Early next morning before breakfast and while Tom and Wendy were milking, Bradley (true to his word) let the children canter around the saddling paddock on Chester. Their beaming faces attested the pleasure they derived from riding the big sorrel. At first he attempted to dislodge Freddie but Bradley soothed the stallion before letting the boy take full rein and Chester understood that while his master was present, he had better behave. The mantel clock had just chimed eight as Tom and Wendy bade safe journey to the three riders, as they set forth with old Barney the grey plough horse, acting as pack animal. Barney was such a wise staid old fellow, that he would willingly stand unperturbed while children danced on his broad back; as it had happened many times.

"Now you two behave well for Uncle Bradley and remember your manners at Grandpa's!"

Tom put his arm around Wendy's waist and squeezed her to him as she warned her brood.

The ponies the children rode were dwarfed by the big sorrel but were well bred and broken, they would give little trouble, if any. Both children had been riding since they were quite young and were very accomplished equestrians. Both had won placing's on their mounts at the annual show at Binnalonga and their ribbons were proudly displayed in their respective rooms. As the dairy-farm disappeared from view when the trio began the ascent of the hills beyond the far paddocks, Justine murmured.

"'Bye Mummy and Daddy, hello Gramps and Grandma!"

"Gee it is going to be fun Uncle Bradley; maybe we can ride Chester every day while we are there?" Freddie looked inquiringly at his guardian.

"No! He will get spoiled, maybe once a week if you are well behaved."

The hills over which they travelled were usually heavily timbered but the cattle and wild animal tracks were abundant, so there was no difficulty for the four horses to traverse them with comparative ease. When down to the flats, the urge to canter was strong but common sense prevailed as old Barney was only a plodder these days. However, Bradley let the youngsters canter ahead at times to particular objects he would pick out. Usually a large tree that stood at the end of a straight stretch of pasture. It was slow travelling inasmuch as they were obliged to use gates every time they came to fences, again because of old Barney. Fortunately, as they lived in the remote outback of Australia, there were not many fences. It was half an hour before noon when they came in sight of the fence upon which the fencing gang were working. The cook-fire had first been spotted by the keen eyes of Freddie. Bradley was in two minds whether to call over and talk to the gang again. The cook's warning about Grubber gave him cause for thought. He was still undecided when Freddie tipped the scales by asking would they be calling on them. The children had never seen a fencing gang in operation before, and didn't Uncle Bradley think it would be educational for them to witness how they go about it?

Bradley knew if Grubber got obstreperous, he could handle the man, but he did not want any trouble to be witnessed by the children. Surely there would be no trouble; after all, they would only be in the camp for ten minutes. He decided to take the risk because he did promise the cook some tobacco and he had it with him to deliver. The fencers were about to down tools as the travellers came upon the outmost pair. It was Steve and Wally, they decided the new arrivals were a good enough excuse to knock off for lunch, so they finished straining the wire upon which they were working and tied it off. A barrage of questions by the children were tolerated and answered, usually by Wally. He had children of similar ages to Freddie and Janine. Steve appeared a little gruff and annoyed; Bradley felt a slight tension with him. The fencers walked back with the riders plodding beside them. As they made their way to the camp, the throng grew as others strung out along the line, joined in, giving the usual curt nod of acknowledgement to the newcomers. Wally seemed to enjoy having the fresh faces of the children about and walked between the two ponies the better to answer their questions. Bradley hoped they were not being too cheeky or annoying as he tried to strike up a conversation with Steve.

"How's the fence coming Steve, keeping to schedule?" He asked.

"Hmmpf!" Steve snorted. "Was, laggin' a bit now with the damn arguments!"

Bradley thought it wise not probe dangerous ground and declined pushing the subject.

"Stayin' for lunch?" Steve suddenly blurted.

"Yes, thanks Steve but we brought our own. Just a cuppa will be fine."

When Steve was getting drinks for the children off the cook, Bradley asked Wally in an undertone.

"Been a bit of trouble?"

"Yeah, that blasted Grubber has been stirrin' th' pot, caused a fight and shied off last night—went afoot. He is a bad 'un, watch out for him Bradley!"

Having stayed a little longer than he anticipated, Bradley gave the cook the tobacco as he promised and the trio thanked their hosts and left. The country through which they were riding was reasonably open, although occasionally there were heavily timbered stretches and one such section was ahead of them now. Bradley worried as he noticed the rain clouds were beginning to build up, it would not be good to get caught without adequate shelter and pondered as to the possibility of erecting a small canvas lean-to that was strapped on the pack-horse. Rather than have the children drenched he would ride a storm out under cover–over-night–if need be. With an eye to the weather, Bradley urged his charges on a little more quickly. In the range of low hills yet an hour's ride away, there was an abandoned mine shaft boring into the rocky bowels of the earth. It would make a very cosy retreat for all, including the horses; if indeed the heavens opened up. As the party made their way through the dense scrubby timber, Bradley cautioned the two keen youngsters about the danger of riding into outflung branches. The ponies knew they could trot under but may not take into account the height of their riders. It was not a branch that was the cause of the mishap. Bradley always had the children ride ahead on the open plains, giving them direction on which way to go and he brought up the rear with the pack-horse. In this manner he was able to keep an eye on the entire entourage. In the timbered country, he deemed it best to lead the way and so select the safest route. The children may wander off course if they had the lead through the scrub.

Freddie as ever, being an independent person, was wont to wander off the path made by the other three animals and make his own way through the foliage. He had been cautioned once but impishly, when Bradley was intent on seeking the easiest path, would sneak around the odd patch of bushes or couple of trees.

A distant rumble of thunder hid the slight gasp as the boy had the breath knocked out of him, by a piece of fencing wire strung between two trees, just high enough for a pony to pass under. The boy was winded again as he fell flat on his back on the thick carpet of wild grasses. Grubber, for it was he who tied the wire, quickly grabbed the pony's bridle and clasped a hand over it's nostril to stop it snorting which would cause the others to look and thwart him. With great haste he mounted and reined the pony away to the left, to be soon lost to sight in the dense underbrush. It was but a matter of seconds for the boy to regain his breath and shout.

"Uncle Bradley–HELP!"

Bradley was glancing back trying to locate Freddie when he heard the anguished call; he left Justine with the pack-horse and galloped back. Freddie was just on his feet holding his stomach as Bradley angrily admonished.

"Serves you right, I told you to follow me and watch out for branches!"

"It wasn't a branch Uncle Bradley, a man pinched Roy-boy. He went that way. Quickly please, get him back!"

Bradley then noticed the fencing wire and told Freddie to go to Justine and wait until he returned. He galloped off in the direction indicated by Freddie, having ascertained that the boy was not seriously injured. The muscles bunched beneath the glossy coat of the great sorrel as the two sped after the cheeky horse thief. Bradley was fuming at the audacity of the fencer for putting the child's safety at risk. It was most fortunate the wire had not taken the boy across the throat; it could have broken his neck! As Bradley burst through the last clump of trees and brush, he caught sight of his quarry flogging the stolen pony mercilessly. Gradually but surely the big sorrel gained on them, although stout of heart the pony was no match for the stronger thoroughbred stallion. As Bradley neared he wasted no time in useless talk but knocked Grubber out of the saddle with a well aimed fist behind the ear. The man fell and Bradley grasped the pony's reins, pulling the heaving animal to a stop, then tied the horses together and dismounted. Grubber was on his feet rubbing one ear and with murder in his eyes, rushed at Bradley. Bradley stood his ground and waited—let the fool run himself out of puff—it will be a pleasure slapping him to the ground for what he did to Freddie. The strength of the smaller man was surprising; he barely flinched as Bradley drove a straight right to his chin. Grubber bored in with a flurry of punches that left Bradley gasping as they pummelled his stomach. The taller man stepped back, then as his opponent paused for a breather, lunged in with a rally of his own. Another straight right quickly followed by a short sharp left rip to the body, a stinging right upper-cut that lifted Grubber off his feet, then a final straight left which put the disillusioned thief flat on his back and semi-conscious. Bradley had a drink from the water-bag on Chester's saddle and rode back to the children. Grubber would have to fend for himself and Bradley did not care if he was nearly dead or not, it would serve him right. One thing the tall Jackeroo knew, they would not be worried by Grubber again in a hurry, and perhaps he had learned his lesson. By the time Bradley reached the children, it was evident by the darkening sky and claps of thunder sounding ever nearer, that the trio were going to be caught in a solid downpour if they lingered. Having assured himself that Freddie had no more than a bruised stomach wrong with him, Bradley led the children at a brisk pace in an endeavour to reach the mine shaft before the storm broke. The object lesson of the taut wire put Freddie in his place but Bradley drove the point home by chastising the boy for not following instructions. Freddie's timid.

"Yes Sir!" Was enough guarantee he would not stray again.

The abandoned mine was found well before the rain or the preceding gusty wind that drove the storm along, so Bradley had time enough to check the entrance for safety and leave the children to gather enough dry leaves and wood for a warming fire, in the event the storm lingered. Having made a torch of brush and reeds, they tethered the animals and explored the length of the diggings. The tunnel was driven straight into the side of the hill for seventy five metres. There were two off-shoot branches at right angles, left and right, one of these had an air vent through which the overcast sky could be seen. It was in this off-shoot that they built their fire, the horses were left outside. They would be brought in to shelter at the last minute. Satisfied there were no deep pits in the floor of the mine, Bradley went about the business of boiling the billy, using water from the saddle canteens. The rain began to fall, so the animals were brought in under shelter. They were backed in, it was awkward getting past the string of horses as they stamped and snorted uncertainly in the unfamiliar tunnel. As the storm broke in earnest they settled down more, no doubt realizing they were better off under cover. The storm lasted two hours, during which time the children dozed in front of the warm fire. Bradley covered them with a blanket off the pack-horse; it was intended for use on their picnic lunch.

With sodden country to traverse after the storm, their arrival at Bendenning was extremely late. The concerned Grandparents welcomed the children with much ado.

"We were not really worried Bradley, knowing you were in control but when you were not here for dinner and with that terrible storm, we wondered if you found shelter or not—oh! It is nice to see the children again, hurry and tend the horses while I hot up a meal for you."

Betty Allison fawned over Freddie and Janine as her husband 'Whitey' added, with a firm hand on the boy's shoulder.

"Nice to have you young 'uns with us, we'll get in a good bit of riding together; eh Freddie boy?"

"Sure will Gramps!"

Two days later, Bradley was riding boundary when he met the fencer's truck on its return trip having delivered supplies. Steve, the ramrod and Wally his ganger, were in it with the driver.

"G'day Bradley!" Wally greeted, when the driver stopped so they could chat. "Got back safely I see, how are the nippers did they enjoy the ride?"

"Sure did. We had a run-in with Grubber though!"

"Ah!" Steve exclaimed. "So that is how he got belted—John here—" he indicated the driver, who nodded and Bradley acknowledged "reckons Grubber turned up in town all beat up, came in on a wild brumby he must have managed to catch. I'm glad he got a thumping—been a thorn in my side for weeks—we're on our way to town now for a replacement. Better go, see you next time!"

They motored off. Bradley continued with his work and looked back later as pounding hooves heralded the arrival of Freddie and Janine with their Grandfather.

"How is it going Bradley?" Whitey asked.

"Real good Boss, now that you have brought out the new hands to help, I could do with some assistance."

Janine smiled and Freddie reined in beside Bradley, his face the epitome of importance.

"We are doing real man's work now, aren't we Uncle Bradley?"

"You sure are Pal, won't be long now before you are doing it on your own place, riding your own sorrel, just like Chester!"

THE END.

13   Michele   7/11/78

Lush green grasses cushioned the tiny body as it rolled down the hillside of the still, clear dam. Bronwyn and Lisa shrieked with laughter as they beheld their seven year old sister subside in a chuckling heap as she came to a stop and lay there, trying to get her bearings. It was the umpteenth time Michele had either rolled or been pushed down the grassy slope and had her mother been present, a stop would have been put to the merry frolicking long ago. The flushed face was beginning to pale and her clear blue eyes were just a little too bright, the girl was becoming over-excited. Twelve year old Bronwyn, the eldest of the three girls was made to be responsible for her younger sisters. As she reached Michele, Lisa, the ten year old tom-boy of the family, fell on top of Bronwyn and they became one merry jostling heap. Bronwyn brushed her long auburn hair away from her eyes and noting the pale features of Michelle, called a stop.

"We had better get back to the house." She said. "Mummy will be wondering where we are!"

"Oh, no she won't let's give Shelley another roll!" Lisa urged.

"I don't want to 'cause I'm awful giddy." Michelle complained.

Ignoring Lisa's wish, Bronwyn started towards the house, shouting.

"Come on—I'll race you—last one there is a donkey."

Lisa, ever alert, was off like a flash after her, golden tresses flying but Michelle, not yet recovered, stamped her foot angrily.

"I don't want to race—wait for me!"

Her words were lost in the slight breeze blowing away from the other two, who were well on their way. A common reaction by little girls left behind by elder sisters, is to sit and fret or bawl their heads off; Michelle did neither. As the elder girls reached the house and looked back, they beheld the little one nonchalantly skipping along in their wake, not at all put out, for she was a happy little soul who had learned to plod along behind; as she was forever being left by Bronwyn and Lisa. Elizabeth Berkley was on the verge of chastising the girls for playing too long at rolling the baby of the family down the slope. She had made for the door for that express purpose, when the children began racing towards her. She awaited them at the edge of the veranda, her happy face belying the concern that she held earlier.

"Did you enjoy yourselves?" Elizabeth asked, as the children ran to her.

"Yes Mummy it was fun. Are we going riding today?"

Bronwyn's question was muffled as she wrapped both arms around her mother and snuggled close.

"Please Mummy!" Lisa begged, as she too, cuddled her mother.

"I thought you wanted to make cakes with me today?" Elizabeth stated in mock surprise.

"Oh, we do Mummy but couldn't we do that another day when it is all rainy and wet? It's such a gorgeous day for riding today and I bet 'Snowy' would love it too!"

The now serious face of Bronwyn strained towards her mother, seeking confirmation.

"Please Mummy?" Lisa added her five cents worth.

"I think Daddy and Jack are too busy to saddle up and ride with you today and I do have a lot of cooking to do—I will have to make the cakes and prepare tea all on my own if you girls don't help!"

Elizabeth brushed the pair of bobbing heads and picked off bits of grass as she spoke.

"We could ride all right without Daddy and Jack Mummy, truly. Anyhow, I can saddle Snowy myself; we can manage on our own. Please Mummy, just around the lagoon paddock!" Michelle, arriving just in time to hear her sister's last remark, stated firmly.

"I am coming to the 'goon paddock too—aren't I Mummy?"

"There will be no going to the lagoon paddock on or off the horses or ponies unless one of us is with you. Now get cleaned up girls, we will see what your father has to say about riding during lunch. Scoot!"

Elizabeth clanged the triangle hanging from the veranda. It was a soft sound but could be heard quite distinctly for a great distance in the still, clear country air. The menfolk out in the fields would hear it and return for lunch very soon. Bruce

Berkeley was a stringy man, bronzed by continuous exposure to the elements. Wavy brown shoulder length hair held in place by a plaited cord head-band, Navajo style and a slightly prominent nose and jaw, gave him an indian appearance. Bronwyn and Lisa took after their father, inasmuch that they too, had similar hair colouring and brown eyes. Michelle on the other hand, was a replica of her mother, Elizabeth. Fair hair and blue eyes—but the little one was very much Daddy's girl—she was his 'angel'. Bruce was pondering the question put to him by the three eager children.

"Well yes, it is a good day to go riding, and yes, the ponies could do with a run; however you know Mum would like some help in the kitchen and Jack and I are very busy in the back paddocks with the stumps. We do not have the time to watch that you girls don't do anything foolish, plus the fact that the 'dozer may make the ponies skittish; especially when it is straining. Perhaps tomorrow, you help Mum today."

Their father had spoken, the three youngsters remained silent. Each glum face dejectedly staring at the unfinished sandwiches sitting upon plates in front of them. Elizabeth weakened, her babies looked so despondent, and Michelle's normally happy features now an almost sullen scowl.

"You know dear." She addressed Bruce. "I really don't need help with the cooking; perhaps I can manage on my own."

Her blue eyes flashed a knowing signal to her husband, he stroked his chin thoughtfully. Three suddenly interested faces glanced at him in anticipation, hope arising.

"We are very busy Love, that's why I have left Jack out there and told him I'd bring some tucker out. We must get the grubbing done today, there's shearing all next week!"

Elizabeth considered that information before she suggested.

"Do you think you could forgo cakes tonight dear? Perhaps I could ride with them—just this once!"

Three sets of bright eyes in eager faces had been looking from one parent to the other as each spoke in turn, reminiscent of spectators at a tennis court; anticipation building while the fate of the afternoon's activities was being bandied.

"Could be a good idea Love, you have been cooped up in the house too long altogether. Would do you good to get out for a breather!" Bruce drummed his fingers on the table-cloth thoughtfully. "I suppose Jack won't mind waiting an extra ten minutes for his lunch while I saddle you up!"

Amid a happy chorus of 'thank you Mummy and Daddy', Bruce and Elizabeth were inundated with a shower of hugs and kisses from three delighted little girls. Lunch over and the kitchen spotless in record time, the four ladies of the house retired to their respective quarters to don riding habits. Resplendent, they arrived in nice time at the stables to find their horse and ponies already saddled.

"Thank you Dear that is sweet of you!"

Elizabeth gave her man a peck on the cheek. He fastened a stern eye upon his daughters.

"Do as your mother tells you and no galloping off on your own, do you hear me?"

"Yes Daddy!" The three again chorused.

"Better keep away from the 'Dozer and the lagoon paddock Love take the bush track over to Benson's Flats but watch the pits in the hills going there—have a good day Love!"

Elizabeth rode 'Skipper' a spirited stallion. He was actually her husband's mount but because Bruce was using the four wheel drive, Elizabeth was to give the bay a run. Her own little mare Topsy still had a tender hoof from a sharp stone which lacerated the frog. The children trailed along behind on the easy track away from the house, and Elizabeth thought it best to lead the way, as Skipper seemed a little toey and was inclined to play up for the first ten minutes. Lisa, on Pepper, a dapple grey, and Michelle on Patches, a lovely pinto, were walking their ponies' side-by-side. Bronwyn bringing up the rear astride Snowy, a pure white show pony. Bronwyn had won ribbons at the local county fair on Snowy and under her father's guidance, was destined to become a champion equestrienne. The track to Benson's Flats was straight for a kilometre where it reached the heavily timbered hills. This was a short low range, extensively mined and the bush track meandered haphazardly up and over, past the old ore crusher and then on to Benson's Flats. There it came to an end by a picnic spot at the sandy inlet on the Big River. The steep incline which was the beginning of the climb through timbered country, soon put an end to Skipper's prancing and the four travelled two abreast as they made their ways leisurely along. Now that the bay was more settled, Elizabeth allowed Bronwyn and Lisa to lead while she paired with young Michelle. At fifteen hands, the bay was a huge mount in comparison to the nine hands of Patches. The sturdy little animal had to trot at four paces to one of the long-legged stallion. The quartet dismounted at the ore crusher for a sticky-beak and to nose through the mullock heaps. Elizabeth thought it would be educational for the girls. They had been there before but there was always another interesting something they would come across and ask questions about. Elizabeth did not profess to be a text-book on mining but could answer most of their queries. Having poked about in the ore crusher and scratched about the diggings long enough, Elizabeth announced it was time to go, if at all they wanted to gallop across Benson's Flats.

"Come on girls, mount up!" She called.

Lisa and Bronwyn needed no second bidding and were well mounted before their mother. Elizabeth glanced about for her youngest.

"Where is Michelle?" She asked, and then shouted.

"Michelle, do not dawdle, we are leaving—where are you?"

A frown creased her forehead as she became concerned.

"Where is your sister, wasn't she just beside you two?"

The girls were already looking about for her. Lisa answered.

"Shelley was just with me a minute ago Mummy. We were looking down that shaft over there by the old tin shed." Lisa pointed to the area in question.

"Oh no!" Elizabeth gasped, dismounting quickly. "You two stay put!"

She ran to the pit indicated. With a terrible fear taking over her whole being, Elizabeth grasped an over-hanging sapling and peered into the deep hole, calling urgently as she did so. "Michelle, can you hear me dear? Where are you—Michelle, answer me—you had better not be hiding from us!"

The pit was empty; at least it did not confine the body of her daughter as she feared it may. Why doesn't Michelle answer? She was normally very obedient and knew better than to disobey. Surely she would not keep the prank up this long; where on earth could she be?

"Michelle!" Elizabeth almost screamed. There was still no answer.

"Where can she be Mummy, should we help you look for her?"

It was Bronwyn, the voice quavered in frightened anticipation. They all realized something was amiss; Michelle was not a practical joker that was Lisa's department.

"Yes girls, dismount and have a look around but do not go near the pits, I will check them out. You look through the crusher and the bushes. Watch out for snakes and don't go too far. Oh dear me, where is that girl?"

Fifteen minutes of fruitless searching failed to find any trace of the missing child. It was now obvious that Michelle had indeed fallen into one of the many mine-holes abounding in the area. Fear of her youngest lying critically injured or worse—dead—at the bottom of a mine-shaft, had tears coursing down the mother's cheeks as she bade Bronwyn and Lisa ride like fury and get their father.

"Hurry but be careful girls and return to the house to wait for us when you have told your father!"

While the girls galloped post-haste, Elizabeth continued her search relentlessly.

"Oh please God, where is my baby?"

She prayed, returning again and again to holes she had already strained to see into, hopelessly, doggedly seeking some tell-tale evidence of her daughter's where-abouts. Elizabeth breathed a sigh of relief as she heard the frantic churning of a four wheel drive vehicle apparently racing at break-neck speed over the rough gravel track. It burst into the clearing and skidded to a stop amid a choking cloud of dust. Bruce fairly fell out and took his wife into his arms, asking.

"Have you found her?"

Elizabeth shook her head, tears bespattering her husband as she explained where Michele had last been seen. Jack arrived with rope and torches from the vehicle. Together the three stood around the shaft, torches lighting the bottom. Debris, old branches, rusted tin cans and rocks; but no Michelle. The search continued, radiating from that pit and those in the immediate vicinity, and then spreading out until most had been discounted. It was not until they returned to the first pit that Jack exclaimed.

"Hey!"

All eyes sought the cause of his exclamation. He was pointing to an indentation amongst the many scattered about. It was an imprint of a man's gumboot. None of the party was wearing gumboots. The girls were wearing riding boots with fairly high heels to lock into the stirrups and the two men were shod in heavy leather boots. It was definitely the ripple tread of a gumboot; as further proof the maker's name was boldly indented into the dampness of a puddle near which the imprint was found.

"Someone else has been here recently!" Bruce stated, his voice strained. "Looks like a man-sized footprint—I wonder—?"

"Not a large man Bruce." Jack mumbled as he studied the ground minutely. "I reckon it is only a small fellow, or maybe a youth!"

"Oh!" Elizabeth gasped tears very evident. "Do you think someone has taken Michelle? Surely they couldn't, we would have seen them about. It—it's not true—is it Bruce?"

Her face appealed as she grasped her man's arm. He patted her hand reassuringly.

"I would not think so, Love. Probably just an old footprint made weeks ago. Michelle has just taken a wrong track and got lost. Come; let us look further a field. You go over that way through the scrub to the road; we will branch out on this side."

The men waited until Elizabeth was on her way before they exchanged concerned glances and scouted around for more gum boot tracks. If possible they would back-track. Each held grave fears for the safety of the seven year old girl but did not want to transmit their fears to the mother. Jack it was who found the next print and it was just five metres from the first but was on softer ground away from the packed gravel of the pit-heads. They followed the now easy-to-see tracks which they had not noticed before, as they were seeking a little girl then.

Proof that Michelle had also gone that way, came when Bruce found her riding cap. Now it was obvious—Michelle had been kidnapped. While Bronwyn, Lisa and their mother were busy studying the crusher mullock heaps, Michelle, independent as usual, had strayed slightly to the remains of an old tin shed. When in its heyday, the shed was used to house tools and explosives used in the mining operations. She was picking up coloured rocks from near the back corner of it, when a hand was clamped over her mouth and she was bodily hoisted up and out of sight of her mother and sisters behind the concealing shed. Michelle tried to scream but the hand was firm over her mouth and the struggles were in vain, against the greater strength of the person who held her. She was quickly carried away through the thick scrub, the shed always between them and the others who were now beginning to call her name.

Again the youngster vainly attempted to wriggle out of the tight grip and scream. It was useless and Michelle was panic-stricken, more so when she heard the strange laughter and mumblings issuing from the throat of her captor.

"Hee-hee, I did it—I've got her—she's mine. Har-har, I showed 'em—clever me. Hee-hee-heee—I've got a playmate—har-har har!"

It was the ravings of an irrational mind but the little girl did not know that yet. All she knew was that someone was taking her away from mummy and her sisters and Michelle did not want to go! Her continual struggling annoyed her captor, he slapped her leg. "Stop it!" He chastised. Michelle was now convulsing with sobs she was unable to release and began choking. Her captor removed his hand from her face, as he knelt behind a thick bush and stood the girl before him.

"Please don't cry playmate."

He soothed as he put his arms around Michelle and hugged her close, rocking as a mother would to lull a baby.

"I won't hurt you—true. I just want a friend to play with!"

Michelle got her first look at the stranger who dared to take her from mummy, as she drew in gasps of air. He was

136

a youth of about sixteen or seventeen but to the small girl he was a man. His mongoloid features frightened the child and now that her mouth was freed, she would have screamed anyway. The girl had just taken a deep breath and screwed her face up to let forth the biggest scream she could muster, when the youth again clamped a damp hand over her face; effectively stifling it. This time he looked into her eyes as he pleaded.

"Don't yell playmate, 'cause then I'll have to slap you—I want to be friends!"

Michelle kicked at him. His face reddened and his eyes blazed as he shook her unmercifully, the scream she would have voiced became a muffled ur-ur-ur-ur as the fair head bobbed about willy-nilly. The youth stopped shaking her and held a threatening hand aloft, ready to strike if she should again try to scream. Michelle glared at him but did not attempt to voice another protest. The tears just trickled down her cheeks.

"Hee-hee-hee."

The youth giggled. He wiped away her tears with a forefinger, then taking the little girl by the hand, hurried away deeper into the scrub. Michelle sniffing as her little legs travelled two to his one over the rotted leaves and twigs. It was perhaps only ten minutes after the youth had stolen Michelle but to the girl, it seemed ages before they came to the ruins of an old building. There was no roof and not quite three walls were still standing. Fallen bricks and broken bottles were strewn about but behind the walls there was a little privacy and shelter from the slight breeze. The mid-afternoon sun smiled down on the peaceful area as the youth sat with his back to the wall and studied his prize. Michelle, between sniffles, eyed him reproachfully in turn. He was short and solid of build, unruly straw-coloured hair that stuck out straight in places, gave him a scare-crow appearance. His denim trousers were stuffed into what appeared to be brand new gum boots and a tattered shirt that was not fully tucked in, was stained with dirt and food.

"Want to play horsy? I'm a good horsy, hee-hee-hee-har— giddyup!"

He yelled as he suddenly jumped up and galloped around the startled little girl. Michelle was becoming giddy just watching him circle around her, slapping his side. He just as suddenly said. "Whoa!" And sat down again.

"Why don't you ride the horsy?" He asked a huge grin evident as he cocked his head to one side. "Ha ha! I'm a very good horsy, don't you think?"

"I want to go back to Mummy, my Mummy will smack you!" Michelle firmly stated.

"Yes, mummy." The youth said, vacantly staring past the girl; then suddenly was beside the girl on hands and knees.

"Ride the horsy first, come on, mount up!"

Michelle shook her head and stood firm. The youth raised a hand, eyes blazing again.

"I'll smack you—mount up!"

Michelle clambered on to his back, softly sobbing. The youth took off on all fours around the ruins and then out onto the grass, the youngster hanging on to his shirt collar. The tears stopped to be replaced by an odd giggle, which slowly increased until the little girl had forgotten her fears in the ecstasy of this new experience that was a lot of fun. The youth fell over, exhausted. Michelle tumbled to the soft grass but she was used to that and quickly hopped astride the heaving back of the prone youth, laughing and gasping at the same time.

"More, I want more, giddyup horsy—giddyup!" She hammered her heels into his ribs.

He lay there ignoring her.

"Giddyup horsy, I want another ride!"

Michelle slapped her hand against his rump and the youth struggled to all fours and took off again. This time the ride did not last a long and they both sat against the wall to catch their breaths.

"Aren't I a good horsy?" The youth grinned idiotically awaiting her praise.

Michelle nodded, still remembering the thrill of the ride.

"Can I go home now? I have played with you!"

"Thirsty." The imbecile answered. "I want a drink!"

He left Michelle and hurried down to the Big River which was but a hundred metres away. Michelle, also very thirsty, trailed behind.

The old ruins were situated a kilometre away from the sandy beach at the end of Benson's Flats. The pair were on a slight rise well hidden by the thick vegetation. When they had quenched their thirst, the two walked back hand-in-hand. Michelle was no longer afraid of the youth, her small mind realized he was not as other people and she sensed he was to be pitied. On the other hand, she also knew he was unpredictable and may turn on her threateningly if she went against his wishes. She knew it was best not to rock the boat. When they reached the ruins, Michelle again asked.

"Can I go home now? I will get into most awful trouble!"

"I need you to have fun with." The youth giggled to her. "We can stay here and play forever!"

Bruce and Jack followed the trail of the gum-boots as far as they could. Neither man was an expert tracker and they had done well to follow the trail so far, now however, they were stumped. The two men had branched out again and again but could not pick up the tracks. They hurried on in the direction they were led by the signs of their quarry but could not be sure whoever it was who had abducted Michelle, had gone straight ahead or not. He may have veered off one way or the other, may even have thrown the girl down one of the many shafts that riddled the area; heaven forbid! Their calls remained unanswered, so Bruce thought it best to return to the crusher for his vehicle and hurry home to organise a search party. As the duo retraced their steps, Elizabeth could be heard calling for them. They raced back expectantly—perhaps Michelle had been found! The first thing Bruce and Jack noticed as they approached the crusher was a land rover. They recognized it as belonging to Lance Gibney, a cattleman and neighbour. He was in earnest conversation with Elizabeth, who hurried to her husband as she saw them emerge from the scrub.

"Oh Bruce! Lance thinks Michelle is with his nephew—he—he is a little retarded. Oh dear, I don't know what to think about it. Do you think he would harm a little girl?"

Bruce held his wife close as he tried to calm her.

"Now let us not panic Dear. We'll get her back safe!"

Lance was now beside them explaining.

"I am sorry Bruce; I did not think Gerald would have the opportunity to do anything like this out here. My sister-in-law wanted a break from him for a bit, so I brought him out to the farm. Didn't think he could possibly get into any trouble out here, he usually plays around old Benson's ruins—didn't expect he would come up here. I was just looking for him when I ran into Elizabeth and she told me young Michelle went missing. I reckon we will find them both at the ruins!"

"Then you think it is definitely Gerald who has her?"

Bruce asked, greatly concerned of course but feeling a little easier in his mind. Visions of the little thing at the bottom of a pit now disappearing.

"Oh sure! He will have her all right but I do not think he will harm her though!" Lance hastened to add. "Gerald is always looking for little kids to play with; he only has the mind of an eight year old. We better not waste any time just the same—he switches on and off a bit—unpredictable, you know?"

The two vehicles sped down the overgrown track to the turn-off that used to be the driveway to the once staid and stately home of Horace Benson. He had made a fortune on the goldfields and put it into land and cattle, but, as he never married there were no heirs and the flourishing cattle farm he built up, withered, died and went back to the wilderness; no one wishing to take the chances he did so far off the beaten track. Fallen trees and heavy timber made the roadway impassable but the ruins were only a matter of a couple of hundred metres, all hurried the rest of the way on foot. Elizabeth heaved a great sigh of relief as the happy chuckles of her baby were borne to her on the slight breeze blowing from the direction of the ruins. When the party burst into the clearing, they beheld the spectacle of Gerald Gainey happily prancing on all fours with Michelle astride his back; merrily whipping him along with a sprig of gum.

"Gerald." Lance scolded. "Come here right now!"

Gerald either did not hear or was not interested, he just kept on going, mouth agape and giggling stupidly. Michelle, on the other hand, upon hearing the voice and catching sight of her parents, scrambled from the unfortunate's back and raced over; screaming in joy.

"Mummy–Daddy!"

They both fussed over their baby, Bruce asking.

"Are you all right, did he hurt you Angel?"

"No, I was frightened at first–I didn't want to go away Daddy–I'm sorry. Are you going to spank me?"

"No Darling!" Elizabeth broke in. "We know it was not your fault Love. Are you sure he didn't hurt you?"

It was difficult for the child to answer with her head snuggled into her mother's bosom, but a muffled reply came.

"He smacked my leg and he shookeded me but we had lots of fun Mummy; he gave me horsy rides!"

Lance Gainey realized the futility of reproaching his nephew but as a token gesture, reprimanded him anyway. The youth just stood with a stupid grin, then stated.

"I got a playmate Unk!"

Lance again apologised for the unfortunate incident and the terrible fright it gave the Berkley Family, vowing that Gerald would not be allowed so much freedom in the future–would they be so kind as to not press charges? The Berkley's had been friends of the Gainey Family since they moved into the neighbourhood and of course, they would not press charges. The child was unharmed and but for a severe fright all round, no damage was done. Perhaps with the exception of a half day's work lost, not to mention the family outing ruined but they understood the situation. But please could Lance keep a better eye upon his nephew.

Lance offered to assist with the grubbing of stumps to help make up for lost time, but Bruce waived the offer aside with thanks. They realized Lance had his hands full with Gerald and would be finding it difficult enough to manage his own farm. When the Berkley's had returned to their house and the children were reunited with each other, Bruce gave them all a lecture on the dangers of wandering off anywhere on their own. Next time they were at a place like the crusher, they must keep together and not wander off as Michelle did.

"Shelley had fun though Daddy and we didn't get to Benson's Flats!" Lisa argued.

Her father placed a stern look in her direction as he sat in his reclining chair and beckoned them all to come closer. When they stood before him, half expecting a blistering tirade at Lisa's temerity, he softly spelled out the dangers and spoke of how fortunate Michelle was, not to have fallen into a pit with Gerald.

"You see girls, he is still only a boy himself and his mind has not developed—it may never get any better—he does not have enough sense to be a responsible person and could easily stumble into one of the pits himself. He is not capable of looking after himself, let alone a small person like Michelle. There are some strangers who might take a little girl away and her parents would never see her again. If you are always together you will not be so easily tricked or give any nasty person a chance to take you away."

He paused to let that sink in, and then continued.

"As for Michelle having fun, that only lasted a little while and she also had a very big fright. You can have just as much fun at home and with friends!"

Michelle sidled up to her father and touched his knee.

"I won't play on my own again Daddy. I am always going to stay with Bronwyn and Lisa! "That's the girl!" He smiled. "Do you know what?" Three heads shook together.

"I have been working too hard lately. I think the whole family should pack a hamper and ride to Ryries Falls for a happy day out and to forget bad memories!"

Three happy little girls raced to tell their mother the good news.

THE END.

H. Reede-Pelling.

142

Nineteen forty four the world was still at war. The Allies were pushing the oppressors ever back as the weight of Russia tipped the balance and V.P. Day was drawing near. There was still another year of war to come before the would-be world dictators were finally crushed. On the home front, every man, woman and child were doing their utmost to help the war effort. Howard Reede was just fourteen and his brother Sidney, two and a bit years his senior. Their mother had taken ill and could no longer manage to make ends meet at home, even though the boy's stepfather had steady work. The doctor advised a complete rest necessary for Missus Smith (Reede), as a breakdown was inevitable under the stresses of war-time shortages and two agile, somewhat boisterous teenagers. Sidney was always pestering his mother to allow him to visit friends in the North of the state. For the better part of a year Sidney had been asking and cajoling. His mother could not afford the costs that would be incurred, but, when there were few menfolk available to harvest the fruit crops, youths and even children were being employed with free government subsidised transport to the vineyards. Missus Smith gave her consent for the boys to go. One of the conditions of the trip was that he would have to take Howard along too and look after him. It was an exciting morning when the two boys climbed aboard the 'Fruit pickers Special', a long train packed with rowdy loud-mouthed itinerant workers. Seasonal farmhands for the most part, shearing in season until they had a pocket full of money and drinking until they spent it; then back to the next seasonal job be it droving or ploughing. This time it happened to be fruit-picking. Howard and Sidney, two fresh-faced youngsters from the big city were among them; a rough, tough, swearing crew. Although children and youths were called for in the advertisements, there were not many youths and Howard was the only one who could still be called a child; he was the youngest on the train. Sidney himself was only a novice among men and put up a good showing as protector of his younger brother.

There were many times aboard the train that he defiantly defended young Howard from the raillery of the rough and ready mob. The two became somewhat of a laughing stock as the few heartless larrikins took a rise out of Howard, just to get a laugh out of Sidney with his shackles up. If it had not been for a few of the more sensible men aboard, the trip would have been almost unbearable for the two youths. A particular incident that sparked up a worthwhile friendship for the boys with one of the men who stemmed their torment, happened towards the middle of the day when young Howard was walking the length of the train trying to find a drinking fountain that worked. Most of them had been broken by hooliganism and the one or two that were still functioning, were jealously guarded by the travellers in the immediate vicinity. Howard had tried to get at a particular fountain but each time was jostled aside by one person or another and more than once, by one man in particular. He was about nineteen or twenty and wore a perpetual sneer accentuated by a thin wisp of a moustache; his brittle black eyes bored into Howard as the youth reached for a cup.

"Back to your own carriage Kid–this one's ours–hoppit!" He snarled, again pushing Howard aside.

Sidney was still in the other carriage towards the front of the train, minding the seats. The two had to take turns in going for a drink or they would return to find another occupant in their seats. Not having his brother present on this occasion, Howard was on his own but still full of cheek.

"Its not yours, it belongs to everyone!" He said, defiantly.

"Run off son or I'll thump you one!" The bully retorted.

A stocky bystander who had witnessed these events, quietly interposed.

"Leave the boy be, he is entitled to a drink!"

Howard thankfully glanced in the direction from which the voice came and took an immediate liking to the young man who interfered on his behalf. The bully's attention was now upon this other party in the dispute, so Howard took the opportunity it afforded to quench his thirst, the while he watched the melodrama being enacted before him.

"Mind your business twerp!" The bully sneered.

The response was immediate. The young man took two paces which brought him within reach of the insolent one and allowed him to administer a short, sharp, solid punch amidships to the unfortunate bully, who doubled up in pain only to be straightened again by a vicious uppercut. As is typical of most bullies, this one chickened out when challenged and moved away, cursing them both and vowing revenge. Howard, slightly frightened by the show of force, was still waiting for his savoir to move aside so he could return to Sidney. The young man asked the boy his name as he allowed him to pass. Howard told the man, adding.

"Excuse me but I have to get back to my brother—and—thank you!"

He ran off. The young man nodded as he smiled at the boy from beneath unruly fair hair, then fell to studying the knuckles of the hand that delivered the blow. When Howard related the incident to Sidney, it was decided they had better stay away from that end of the train for the remainder of the journey. Even if it meant going thirsty, it would be better than to risk the wrath of the bully. When in the late afternoon, the 'Fruit picker's Special' arrived at its destination, the whole 'entourage piled out and waited about the station for the various vineyard owners and managers to select their gangs. Most of the pickers had prearranged to work at particular vineyards; Sidney and Howard of course, were among these. It was a condition of their going that they be supervised at all times as it was a Government Sponsored work party. By this means the fruit growers were able to organize a special train. The parents of course, would not allow youngsters to wander at will in the unfamiliar fruit growing areas. Sidney and Howard were anxiously seeking the red haired owner of the 'Almonde Vineyards'. They were supposed to await him by the telephone box outside the station and were beginning to think he had forgotten them, when a three ton truck with the name emblazoned on the doors; careened around the corner. Howard was very surprised to see that the driver was none other than the fair-haired stocky young man who came to his rescue aboard the train. The truck slewed to a stop beside the youths and the young driver called to them.

"Well, fancy meeting you again Howard! Are you two named Reede?"

His happy smiling face heartened the brothers. Sidney, taking note of the name on the truck, introduced himself and Howard before asking.

"Are you Mister Albert Monde? We were told he was red-headed!"

"He is mate, and with a temper to match. I am Johnny Farren—everyone calls me 'Snowy'—so you might as well. I'm his foreman, just been to the depot to get the truck here, now I have to pick up the pickers—there's a pun for you—they will be at the pub quenching their thirsts. Al said I was to get you young 'uns first, in case you strayed or got lost. Throw yourselves and your bags in front here with me, you will be lucky and get the soft ride out to the vines. Snowy proved to be a bonzer bloke and Sidney thanked him for what he did for young Howard on the train. Snowy brushed his thanks aside, saying it was just part of his job to keep order on the trains and to put bullies in their place. He explained how the boss expected everyone to behave well, work hard and not get into any mischief. If they all did this, the rewards would be great, because the crop could be harvested quickly and everyone would benefit. As they were talking, Snowy had driven to the hotel just a matter of a hundred yards from the railway station; they stopped under a shady tree within sight of a milk bar.

"You blokes got any money?" Snowy asked as he alighted.

"Just a quid, for emergencies!" Sidney informed, suspiciously.

"Well, you had better hang onto it 'til you are settled. Here, here's a couple of bob—get yourselves a cold drink, then wait in the truck for me. You can pay it back later when you get your wages if you like.

"Gee, thanks!"

The two made haste into the Milk Bar. As they enjoyed the refreshing liquid, Howard could not resist pushing the virtues of his new-found friend.

"Told you he was a great guy Sid, didn't I?"

"Yeah, he is all right. I just hope the others are!" Sidney worried.

A good ten minutes passed by before Snowy left the pub, followed by eight rough-looking characters, mostly in their late twenties. There were two men well into their forties, in fact, the one wearing a battered old felt hat could well be in his fifties. He was very tanned and it would seem, must have spent the better part of his life out-doors. Howard later learned the man's name was Herbert Stevoric and the lad was to become very perturbed by this man.

The youths were seated and waiting when the noisy pickers clambered into the back of the truck. Snowy swung up behind the wheel and was driving off before some of the men had settled themselves. Amid a chorus of foul language and thumping on the roof, Snowy inquired if the two beside him had enjoyed their drinks; completely ignoring the clamour from the indignant pickers in the back. The boys assured him they had, as they clung apprehensively to whatever handholds they could find within the cabin. Snowy drove with a careless disregard of himself, his passengers or the vehicle. The Almonde Vineyards were ten miles out of the township and the approach driveway was lined with an avenue of almond trees, each with bagging spread around the base and supported by short posts to keep the bagging high and dry. These were 'catcher' nets and their effectiveness was evident by the large quantities of nuts lying in them. Howard thought that perhaps the vineyards got their name because of these almond trees but Snowy told him, when asked, that the vineyard name was an abbreviation of the owner's name—Albert Monde. The almond trees were just co-incidental. When the crew arrived outside the bunkhouse destined to be their home during the grape season, the owner was there to greet them. He could not be mistaken, the fiery red hair stood out like a beacon atop the six foot two inch frame.

"Where the hell have you been, Snowy? You should have been here hours ago! Think I got nothing to do but stand in the blisterin' sun?"

The tirade had Sidney and Howard a little scared, they were to find out his bark was worse than his bite. Snowy cheekily answered back as the crew alighted.

"Damn it Al, I had to round them all up and you know the road's not the best!"

The big man was not even listening as he welcomed the known pickers of previous seasons and was introduced by them to the new ones. He scratched his chin thoughtfully as he eyed the two brothers.

"So, you are the Reede boys eh? Only a bit of a nipper aren't you young 'un?" He said as he fastened his piercing gaze on Howard. "Still, you can pick same as anyone else, you got hands aincha? Just do as you are told by me an' Snowy here, an' you'll do okay. Now get yourselves settled in the bunkhouse an' I'll give a talk to the lot of you at mealtime!"

He strode off with Snowy, both in earnest conversation as they went to the house.

The bunkhouse was a large barn; a separate room was built at one end to be used as a kitchen. There were ten bunks along each side of the building and privacy was at a minimum. Sidney and Howard were left a choice of four bunks at the kitchen end; evidently the greasy smelly kitchen area was not a desirable resting place. Perhaps because of the continual passing traffic as the residents made themselves snacks and cups of tea or coffee. The lads would not have many early nights. In all, there were fifteen pickers and the cook living in the bunkhouse. Four old hands lived there full-time as they tended the vines and maintained the vineyard during the 'off' season. The cook was a regular who arrived a week ahead of the seasonal workers, to make the necessary catering arrangements. When the evening meal was in full swing, the boss (true to his word) gave the men a quick summary of their wages, conditions and what was expected of them. He also paired them off into working gangs and informed that they would begin work at six-thirty or first light in the morning—which ever came first. The wages structure that was outlined was extremely good and all were eager to get to it and make their fortunes. Sidney and Howard were paired off with experienced pickers, so they would be separated during working hours. This was no great worry to Sidney as he knew no real trouble could befall his young brother, just picking grapes. In this he was wrong. The wages earned was on the number of 'buckets' filled with grapes that each person picked. They were issued with a small, sharp knife and each pair of pickers would relieve the vines of their fruit, one either side of the row of vines. The filled buckets would be collected by Snowy, who would tally them against the picker's name. Howard was paired with the older man he saw coming from the pub. It was Herbert Stevoric!

Two days of intense heat and hard work left Howard a quiet, solemn lad. He was too tired after the big days work to act the ninny and frolic as was his wont as a rule. His workmate proved to be a little frightening, as he had a bad habit of coming through the vines to Howard's side when he wanted a smoke. This in itself was no worry but he kept patting Howard on the shoulder and often tried to talk the youth into having a cigarette with him. Howard always politely refused and moved away but Herbert persisted in annoying the lad. Howard was also becoming suspicious of his bucket tally. Herbert insisted that the lad work ahead and take all the big bunches of grapes and leave Herbert to clean up the left-overs, as perhaps Howard may not get them all. The lad was sure Herbert was taking some of his buckets through the vine with him and so enhance Herbert's own tally to the detriment of Howard. When Sidney was told of his brother's fears, it was decided they should ask Snowy's advice in the matter, after all, he was foreman and it was his responsibility. Also, Howard felt, Snowy would help him even if he was not the foreman; he liked the stocky young man and felt it was mutual. Snowy was genuinely concerned when suspicion of the pilfering was voiced. He declared that he could do nothing on hearsay, he needed proof. Snowy suggested that in future Howard should stack his buckets in groups of five, then perhaps it would be noticed if the stacks were not uniform. Even if the whole stack of buckets were taken at the one time, it would be noticeable because of the greater distance between stacks. This would make it obvious that they were being pilfered and then suspicion would fall heavily on Herbert. Howard felt happier with this new arrangement and looked forward to the next day's tally as being his best yet. At the lunch break on the following day, Snowy sought young Howard.

"Hey Son, couldn't you carry the buckets to stack them in fives?"

Howard looked surprised as Snowy sat beside him.

"But I did!"

"True?" Snowy eyed the boy dubiously.

"Three on the bottom and two on the top like you said."

"You sure pal. Not kidding me are you?"

"No truly, I made a special effort, I even counted them. I cut eighty-two buckets this morning. That is honest Snowy!"

"Well, your tally was only sixty-six. They were in lots of four, sixteen stacks of four and an odd two. I think I better have a talk with Herbert!"

Herbert was a little late getting to work after lunch and when Howard did see him, the man was flustered and looked very angry. He kept away from the youngster for the better part of an hour, but came back when he usually knocked off for a smoke. Howard quailed as the man approached a slight sneer on his face. The lad instinctively backed off into the vines as Herbert deliberately stood so close in front of him that Howard could not get away if he wished.

"So, you set your dog on me did you?"

With cigarette drooping from tight lips, the man poked Howard in the chest with a forefinger.

"But–they were my buckets you were pinching!" Howard managed to splutter.

"I ought to break your bloody little neck, makin' me look bad with the boss."

Howard just stood, waiting at the man's mercy. Herbert, though smoking, took out another cigarette and thrust it at the terrified lad.

"Here, have a smoke." He ordered.

Howard shook his head but reached out for the cigarette as the man raised a threatening hand and his jaw muscles bunched. Herbert lit it and smiled grimly as Howard puffed and coughed. It was not as if the lad had not smoked before, he had. Both of the brothers and a friend 'acquired' some cigarettes one day and had a sneak preview. This was different though—he was being forced on this occasion and he was quite scared of what the man might do to him.

"Come on, puff harder!" Herbert ordered.

Howard obeyed, the smoke making his eyes water.

"See, not so hard is it? You kids are always sneaking a puff; you should enjoy me letting you smoke!"

"Please—can I stop now—I don't want to smoke any more!"

"If you can stop telling tales you can stop smoking—I have plenty of cigarettes. You gonna tell more tales?" Herbert eyed him belligerently.

"No, I promise!" Howard offered the cigarette back.

Herbert took it and stamped it out underfoot, then clawing each of the lad's shoulders with a strong hand, said chummily.

"I don't want to hurt you son, we should be friends, you sure you won't be telling tales again?"

The man had Howard terrified and the lad thought it best to go along with his wishes. What were a few buckets of grapes anyway? He would be better off with his neck intact.

"Can I go back to work now?"

Howard tried to wriggle free. Herbert held him firmly; a triumphant grin creased his tanned face.

"Just remember, you can't get away from me too easily son. I don't want to hear any more about missing buckets—okay?"

As he let Howard go, the man gave a knowing wink. What Herbert meant, the youngster could only guess at but the way he emphasised 'friends', made Howard determined to get away from him. Perhaps Snowy would let him change places and pair up with another picker, he would ask tomorrow.

The youngster worked hard for the rest of the day in an effort to keep as far ahead of Herbert as he possibly could. The sun beat down mercilessly and the temperature was in the high nineties. Howard had dropped his wide-brimmed protective hat where he had been jostled and had no desire to pass Herbert again to retrieve it. He should have, for to the city boy, unused to the dry country heat and with his blood already 'steamed up' by the fright he was given earlier; the vines were beginning to jump up and down. Finally the vines began to spin around and Howard felt he was falling into a bottomless pit, would he never stop falling? He reached out his arms to arrest the falling but he did not know he was already on the ground, arms firmly pressed to the soil. Howard was sunstruck, he had fainted. When Howard woke, he was looking at unfamiliar walls with old-time photographs of stern-eyed people of a time long gone. An old oak sideboard with a large vase of roses that gave the room a beautiful scenty aroma and the old time-piece hanging from a wall giving forth a quiet rhythmic ticking, made for a feeling of peace and serenity. Howard just lay back and rested, puzzled at how he came to be there. He remembered the vines spinning and a very sick feeling in his stomach but what happened after, he did not know. A lady came in to the room with a glass of orange juice and a damp cloth, she smiled as she placed the drink within Howard's reach and dabbed his brow with the cloth; it was very comforting.

"Feeling better Howard?" She asked putting the cloth aside and offering the fruit drink.

"Yes thank you. What happened?" He asked.

"You silly old duffer, you went and fainted with sunstroke! Just rest for a bit and you will be good-oh. Mister Monde thinks the work is too strenuous for you–being a city boy–so he is going to work you at the drying racks.

Howard was very pleased with his new situation, for he was now in regular contact with Snowy. He was stationed at the caustic dip–a huge vat of caustic soda into which the buckets of grapes were dipped to cleanse them of bacteria and hasten their maturity. Howard's job was to pass the buckets from the collection wagon when Snowy arrived from his rounds and give them across to the other 'older' man, he had noticed coming from the pub with Herbert Stevoric. He only knew this man as Ben. Ben was a quiet man who spoke seldom and then only to issue orders. He would take the buckets from Howard and dip them, then set them on a draining board. When Snowy went off to gather another load, Howard and Ben would spread the drained fruit on to the long drying racks. It was hard work for perhaps half an hour, and then while waiting for the next load, they could sit and relax. Ben was better company than Herbert because he left the lad entirely alone to do what he wished until the next load arrived. Two weeks of hard work in the hot climate passed without further incidents and the youths were happy with their lot. They were amassing more money than they had ever owned before and Sidney sent some back home to help their ailing mother. Sidney's chance to visit his friends in the area came when a cold front moved over the vineyards. A heavy downpour effectively put an end to the picking, as the fruit could not be dipped and dried properly. The pickers were given a day off. Snowy could not help the youths to get to the friend's farm as he had to drive the pickers into town, they preferred to have a day at the pub; Snowy would join them. It was Albert Monde, the boss, who kindly offered to take them the six miles to visit Sidney's friend, Gerry Tencliffe. The lads were old school mates and Sidney had always vowed he would come up and visit when Gerry moved to the country. It happened that Gerry's father and Albert Monde were also great friends, so the visit would skin the rabbit from both ends—so to speak. After the preliminaries of introductions and so forth were over, Howard was virtually left to his own devices as the older boys got by themselves to talk over old times and what new girl friends they knew. Howard felt a little left out of it so he decided to nose around the farm. It was not a large farm by any means, Howard overheard when the adults were talking and gathered it was a cattle farm with only eighty head of stock. It did have twenty acres of vines however and could manage to get but two pickers. When the youth wandered to the bunkhouse he met one of them coming out with a bucket.

"G'day son, where'd you come from?" The man asked a grin evident.

Howard explained that he was visiting, with his brother. The man "Hrumpfed" and stalked over to the water tank where he proceeded to fill the bucket. Howard poked his face in through the open bunkhouse door.

"Hey you—come over here!" A rough voice demanded from within.

Howard fancied he had heard the voice before but could not remember where; the fellow who spoke was at the end of the room in the shadows. The youth tremulously made his way there in response to the demand. He stopped short when the man stepped out into the better light by a window. It was the bully from the train! A resounding whack sent the youngster sprawling and he fell back holding a stinging cheek, shocked more than hurt by the sudden onslaught for no apparent reason.

"Why—why did you do that?" A bewildered Howard asked—knowing it was retribution—deserved or not.

"You bloody well know why you damned little trouble-maker."

Those fierce eyes blazed at him and the youth worried that the bully would strike again. The man with the bucket arrived; he had witnessed the attack from the doorway and hurried up to them.

"What's up Joey, why did you clobber the kid?"

"Arrgh!" The bully spat out. "Th' little bugger caused me some trouble on th' train—hop it kid—'fore I whack you again!"

He took a threatening step forward. Howard hastened away, angry at his unfair treatment and angry at himself for not at least kicking the bully in the shins. As the youth made his way to the house, he pondered as to whether he should mention the incident or not. No good could come of it even though he felt revenge would be sweet. On consideration Howard deemed it better to just let the matter drop. It would only upset people and may cause a rift between Sidney and his pal, Gerry. Also Mister Tencliffe and Mister Monde may feel embarrassed over it. There was no reason for Howard to return here, after all, he had nothing in common with Gerry Tencliffe, and he had only just met the family. They were Sidney's friends. But for the advent of Snowy, Howard realized he did not really have a friend up here and all he did was to work hard; no play whatsoever. Then there were people like that bully Joey and that creep Herbert Stevoric, Howard hated that man and was very frightened in case he should be in a situation where he would be alone with him. Howard made a mental note to keep as much with Snowy as he could, Snowy would watch out for him. It was a pity that it was not Snowy who came in with the bucket of water, he would have belted Joey. Howard sought his brother and Gerry, keeping close by them until it was time to return to their own vineyard. They reached it just in time for the dinner gong to summon them to the evening meal. Work began in earnest the following day, it was hard going too. The rainstorm had passed as suddenly as it sprung up but left in its wake, sticky clinging mud. The picking slowed down accordingly. Although each picker was determined to catch up on the lost day's quota, they were hard pressed as their footing slipped and the buckets stuck in the syrupy goo. The buckets were heavy enough for

Howard when fully laden in the dry weather but with the sticky mud on the bottoms, making the grapes adhere to the bucket or the bucket to the floor of the truck; the young fellow was having great difficulty indeed.

Another hardship was that each bucket had to be dipped twice, once in water to wash away the mud, then into the caustic soda. By the end of that day Howard was absolutely pooped and sought a shady spot to rest under one of the almond trees that lined the entry into the vineyard. The spot he chose was at a bend where the vines grew close in to the trees keeping plenty of shade on the soft grasses that grew in profusion under the bagging. It was further secluded by the two or three flowering shrubs picturesquely placed for decoration. Howard was almost asleep when he felt the presence of another. He lazily opened an eye to behold Herbert Stevoric smiling down at him! Howard made to rise, he felt trapped beneath the bagging. Herbert restrained the youngster with a firm hand upon his shoulder.

"Stay there son, I just want to talk for a bit. You have been avoiding me lately; I don't see much of you any more!"

It was almost an accusation. Howard fumbled a reply.

"I–I've been very busy."

Herbert nodded, thoughtfully.

"Yes, I know, you are a good worker."

Herbert sat on the grass beside the boy, neither spoke for a while and Howard was becoming quite nervous; wondering what was in the man's mind. Why did Herbert single him out? Was the man going to force more cigarettes on him?

"You don't like me much, do you Howard?"

Embarrassed, Howard blushed as he tried to avoid the issue. After all, he was at the man's mercy.

"I never thought much about it, I mean–I–er, I don't get to the vines now. I don't see you 'cause I work with Ben."

Herbert nodded absently, and then said, apologetically.

"I'm sorry I frightened you the other day, I was angry you dobbed me in–it's every man for himself out here–that's why I pinched your buckets. I am in a lot of debt and need all the cash I can get!"

Again they were silent. Howard stirred.

"Excuse me, my brother will be wondering where I am!"

"You don't really have to go do you Howard? I came looking for you especially, wanted to ask you something!"

Herbert lit a cigarette as the youngster asked querulously.

"What?"

Carefully blowing the smoke away from Howard, Herbert surprised him with.

"The boss said I could borrow the truck tonight to take some money in to a friend in town, I was hoping you might like to come along for the ride!"

"I don't think Sid would let me!" Howard fenced.

"I already asked him, he said it was up to you. Come on son, I want to make up for giving you a fright and it'd be nice to have some company!"

Howard scrambled to his feet before he answered.

"No! I don't think I'd better, thank you!"

Suddenly Herbert wheeled about and hurried off, calling back over his shoulder.

"Suit yourself son, I just wanted to make it up to you, pinching your buckets an' all!"

As the man went off, Howard stood in the deepening gloom, for now the sun was well set. 'Perhaps' he thought 'the man wasn't so bad after all, he seemed genuine and he did apologise.' Thinking further, Howard realized that the old picker did not do anything damaging and the stolen buckets were returned to Howard's tally. The truck left the yards and made its way towards him along the drive. On the spur of the moment Howard stepped to the side of the road and hailed the driver. The vehicle stopped beside him, Howard stood on the running board.

"I want to come but I'm frightened."

"I won't harm you son, promise!"

"You sure Sid said it's okay?"

Herbert studied the boy's face awhile, and then admitted.

"No Howard, I made that up. I just wanted to see what you'd say. Didn't think you liked me enough to come. Will we go back and ask him?"

It was Howard's turn to study the man. He was glad Herbert was honest with him.

"All right!"

Herbert smiled.

"Good lad—hang on tight!"

He reversed the truck at great speed to the bunkhouse. It was a matter of moments for the youngster to locate his brother and convince him that he would be all right with Herbert Stevoric now. Dubiously, Sidney gave his consent saying he would explain to Mister Monde where Howard had gone; and with whom. The ride into town was exciting for the youth. The twin beams of the masked headlights barely made the road visible, but it mattered not for a full moon bathed the countryside, lights were almost unnecessary. Howard marvelled at the night life they witnessed. Every now and again, a rabbit or two would scurry across the road and they ran over a snake on a straight stretch just after turning a bend in the road. It was hard to tell what kind of snake it was in the gloaming but Herbert assured Howard it would have to be a brown. This was brown snake country and tiger snakes usually inhabit the swampy areas and riverbanks. Those were the two most common snakes of the state. Very little was said between the two until the buildings of the township came into view in the moonlight. Being war-time, all lights were heavily masked as a precaution against air-raids.

"You will like my friends here Howard. Tom has a boy—his name is Tom too—they call him Junior; he is about your age. We won't be stopping long; we have to rise early in the morning. I'll just get my business done and have a drink, and then we will be off."

It was just as Herbert said it would be, the business he had took little time and while the men enjoyed their beer, Howard and Junior had a milk-shake each; made by Junior's mum. They spent a small amount of time in his hobby-room looking at model boats and aeroplanes. All too soon for Howard, the time slipped by. They bid Junior and his parent's adieu then set off back to the vineyard.

On the return journey there were many more rabbits to be seen on the roadway and they even saw a large possum waddling along the gravel edge. Noting the eagerness with which the youth beside him was taking in this new experience, Herbert was moved to ask.

"Enjoying the outing son?"

"Yes, it's great thank you."

"Not scared of me any more?"

"No."

It was almost ten in the evening when they finally crept into the bunkhouse. It would be unfortunate if they woke the others, as fruit picking is a tiring job and rest was golden. Howard undressed carefully so as not to disturb Sidney but he was still awake.

"That you Howard?" He whispered.

"Yes."

"Goodnight!"

"Goodnight Sid."

Howard could not sleep immediately; he was over tired; it had been a big day. He found it difficult to woo sleep, visions of Herbert standing over him, then having an almost about-face and becoming good friends, disturbed him. 'The man was in debt and worried, perhaps he could be forgiven for frightening me.' Howard thought. Eventually nature won out and the boy slept. Morning found Howard still asleep; he slept on as the others went to work. When he eventually did waken, he shamefacedly reported to his post. If he was not there it would slow the work down, each person had a place and a job to do, if a link collapsed then the chain broke and work would be held up. The youngster was surprised to find

Herbert Stevoric in his place, doing his job. 'I've been sacked' he thought 'for sleeping in.' Herbert jumped down from the dip when he saw the boy.

"Here you are son, I have been filling in for you, my fault you slept in!"

Howard took his place as Herbert departed for the vines. The man was heavily in debt and needed all the cash he could earn, yet he had waived that aside and filled in for Howard so he would not get into trouble with his friend Snowy; or the boss. Howard knew he had made another friend. A happy time at the vineyard was assured now–he had no one to fear–the future looked rosy!

THE END.

Howard Reede-Pelling.

15   Scotty   19/12/78

It was a beautiful morning; Scotty loved these warm summer mornings. The grass in Swamp Park always smelled good on a summer morning, the dew made it fresh and springy to walk upon and there were always children playing at the pond. They would fish for yabbies and tadpoles, sometimes they just threw rubbish into the water to watch it sink. Scotty did not like children who did things like that, he came from a good home where children were taught to clean up after them. As he ran to the park, he listened for the happy laughter of children. Scotty loved playing with the children, sometimes one would be mean to him, but not often; he nearly always had fun with them. At one time Scotty had lots of children to play with, when he lived in the stately old manor. But the people he lived with sold up the old manor and moved away to some place called overseas. Scotty did not like that place. Oh, he had never been there, it's just that all his troubles started when the family he lived with, moved out of there. Sure, they fussed over Scotty and there were lots of tears. The children wanted Scotty to come too, but their parents were very firm and said, no! Scotty would be well looked after by nice people, he could not possibly come with them. Scotty did not like the new people with whom he was left. Although he had his own kind of friends there, he missed the family. When the gate was left open one day, Scotty quickly ran out and began to look for this place called overseas. He would find that nice family he knew and then, when they saw him back; the children would not let their parents leave him again. Poor Scotty, he looked and he looked but he could not find the family anywhere, they truly had gone. The old manor was still there but the family had disappeared completely. Now Scotty was going to the park where the children always played. He would find them there he was sure, even if those children he lived with were not there, their friends would be and they may take Scotty to where the family went—overseas! As Scotty entered the park he was amazed that on such a nice morning he could not hear the merry frolicking of children. Why, the park seemed quite deserted, not even an adult walking through. Scotty was all alone, still, the grass was lovely and soft and the sweet scent of all the shrubs and flowers, wafted on the warm morning breeze. Scotty felt good–really good. In sheer delight he rolled upon the grass, kicking his legs up in the air ecstatically, then rolled over onto his tummy and just smelled of the lush grasses. Presently Scotty arose and idly trotted over to the garden where the shrubs and flowers grew. He smelled of the flowers and sneezed as the pollen tickled his nose. An early on the job bee buzzed away, no doubt angry at being disturbed at its work. Scotty casually watched it, and then trotted off to peer into the pond. It was most annoying to find the park deserted, he did so miss the family and the children with whom he always played, and they were great friends. Where on earth could they be? What was keeping them inside this morning? The day was too nice to stay indoors. Perhaps it was this Christmas Day thing he heard the children talking about, when they came to visit his other friends at the place where he was left when the family went to that overseas place. Yes, that was it; it must be Christmas Day's fault. The children all sounded happy about this Christmas Day, it must be something wonderful. It was not very wonderful for Scotty, all the children he used to play with; were gone! The park was lonely without any people in it and Scotty tired of walking and trotting about on his own. He found a nice warm spot beneath a huge old gum tree and lay down to snooze. Perhaps if he waited a while, the children would come. However, it was not a child who came, it was a young man; he appeared to be about twenty eight. His clothes were not of an expensive type and the shoes he wore had seen better days but at least he was clean, and he proved to be a gentle kindly person.

His very worried face broke into a sparkling smile as he saw Scotty beneath the tree. He came over and sat down beside Scotty.

"Hello Scotty, how are you this fine Christmas morning?" He asked.

Well now, that was a shock! For a complete stranger, how on earth did the man know the name was Scotty? It was so surprising that Scotty just lay there and only lifted his head in acknowledgement as the man put out a friendly hand towards him. Scotty liked the smell and let the man pat his head. It was a gentle kindly touch and Scotty knew they would get along just fine. They both rested beneath the tree enjoying each others company. Suddenly Scotty became alert, he heard a child's voice, it came from the other side of the pond. Soon a little boy of about eight years came running towards them that was better. Scotty jumped up and ran towards the boy. Upon seeing Scotty, the boy yelled joyously.

"Daddy! It's a doggie—you got me a doggie—you bought me a Christmas present after all. Oh thank you Daddy!"

He fell to his knees and cuddled Scotty, who jumped and danced about happily, thrilling with the excitement of a frolic with the child. His father put a hand on the boy's shoulder.

"Son, it is not our dog. He was just sitting under the tree. I'm sorry Son; we can't take him because he is not ours to take. Dad can't afford to buy you a dog. I have been worrying that I can't get you a nice Christmas present."

The boy held Scotty to him, tears trickled down the flushed cheeks.

"But Daddy—he—he might be lost, maybe no one owns him, I would love a doggy to play with Daddy. Please, can't we keep him?"

The man loved his son, Scotty could see that. They loved each other and Scotty wagged his tail and barked to tell them he would like to stay with them until he found his family again.

"See Son." The man said, grabbing Scotty's collar. "I will read it to you. It says—Scotty! Well now, that is funny—I called him Scotty when I met him, of course he is a true Scotch terrier, so it is natural people would call him Scotty!"

"What else does it say Daddy?" The boy eagerly waited as his dad read on.

"It only says Scotty on the collar Son! Wait, there is a disc hanging on there too with something on it—well now, would you look at that!"

"What is it Daddy—what is it?" The child eagerly asked.

His father's face brightened, a smile appeared.

"You know Son, there is just a chance—a small chance mind you—he might be a lost dog after all!"

"Oh goody!" The boy clapped his hands in glee. "Then can we keep him Daddy?"

"I won't promise Son, but we will take him back and see!"

The man lifted Scotty and carried him under one arm, the little boy all agog with excitement, clasped his dad's other hand and they took Scotty to the place where his family had left him. It was an elated father who placed Scotty on the ground outside the kennels and passed the leash he had been generously given, to his deliriously happy little son.

"It is all right Son; his owners have gone away and will not be coming back, so we may keep Scotty. I think he is a very good Christmas present, don't you? So he is your dog now, you be good and kind to him and have a happy Christmas!"

"Thank you Daddy, you have a happy Christmas too!"

The boy gave his father a great hug, and then did likewise to his dog Scotty.

"And you have a happy Christmas too doggie—my lovely Scotty doggie!"

Scotty WAS happy; he wagged his tail vigorously and licked his new young master's hands and face. Of course he was happy now—Scotty had someone to play with!

THE END

Howard Reede-Pelling.

163

The old lady shuffled across the street, moving against the red light and taking her time as she creaked along, the heels of her faded blue slippers scraping the bitumen. A passing motorist honked angrily at her, she paid him scant attention but mumbled to herself.

"Oh! Bother the horrid things, why don't they use a light sulky or a nice hansom with a good pair tugging at the bits? Don't know how to live these modern folk. Always hurry hurry and pushing a soul about, a body has a good mind to give them the length of her tongue!"

Millie was back on the footpath. She turned her whole body as she searched to the left then to the right, trying to decide why she crossed the road in the first place. Her neck was quite rigid with age and a touch of arthritis these days and she still argued with herself and mumbled as lonely people were apt to do. Her main worry at the moment was whether she had just crossed the road already or was about to; her memory was not the best. A fruit shop two or three doors down the way had its wares proudly displayed and Millie remembered that is why she crossed the road, to buy fruit. Alphonse needed some apple and Millie also liked a little, although she never ate much herself, sometimes the whole piece that was left after she had put the best half into Alphonse's cage. He was Millie's pet and best pal, after Smoky that is—no one could take the place of Smoky; her dusty coloured old tom cat. The old feline was in his sixteenth year and Millie knew he did not have long to go, he was already staggering but he was her only love—her mainstay to beat boredom. Millie only had her cat, the canary and her daily walks to keep her occupied nowadays, because at eighty two she had nothing much else to live for, except perhaps the garden—such as it was. She had outlived her two girls and their children, although an accident took one family, the other just died off like her husband Joe did. Joe died twenty five years ago and poor old Millie just plodded along on her own—well, what else could a body do? As she neared the fruit shop, a little boy of about nine years watched her. He had been avidly eying the wares of the shop—perhaps hoping a piece of fruit would fall and somehow he might acquire it. Millie shooed him away, waving her hanky at him, even though the child had not offended her in any way. It mattered not, Millie detested children.

"Go away you horrid little boy—shoo—shoo, scat, be off!"

The youngster, taken by surprise moved back a few paces, then stopped to stare in wonder at this strange old lady. She was not shabbily dressed at all, but then, she was not neat either. Her petticoat hung rather limply an inch or two below the fading black skirt and the pale blue cardigan she wore, was stained with dribbled food. Even so, she did appear fairly clean, thanks to the home-help people and the meals-on-wheels organizations. Of course, the boy did not know that. He was rather a ragged little fellow. Patched denim jeans and a grimy jumper attesting the fact that he was not very well cared for, and, as he was lounging in the vicinity of the fruit shop no doubt looking for a hand-out, could most likely mean he was not very well fed either. Millie fumbled in her purse, the boy already forgotten and purchased three nice apples and five bananas. She loved banana sandwiches; they went well with a cup of tea and a biscuit for the evening meal. As the meals on wheels people only supplied one meal a day, usually a roast with vegies and some nice soft sweets, such as plum pudding and custard or apple pie; Millie had to find the other meals herself. She settled the apples in the crook of her arm and held the bag of bananas in her left hand, clutching the precious purse in the right. As she only had one side of the paper bag, it gave way and the bananas spilled onto the ground. The little boy was there in an instant, gathering them up.

"Oh! You horrid little boy, you are stealing my fruit, stoppit I say, stoppit!"

Millie tugged at the boy's shoulder as he straightened up, the bananas in his hands, offering them to her.

"But lady, I was just picking them up for you; I wasn't stealing them!"

Millie snatched the fruit from him.

"Hrmpf! A likely story that is!"

She shuffled away, ignoring the hurt look on the youngster's face.

"I'm sorry I picked up your rotten old fruit anyway!" He shouted.

Millie stopped, turned about and gave the boy a long look. He faltered, ready to bolt if she looked like coming back. She continued on her way, again muttering to herself. Millie waited at the roadside, turning one way and then the other to see if the way was clear to recross the road. Would the smelly cars never stop? How on earth was a body to cross if they kept coming all the time? Millie still lived in the past. New innovations such as traffic lights meant little to her. People kept telling her she must abide by the traffic lights, but for the life of her she had no idea which colour meant what.

"Oh bother!" She mumbled as she shuffled out onto the road. "They can jolly well stop for me!"

A screech of rubber as a vehicle slewed to a stop and a blaring motor horn accompanied by profane language, had Millie hastily step back on to the footpath again. She was a little ruffled, for the sudden commotion gave her a fright. The motorist continued on his way, glaring at the frail old fool who did not have sense enough to wait for the green light. Millie was shaking, how was she to cross this terrible road? Again the little boy caught her eye; he was still standing wide-eyed at the fruit shop. He had fully expected to see her get run over, now she was waving her hanky again and calling to him; was she shooing him off again, or what?

"Little boy, come here this minute!" She demanded her cracked voice hardly audible above the noise of the traffic; it was his duty—he should come when his elders spoke. The boy came, somewhat timidly and stood his distance from her.

"Yes Lady?"

"How do I work this silly contraption?"

She waved her handkerchief at the pole upon which the traffic lights were mounted.

"But lady, the lights have been green twice while you have been standing there!"

"Tush! Stuff and nonsense—blue—green, what's it matter? How do I stop those terrible cars—come boy—show me!"

The lad pressed the button on the pole, old Millie grasped his shoulder and began to move.

"Do we go now, boy?"

"No lady—wait! The light's still red!"

The lights changed, the cars stopped.

"Now lady, I'll walk across with you."

Awkwardly, he led her over to the other side of the road. As they reached the footpath, Millie released her grip on the boy's shoulder and shuffled off, ignoring the boy completely.

"That's all right lady, it was no trouble!" He cheekily called after her.

Millie stopped and turned around.

"Eh, what's that?" She glared at the boy, who reddened, realizing he had been cheeky.

"Come here boy."

The youngster thought he would be berated and glanced at the traffic lights. Had they been green he may have bolted, but they were red. The old lady waited. He walked up to her.

"Yes?"

"Boy—do you want a banana?"

"Oh, yes please." His face broke in to a huge grin, the usually sombre eyes sparkled.

"Thank you lady!"

Millie passed the fruit to him and when he began wolfing into it; she turned and shuffled off home.

It was two days before Millie ventured out to the shops again. She had to get some fresh meat for Smoky, he loved sheep's heart and liver. Usually the butcher left enough with Missus Smith next door but as the Smith's were away for a fortnight's holiday, with their children, Millie was left to get the meat herself. She would have to cross that terrible road again and had barely turned the corner of the street into the shopping centre, when a familiar voice said.

"Hello lady."

Millie stopped and peered through dim eyes at the same horrid little boy who tried to steal her apples—no—it was bananas. Come to think of it, he didn't try to steal them at all; he picked them up when the bag burst. Still, Millie did not like children, they were nasty little brutes. Always throwing stones at Smoky or playing in her garden.

"Shoo, little boy, shoo!" Millie walked on.

The boy, aware of her mannerisms, tagged along.

"Should I cross the road and get your bananas for you lady?" He asked, hopefully.

"Bananas, bananas?" She mumbled. "I don't want bananas do I?"

She stopped, pondering her situation.

"Now what did I want? Alphonse has enough seed, I have another apple, and Smoky has plenty of milk. Oh, Smoky! Smoky wants his fresh meat so I have to go over to the butcher—drat and bother!"

"I could go over the road for you lady. Are you sure you don't want any fruit?"

The lad eagerly asked.

Millie stood, considering the boy. Yes, he could cross that horrible road. He knew how to make the traffic stop, he could work that traffic post thing. Millie dived into her purse and pressed some silver into the boy's outspread hand.

"Three lambs hearts and half a pound of liver, can you remember that? And be quick, now off with you!"

"Yes lady."

The boy ran to the lights, they changed as he arrived and he crossed the road and disappeared into the butcher's shop, next door to the greengrocer. Millie sat on the nearby bus seat, eyes glued to the shop. It never occurred to her that the youngster might just run off with her money. Such a thing was not in the boy's mind either. He reached over the counter and placed the silver down. The butcher smiled and asked.

"Yes Greg, what can I do for you?"

"Three lambs hearts and half a pan of liver, please!"

The butcher scratched his head.

"Half a pan of liver, what the ding-dong is half a pan of liver?"

Gregory peered over the counter, his jet black hair bothering his vision.

"I don't know, some old lady said I was to get half a pan of liver; that's all I know."

The butcher smiled knowingly.

"Ah, that'll be old Millie there, sitting on the seat, she still lives in the past. Half a POUND of liver is what she wants, don't you know the old weights Greg old son?"

The boy shook his head, the butcher explained.

"A kilo weighs in at two point two pounds, so if old Millie wants half a pound—how many kilos is that?"

"Just over a quarter of a kilo?"

"Smart work Greg, yes, point two, five seven of a kilo!"

As he was talking the butcher weighed and wrapped the meat. He passed it to Gregory and gave the boy the due change.

"Bye." Gregory cheerily waved as he departed.

Millie rose as the youngster returned and held out her hands for the parcel.

"Did you get the change boy? You didn't forget the change did you?"

"No lady, fifteen cents!" He passed it into her hand.

Millie considered the boy. Maybe this one was not so bad, at least he had not thrown stones at her Smoky and she could not recall him running on her garden. It was mostly those nasty Smith children next door. If it had not been for Violet—their mother—getting the meat for her, she would have got the police to them long ago.

"Here boy, spend it wisely!"

Millie handed the five cent piece to the boy and put the ten cents in her purse.

"Thank you lady—do you eat liver?"

"Of course boy, doesn't your mother teach you anything? It is called lamb's fry; but this is for Smoky!"

"Who is Smoky?"

"Who is Smoky indeed? Smoky is my dear friend, my lovely big old Persian tom cat. That's who Smoky is!"

Gregory eyed the old lady wistfully.

"I love cats. Mum won't let us have any pets; she says they eat too much. What is a Persian?" Millie studied the wide-eyed face; the boy seemed genuinely interested in her dear old Smoky. "A Persian? Well, it's just a cat with long hair—you must know what a Persian is—don't be stupid boy!" She began shuffling off.

169

"I must go and feed him; he will get cross if I don't hurry."

The boy walked along beside her.

"Please lady, could I pat him? I like cats."

"Pat him!" She snorted. "Pat him indeed—more likely you will throw stones at him or pull his tail!"

"Aw gee lady! No I won't, truly, I love animals—just let me see him—please!"

They arrived at the gate of Millie's house. She entered and shut the boy out.

"Please!" He begged.

"Does your mother know where you are, little boy?" Millie squinted as she asked.

"No, she doesn't care where I am, long as I get home before Dad does. It'll be all right, I won't be any trouble and I'll go more messages if you want me to—please!"

"Oh, all right. But you go straight home after and you mustn't touch him while he is feeding—promise me boy!" Millie opened the gate.

Gregory entered eagerly, saying.

"Oh beauty, I'll behave, true I will!"

The boy followed the old lady around the sideway and onto the back veranda. Millie lifted a flower pot and retrieved a key from under it, then opened the door. A half-hearted meow came from beneath a lemon tree behind them.

"Stand aside boy, so you don't frighten Smoky. Here Smoky, where's mummy's boy then? Come and get your dinner!"

The old tom casually limped over, paused as he eyed the excited youngster, and then sedately followed Millie into the house. Gregory followed.

"Wow!" He breathed. "Isn't he beautiful?"

He could not have struck a happier note in Millie's heart.

"He's my little baby." She said, pridefully.

It was the first time the boy had seen her smile. Millie sliced one of the hearts in half, and then chopped one of the halves into small cubes. She placed them on a plate specially set aside in a corner of the room. Smoky sniffed, licked the meat, and then squatted down to eat. Gregory watched with interest, and then asked.

"What about the liver?"

The old lady nodded absently.

"The liver—oh—yes, the liver. No, I give him some of that tomorrow mixed with some more heart. Smoky likes a change of diet. She placed the kettle on the stove.

"Do you drink tea boy?"

"Yes lady, are you going to make a cup of tea?"

"My word I am. A body can't live long without a cuppa—and a scone—do you like scones boy?"

At the mention of food, Gregory wrenched his admiring gaze from the cat, to look at Millie with renewed interest.

"Yes, I think so. I think we had some at my Aunt's place once."

"Well, get some cups—don't just stand there—in that cupboard."

Millie indicated the one in question as she got milk from her old refrigerator. It was one on the few 'modern contraptions' she had been talked into acquiring. Gregory's eyes were never far from the carton of milk as Millie placed it on the table.

"What is the matter boy; you have seen milk before, haven't you?"

Again Gregory blushed.

"Yes lady but we don't have much at home. Mum says she can't afford to be buying carton after carton just so we can guzzle it down."

Millie "harrumphed" as she spread butter and jam onto the halved scones she took from a tin.

"Get a glass, boy. Perhaps it would be better to give you milk, you have a lot of growing to do!"

"Yes lady, thank you!"

Gregory selected a glass from the cupboard and they sat and enjoyed a snack, the boy taking in all he could as his gaze wandered around the room. Smoky had his fill and was contentedly licking himself, when a shrill trill suddenly sounded from an adjoining room. Gregory looked up in surprise.

"It's a bird!" He stated.

"That's Alphonse, he thought you had gone. He does not whistle when strangers are around. Hurry and drink your

171

milk boy, you must be getting back home or you will get into trouble." Between mouthfuls, Gregory gulped.

"No I won't, Mum doesn't care—oops?"

He was interrupted as Smoky managed to jump onto his lap and curled up, purring. The boy eagerly but gently, stroked the animal. Millie smiled again as she saw the radiant face of the happy youngster.

"He likes you, boy. He won't go near strangers usually, you should be honoured!"

"Oh I am, I am!"

Because her pet was settled and contented, Millie let the boy dally a little longer but came the time when he had to go, Millie walked with him to the front gate.

"Goodbye lady and thank you, could I er, could I come again one day?"

Millie gave him a long look before answering.

"You are not really a nasty little boy, are you? And Smoky does like you; perhaps you could ask your mother if you can come again tomorrow. I might need a message or two!"

As she watched the boy skip joyfully away, Millie mumbled to herself.

"Don't know what has come over me, tolerating the horrid little urchin. But he was gentle with Smoky—now what messages do I need tomorrow?"

THE END.

Howard Reede-Pelling.

17   Frosty   11/3/79

Frosty Lentiss clawed grimly to the vibrating steering wheel as his land rover jolted awkwardly down the treacherous steep incline. Cursing as he fought to keep the runaway vehicle to the narrow confines of this rarely used track, which led to goodness knows where. Frosty urgently plotted the most likely path among the loose rocks and boulders that had fallen and were strewn as monolith marbles; to bar his way. It appeared at first when he breasted the rise that the track he was following veered to the left but alas, as he steered that way the track could be seen leading off to the right. Trying to correct, Frosty had turned the wheel sharply and unfortunately a large rock came into contact with the inside of the off front wheel, tearing away the fluid line to the brakes and rendering them useless. Frosty had strained the manual brakes to the rear wheels on to their full extent, but weight of the vehicle in conjunction of the steep incline down which he was plunging, made an arrest of the land rover an impossibility. His only hope for survival was to point the vehicle straight down and hope he could dodge the trees and boulders. As luck would dictate, Frosty had the land rover bounding down a cattle track and he prayed that it kept leading straight and did not circumnavigate the hill horizontally. Leaving the gears engaged, Frosty switched off the ignition, trusting the combustion to work in his favour and have a braking effect. He could not steer clear of all the rocks and fallen limbs, so it was that one particular bump he was unable to avoid, caused the stricken vehicle to bounce off what little track there was and plunge headlong over a hump where it came to rest astride a dry watercourse. The nose firmly embedded into the opposite bank and three of the four wheels were left airborne. Frosty was jolted out of the door where he landed heavily, precariously balanced atop the embankment. It was not a very deep watercourse and should he slide off onto the rocky bed, he would not be in great danger of being hurt. However, luck was slightly in his favour and he did not fall heavily. He was quite winded though and lay where he fell, recovering his wind and his senses. As Frosty lay, his gaze wandered back over the rough terrain down which he had plummeted. The skid marks at the top were quite clear and he shuddered to think how lucky he was, not to have his land rover overturn and possibly kill or seriously injure him. That he managed to steer clear of the trees and huge rocks was nothing short of miraculous. That he and his vehicle survived that mad jolting journey off a virtual cliff-face; was unbelievable. Even if he somehow managed to winch the land rover out of its present predicament and repair the damaged fluid-line, one look at that fierce cliff down which he plunged, convinced Frosty that he could not possibly return that way. A though struck him, what of Estelle? When he did not return on time how she would worry. What a girl she was, the best wife a man could have, he must not let her worry unduly. Frosty eased himself erect and tested his limbs, yes he was quite all right; no breaks. The poor land rover was another matter though. He had no qualms about getting the sturdy little vehicle out, it's built in cables would see to that; providing the engine was not damaged and there was the possibility of the radiator being pushed in. If it were, that could make things awkward. Also, was there a tree handy that was solid enough to use as an anchor for the winch? He would need it as a bastion for his block and tackle. Yes, there was one just behind, how he missed it on his way down he would never know! The first thing to do Frosty realized was to fix the brakes if possible. He checked and felt sure the vehicle would not settle any lower or fall from its elevated position while he did the repairs. One good thing, suspended like that, the land rover would be easy to work on. It was perhaps about an hour before the repairs were completed but Frosty knew the brakes would still be inoperable, as he did not carry any spare brake fluid. He would have to trust to the gears and hand brake and not travel at any great speed. Having the fluid line repaired would ensure that no more dust than was already there would get in, while he attempted to extricate the land rover from its predicament. A careful check and Frosty was sure there was no damage to the radiator or engine. Although he could not get at the winch from the front, as the vehicle was well stuck by its bull bar into the dry wash, Frosty was able to release the cable from beneath and pass it up through a tiny aperture under the chassis at the rear. It was but a matter of minutes and he had a pulley attached to the tree. He put the cable through it and returned to the hook on the back of the vehicle. The next step was to gather as many logs as he could find and pack them under the land rover to build up the floor of the wash, so that when he began to winch, the vehicle would have some sort of support and not fall too far. It was suspended by both ends, front and rear. The crucial moment came, Frosty turned on the ignition. After a few revs, the engine burst into life. He let it warm up a little. Gingerly, the lever was operated and the winch ground in to motion. The vehicle shuddered as the cable lost its slack and the full weight of the land rover was taken as Frosty 'revved' her up. At first nothing appeared to be happening, and then all of a sudden, a backwards motion accompanied by the awesome drop of the nose as it was dragged clear and fell the few decimetres onto the logs; heralded the beginning of its extraction. The sturdy motor ground on and before long, Frosty was uncoupling the cable and packing it away, the land rover once again on solid ground. Gingerly he edged the battered work-horse along the edge of the dry water way, grimly studying the walls above; seeking a possible means of ascending. Estelle would be worried sick. Frosty promised he would be home for the evening meal and already it was well past his expected time of arrival, in fact, he must find a way out soon; the sun had set and the night time was beginning to close in!

Estelle Lentiss was concerned. As a rule Frosty was very punctual, it was most unusual for him to be as late as this. If he were unavoidably detained he would have 'phoned. Perhaps the land rover broke down; yes that is what must have happened! She had already put aside one half hour, then another and even waited for him at the front gate. He was not in sight. Estelle finally plucked the receiver from its cradle and dialled Bob Mattron at Konbillie, the little township some thirty kilometres away. Frosty and Bob were great mates and it was to return Bob's trailer that made the trip necessary. Perhaps Frosty had got too deeply into some agricultural subject with Bob and time just slipped away unnoticed. She would ring Bob and check. Mentally noting that she must chastise her man for causing this concern, she anxiously awaited the other end to answer. At last the call got through, a small childish voice spoke. "Huwwow–vis is me–'Lisbef. My mummy said I should hang on to you 'cause she's cooking tea!"

"Oh! Hello Elizabeth Dear, this is Missus Lentiss. Is daddy there?"

Silence echoed the question, and then a loud whisper could be heard.

"Mummy, it is Missus Wensis. Her wants my daddy."

"Who's on the 'phone Love?" A loud voice boomed.

It was Bob Mattron who had evidently just entered the room. Confused whispering by Elizabeth as he took the receiver, then.

"Hello, is that you Estelle? Just been making room in my shed for the trailer. Frosty get home okay?"

"He has left then?" Estelle querulously asked.

"Why yes, two–three hours ago, don't tell me he's not back yet, Estelle!" There was a concerned note in his voice.

"Didn't call on anyone else on the way home did he?"

"No, I would not think so." Estelle shook her head, notwithstanding the fact that Bob could not see her. "He would have 'phoned. Oh Bob, I am terribly afraid he has had an accident, it should only take an hour to get here. What should I do?"

Bob pondered the situation.

"Now don't go off half-cocked Estelle, you stay put so I can ring when I find him. I'll back-track to your place; he is probably broken down somewhere. Don't worry, I will find him!"

He hung up and Estelle made herself a cup of coffee, to sip and worry over. Bob Mattron left immediately and it was only forty minutes later that he pulled up outside Frosty's home. The strain and worry could be seen on Estelle's face as she opened the door to him.

"You didn't find him?" It was an accusation. Bob frowned.

"He's still not home then? He was not broken down on the highway anywhere; he must have turned off some place!"

"Oh Bob! Estelle grabbed frantically at his arm. "Something terrible has happened, I just know it, and we will probably find him overturned in a ditch somewhere. I'll come with you; we'll search the side of the road!"

Estelle made to pass. Bob held her back.

"No Estelle! Not so fast, you are beginning to panic. If we both go he will probably turn up when we are gone and wonder where you are, then he will get worried. End up like a dog chasing its tail. It is best if you stay, I will go slowly and check the side roads. He may be broken down along Hogan's Road, we were talking about a property out there and I will bet that is where he is; checking it out. Don't worry, I will find him!" Bob ushered her back indoors. "Now you sit by the 'phone—no—better still, get a nice hot meal ready for him. I will have him back in a jiffy!"

"But—?"

"No buts do as I say; promise?" He gave her confidence, she nodded agreement.

"Yes, you—you're probably right, I do tend to panic a little. Oh, I pray you'll find him safe—go—please hurry!"

Bob was not at all sure he would find Frosty safe, the time lapse was too long; still he saw no sense in giving Estelle the additional worry by telling her of his fears. No doubt he had spoken truly of Frosty's whereabouts; he could only have gone to inspect that property. After all, it was on his way home but should only have taken him an extra quarter of an hour. It was very obvious that he must be broken down or in some kind of trouble with the land rover. Bob only hoped that it was not too serious. When Bob entered the turn-off and sped along the gravel road that led to the property where he expected to find Frosty, he beheld the glare of headlights approaching from behind the next rise. It was by now, quite dark. It had to be his friend, Bob stopped to await his coming. When the vehicle came within an appreciable distance, Bob dipped his headlights two or three times. The oncoming vehicle responded and pulled up beside him. The welcoming smile vanished when Bob realized this was not Frosty or his land rover, this was a gravel-truck! The burly driver asked.

"What's up Mate, broken down?" Bob shook his head.

"No, I am looking for a mate. Didn't happen to see a snowy-haired bloke in a brown and white land rover, did you?"

The bewhiskered driver pouted as he solemnly shook his head.

"No mate. Thought I heard one whining down in Fraser's Valley a coupla hours ago though, dismissed it as echoes. Even a land rover couldn't get down there!"

"Where's Fraser's Valley, is there a chance he could be in it?"

Bob's concern had the truck driver interested.

"It is down an off-shoot track about half a kilometre back!" He indicated by thumbing over his shoulder. "But there's no way you could drive down there. Old Fraser did start to bulldoze a cutting but it was such hard going he abandoned it–'fraid the 'dozer would tip!"

"I had better check the valley out just the same, Frosty is three hours overdue. I will never find it in the dark, would you lead me to it Pal?"

Bob breathed a thankful sigh as the truckie locked his vehicle and hopped into Bob's car. Bob followed his directions to a turn-off and they proceeded along what was little more that wagons track. Though mostly straight it did wander in and out amongst trees and rocks somewhat, luckily the truck driver knew the track fairly well and they proceeded at a brisk pace. When they finally stopped, the burly truck driver pointed to the cutting that Fraser had begun many years ago and quite distinctly in the glare of the headlights, could be seen fresh wheel marks leading downhill.

"He has been here!" Bob exclaimed, pointing to the evidence. "God, I hope he isn't killed!" Bob grabbed a torch from the glove compartment of his car and they proceeded to follow the wheel marks. They had travelled perhaps thirty metres, when the truckie held Bob back.

"Listen, what's that?"

They stood in silence for a moment, then the call the bewhiskered truckie heard, was repeated. Faintly from above, somewhere beyond the perimeter of the hill in the vicinity of the track they had been following; came a frantic cry.

"Hey there! Hang on a minute—help!"

The two scrambled hurriedly back to the vehicle, and then ran along the track in the direction from which the cry came. They beheld a very dishevelled Frosty, panting along in the dark at a brisk trot. He collapsed, exhausted at their feet.

"Thank God someone came. I've been wandering around in the dark for hours!"

"Frosty, are you okay? Thought you must be dead when we found you went off the cutting!" Bob worried.

"Bob!" An exuberant Frosty exclaimed upon recognizing his mate's voice. "How on earth did you find me?" He grabbed his pal's hand and shook it vigorously.

"Wouldn't have only for our friend here, he knew the area and led me to the spot." Introductions were made all around and then Frosty explained what happened, finishing with:—"so I drove back and forth along the valley until it got too dark. Decided to leave the 'rover and hoof it but with all the ridges and no moon, I soon got lost. Then I stumbled on to the track and boy—was I pleased when I saw your headlights. Have to leave the land rover 'til tomorrow, damned if I know where I left it. One thing for sure, I won't be buying that valley. Let's go home; poor Estelle will be frantic with worry!"

Happily, the three made for home, Frosty still reliving his frightening experience.

THE END.

Howard Reede-Pelling.

18   Gerry   14/4/79

The dust hung like a cloud over the still air on this glorious summer day. It was the second week of the annual school holidays that mothers dread and as with other families at this time of the year, the children were beginning to wear mother's patience and had been sent out to play. That is why the dust hung in the air. Four boisterous youngsters were sliding down the steep side of a hill, some one hundred metres to the rear of the old tin and weatherboard house, tucked away in the backblocks of outback Australia. That the dust clouded the air, attested to the fact the shenanigans had been progressing for some time. It would seem that their mother believed in the fact that, if the children were noisy, they were well and healthy. These certainly were a healthy bunch of children. All were covered in dust from head to foot and that included inside their clothes and shoes. The sheets of tin that were being used as toboggans, should have made their parents shudder with the fear of having tiny fingers to mend and bandage. Perhaps their philosophy was, if the children were foolish enough not to watch what they are doing, then they deserved to be cut and bandaged. David slid to a stop at the end of his umpteenth slide and tossing aside the jagged chariot that had served him so well, called to Benjamin, his six year old brother.

"C'mon Ben, I'm tired of sliding, let's go to the dam and catch some yabbies."

Benjamin was but an elf and would be in anything that David suggested so with a yelp of

"Yair, let's." They were off, leaving their two older brothers to themselves.

The boys, having lived in the area all their lives, knew every waterhole, niche and dry wash in the neighbourhood and had explored them thoroughly. Hence it was not long before they were bored with yabbying and sought new worlds to conquer. They wandered off aimlessly barefoot, as they had left their gumboots at the edge of the dam, having taken them off to ooze the mud through their toes. The children were in trouble with mum and dad if they went a field without gumboots, because of the danger of snakes and the incidence of the prickle plague that was being experienced throughout the district. However, around the house and its near vicinity they were normally barefoot, so to forget to put the gumboots on was a usual practice. David and Benjamin wandered aimlessly along the outer fence of the chicken coop, idly throwing stones at the thistle stems growing in profusion and before long, found themselves at the dry creek bed. Well, it was not completely dry, there were many deep holes brimming with clear water but the creek was no longer running. There had been no decent rain for nearly three months and the situation was becoming desperate for the people of the district. The boys walked up to one of the many deep holes, peering into the water as they did so, hoping to catch a frog or some tadpoles.

"Hey! There's a fish!"

Benjamin was excitedly pointing to the bracken and driftwood clogged at the bank of the deep hole.

"Let's try and catch it."

David looked about for a stick or a tin, something with which he might trap the elusive fish. The two set about their task with enthusiasm.

Back on the dusty hill, fourteen year old Timothy and his younger brother by two years, Patrick; were also tired of sliding down the hill. It is not that they could not take more of the sliding but to do so, necessitated a stiff climb back up, dragging a cumbersome piece of tin; so they desisted and took to the dam.

"Hey Pat, I'm dusty, how about a swim?"

"Yair!"

The boys divested themselves of their clothing and were soon splashing merrily in the muddy dam, naked as the day they were born. They were sunning themselves dry on the rough dead grass below the dam walls, when Patrick suddenly shouted.

"Hey Tim, Dave and Ben nicked off and left their gumboots— gee—they will cop it!"

"Argh, don't worry Pat, we can take them home and Mum won't know the difference!"

"Yair, I s'pose!"

The boys lapsed into silence and were almost asleep, when a motor could be heard droning in the distance. Timothy jumped up.

"Pat, wake up–Dad's coming–quick, get dressed!"

Both boys managed to get home and put their younger brother's boots away and were racing to meet the truck before it came down the driveway through the evergreen cedars that lined the entrance to the property. Gerry Kendicer stopped the old truck when he saw his two eldest boys racing towards him. They were ever keen to stand on the back looking over the cabin as their father drove the last hundred metres to the house.

"Hello boys." He greeted. "Hop up quickly and hang on!"

They returned the salutation and clambered aboard. It was hardly worth the effort, for the short trip was over almost before it began. The youngsters did not mind, as the ride broke the monotony of having little to do. They alighted as the truck stopped and fussed about their father.

"Did you go to Barrellan Dad?" Patrick asked eyes alight in anticipation.

"Yes, I bought you all some sweets too. You may have them after dinner. Got something else for us all too!"

"Ooh, what is it Dad?" Timothy eagerly queried, as his father passed parcels out for the boys to carry inside.

"No, I won't tell you yet, wait until we are all together at dinner time. Where are Dave and Ben?"

Both boys shook their heads. Timothy answered.

"Last we saw of them, they went to catch yabbies and frogs at the dam."

Patrick added his two cents worth.

"But they weren't there when we went swim–I mean, when we got there, they'd gone!"

Gerry Kendicer smiled; his son may as well have said it all.

"Well, you boys had better go and look for them and–?"

He was cut short as a shrill scream echoed from the creek. He recognised it and was running towards the sound as David's voice called frantically.

"Help—Mummy—help!"

David poked at the bracken in the water hole where Benjamin said he saw the fish flit out of sight, but the sun's reflection hampered his vision, so he decided to climb the towering bank at the back of the water hole; then try to get down to the water again where he could stand on a protruding tree root. From there he might manage to see the fish. David reached his objective but still could not see the quarry. If only he could reach the stick he was using into that dark ledge under the bank, the fish may swim out into the open. The boy stepped into the water and balanced on a submerged tree root, up to his knees in the water; he still could not reach the cavity. Benjamin was watching the fruitless efforts from the gravel creek bed opposite.

"Ben, grab a longer stick and bring it around. I reckon I can shoo him out if I have a longer stick—hurry!"

Benjamin scouted about and soon had a suitable piece of wood. He clambered up the bank and along the top till he came to where David was waiting. It was an awkward climb for the smaller boy, especially so, as he was hampered by the ungainly stick. He was just reaching the stick down to his brother, when the tuft of grass to which he was clinging, gave way. With a shrill scream he fell on top of David and the pair of them disappeared beneath the surface of the water. David, still with a firm grip on the tree roots, pulled himself up as far as he could, which was only head and shoulders out of the water. Benjamin, having dislodged his brother's footing from the branch upon which he was standing, caused David's leg to become entangled in the tree roots underwater. Benjamin could not swim and David had the presence of mind to reach out for him as the little fellow surfaced. It was David's frantic call that guided his father to their predicament and it was upon that scene he stumbled as he ploughed into the water. He reached across.

"Right-oh David—let Ben go—I've got him!"

The father sat his youngest son on the gravel and left him sobbing as he went to the aid of David. He reached out and ran a hand down the boy's leg until he located the obstruction. Although forced to submerge himself, he could not see, for the water had been agitated and muddy now with all the commotion. It was not hard for the man to spring the supple roots apart and turn the boy's foot so it could be extricated. Gerry Kendicer carried his son to safety. The boy's foot was only slightly lacerated. An angry father turned upon the boys.

"What the hell did you think you were doing playing by these deep holes without your brothers? You know I have told you two time and time again not to go near them without Tim or Pat, you could have drowned yourselves!"

Gerry angrily glared at the errant pair, as he felt of the injured ankle.

"Ben fell on me, Dad! I didn't go in on purpose!" David defended.

"It wasn't my fault!" An indignant Benjamin explained. "The grass broke!"

"Never mind whose fault it was, you are both to blame for playing near the deep holes without your brothers. Now off home and get into some dry clothes, scoot!"

Timothy and Patrick were close on their father's heels and assisted the hobbling David.

Marilyn Kendicer awaited her family at the back gate. She had been disturbed from her cooking by the sudden commotion and arrived at the door to see her husband and the two older children running helter skelter down to the creek. She too heard the screams and had come to investigate. Marilyn called as Gerry returned.

"What is going on, is someone hurt?"

"No Love, Ben and Dave took a ducking, that's all."

Gerry was wringing his wallet and handkerchief out as he walked back.

"Hmpf!" Marilyn snorted. "Looks like they weren't the only ones either; did you have to go in clothes and all? Just look at your good pants and shirt!"

"Sorry Love. Better to be on the safe side, made a mess of the papers in my wallet. Just as well I had my jacket off, the cheque books in the pocket!"

It was some little time before the drenched three were in dry clothes and Gerry had his private papers on the way to recovery, drying on a piece of plywood atop the old one-fire stove. The Kendicer Family, for a change, were quiet as they sat about the dinner table. The two younger boys were in disgrace for causing their father to take a ducking in his good clothes, the elder two, also apprehensive for allowing their younger brothers to wander off and get into the dangerous situation that caused the ducking. Each child expected to be berated by the parents, so a rather tense atmosphere prevailed.

"How did the trip to Barrellin go dear?" Marilyn asked as she piled salad high on each plate.

"Very well Love, it was exceptional really. The pigs brought a higher price than I expected and I got rid of all the vegetables, I knew we were not planting too many."

He turned sharply to Timothy and Patrick.

"Did you boys put those parcels in our room?"

"Yes Dad." Both replied simultaneously.

"Didn't peek did you?"

"No Dad!" Timothy answered as Patrick shook his head.

"Should I ask what is in the parcels Dear?" Marilyn queried.

"Something special for you, My Love. When the boys have done the dishes, we will all enjoy the surprise."

"Dad." Timothy querulously asked.

"Yes Son?" "Are you—are you still mad at us, I mean, about Ben and Dave?"

"Of course. You did not act responsibly!" He tried to keep a stern expression as he watched the solemn faces.

"Does that mean we will not get the surprise you promised us?"

Gerry considered a moment before replying.

"No, but I do expect you to make up for it in other ways, like helping Mum and me around the house and garden and keeping out of the way when we are busy!"

"Gee, we will Dad, won't we Pat?" The boy turned to his brother for support.

"Promise we will Dad—what is the surprise?" Patrick eagerly asked.

Marilyn looked up with interest, as did all their sons.

"Uncle Arnold is coming to stay for a couple of days and he is bringing his speed-boat and water skis!"

When the excited babble had died down, the dishes washed and put away, Gerry had the boys bring the parcels out of his bedroom. He placed the one with the pretty ribbon on Marilyn's knees and all waited expectantly as she opened it.

"Goodness gracious, Gerry! A swimming costume, I'm past all that–but it is a bit daring–don't you think?"

"Nonsense Love, It is not too daring and you are by no means past all that! It is high time we had a holiday as a family, we have worked very hard to get the crops in and we are going to enjoy life a bit. Arnold can be very persuasive at times and this is one time that he is right. Now hop into it and see if it fits!"

"Have you got a parcel for us, Dad?" Young Benjamin piped up.

"Yes Ben, there is one for each of you and one for me. Now all try your togs on and see if they fit."

Four eager lads needed no second bidding as they frantically tore their packages open amid a chorus of.

"Wows" and "Thanks Dad!"

From early morning the next day, the four Kendicer children were anxiously awaiting the arrival of their Uncle Arnold at the gate leading to the avenue of cedars. Their father thought that they would be more interested in his boat, than in Uncle Arnold and in this, he was probably right. The cheers of the children as they detected a cloud of dust in the distance brought their parents to the front door, where they awaited the arrival of the vehicle. A disappointed moan was heard as the children noted that there was no speedboat being trailing behind. It was a false alarm, the driver being a stranger asking directions to a neighbour's place. The children settled down to wait again. It was another half an hour before the next cloud of dust appeared. This time the vehicle could be seen to have a trailer.

"It's a boat, it is Uncle Arnold. Hey Dad–he is here–Uncle Arnold is here and he brought his boat!" Timothy yelled, loudly and clearly.

Gerry and Marilyn walked arm-in-arm to the front gate to await Gerry's big brother. The car was quite a time at the entrance as Arnold made sure his nephews were safely settled into the boat atop the trailer. They did not spare him much more than a quick.

"Hello Uncle Arnold, can we hop in your boat?"

He ruffled each head as he hoisted them up, with strict instructions to sit still or they would have to ride in the car, then he slowly drove to the house and a friendly cuppa. Arnold Kendicer was a tall, athletic man whose physique belied his age. Though greying on top and at the sideburns, the quick twinkling eyes and ready smile, gave him the impish look of youth. Gerry could have been his twin but for the fact he was shorter and no grey was evident whatsoever. As they sipped tea, the three adults planned the afternoon's activities and decided that if everyone pulled their weight, they could be on the road to Griffith and Lake Wyangan before eleven-thirty. While Marilyn set to preparing a picnic lunch, the two men enlisted the aid of two of the boys in preparing the truck. Patrick and David were sent inside to help their mother, while Timothy and little Benjamin got to work on the tray of the truck. Old vegetable crates and coils of rope had to be packed away in the shed and the tray had to be swept and hosed, because the pigs had been aboard. Meanwhile, Gerry extolled the virtues of the engine to his brother, the while he checked the oil and battery and generally prepared the truck for the afternoon's outing. At last all was in readiness, Arnold's overnight bag was put in the spare room made available, so the boys could all ride with Uncle Arnold. They drove off towing the boat, the children excitedly jabbering and waving to their parents following in the truck, with the picnic gear. The fifteen kilometres to Barrellan did not take long to traverse and there was only a short stop for fresh milk and bread, before they sallied forth again, on the forty-odd kilometres to Griffith. By one o'clock they were well established by the lake upon which all expected to try their luck at water-skiing. The children were soon exploring the water's edge and had to be threatened before they came back to enjoy the picnic lunch. Having lunched, the boys were eager to enter the water, but their wise parents explained again as they had done many times in the past, that it was not practical to go into the water right after a meal. They must wait and let it settle first. Arnold decided that the hour could be spent taking the eager boys for a ride around the lake in his runabout. When the boatload of happy youngsters set forth across the water, their parents merrily waved them off; then settled down to a quiet cuppa as they nestled together under the protective outflung branches of a shady tree. The hour seemed to flit away and Arnold spent the next fifteen minutes instructing his nephews on the correct method of water skiing. Having satisfied himself that they had learned enough on dry land, he set the eldest–Timothy–the task of leader.

"You show them Tim!" He urged, as he eased the boat forwards gently.

Marilyn remained on the shore with Patrick and Benjamin. The boys would take it in turns so there was less risk of mishaps. While Uncle Arnold managed the speedboat, David would be his observer and the boy's father would act as lifesaver or emergency pilot. The line slowly became taut and as Timothy had his skis pointed skywards in the approved manner as shown by his Uncle earlier, Arnold eased forward, then 'gave her the gun'. Timothy rose, was up–faltered a little–then straightened. Arnold, glancing over his shoulder at the boy, saw he was in control and so increased the speed just a little. Timothy appeared to be going well, then suddenly shot forwards out of his skis, head down and feet up. He seemed to cartwheel before he disappeared under the turbulence of the boat's wake. Gerry waited until the boat circled back, then dived in and swam to his son's assistance. Gerry's anxiety was short lived, for Timothy was happily bobbing about in the water; non-the-worse for his ducking.

"Are you all right, Son?" Gerry queried, as he reached for one of the skis floating nearby.

"Yes Dad, can I have another go?"

"Sure you want to?"

"Do I ever? And I won't fall this time, I betcha!"

Nor did he and his proud mother waved in answer to his shouted.

188

"Look at me Mum!" As he skimmed past, albeit a little unsteadily.

There were many more spills as the smaller boys took their turns at water skiing and although Benjamin could not quite grasp the method of rising out of the water, he had as much fun as his older brothers who managed to skim at least some of the time on top of the water. Eventually the younger pair, David and Benjamin, were left to play around the water's edge with mum keeping a wary eye upon them, so Arnold and Gerry could take turns at skiing, using the older boys, Patrick and Timothy as observers. Inevitably the day had to come to an end but the exploits of all were told and retold by the happy exuberant youngsters. The highlight of the day came when Uncle Arnold took them all to a hotel for a nice roast chicken dinner, with apple turn-overs and cream to top it off. The boys sipped lemon squashes as the adults enjoyed a convivial beer in the quiet atmosphere of the lounge. By the time they reached home, Benjamin and David were fast asleep and Timothy and Patrick were bleary eyed.

Morning found the Kendicer Family up and about early, as they were wont to do. When your livelihood is farming and market gardening, it is second-nature to arise early. The children gave mother a good ribbing for being a 'fraidy-cat' and not going into the water. She smiled their raillery aside with.

"Well, someone had to be with Benjamin and David while you others were enjoying yourselves, besides, I had no intention of getting my nice new bathing costume all wet. I just wanted to sit there and look pretty!"

"And so you did, Love." Gerry agreed. "Now you lot clear out and leave your mother alone, go on–scoot!"

He grinned as he pretended to chase the chuckling youngsters out.

Arnold came into the kitchen yawning hugely.

"Am I ever hungry, what's for breakfast Marilyn, Honey?"

She waved an egg-flipper in cheery greeting as she answered, setting a plate of eggs and bacon before him with the other hand.

"Does that answer your question, Dear Brother-in-law? Plonk yourself down and we will eat with you–tea or coffee?"

"Oh, coffee thanks—black!"

"Suit yourself, Gerry and I are tea-drinkers, so you will have the pot to yourself."

Marilyn prepared the coffee in the percolator and left it simmering, then sat down with the men.

"Where are the boys?" Arnold asked.

"Just fed and went out to play, don't know how they do it. I am all stiff and sore from yesterday's activities." Gerry answered.

"They are awfully quiet. I hope they are not up to any mischief!" Marilyn pondered.

Arnold left his chair and peered out of the window.

"I see them; they are playing on the old dray up on the rise. They'll be all right there won't they?"

"Sure!" Gerry said. "It is pretty well chocked up with stones. They can't do much damage to it."

The men were having a restful smoke while Marilyn washed the dishes. Arnold, upon hearing the distant chatter of the children, again went to the window.

Meanwhile, Timothy had tied a piece of rope to the drawbar of the dray and was holding this as he balanced astride the shafts, one foot on each. He was pretending to be water skiing. The other three boys were acting as drivers and observers on a speed-boat. They were rocking the dray violently, simulating the movement of a boat on a rough sea. Timothy urged them on as they rocked harder. The chocks holding the dray back were jolted out of position and the dray slowly began to move off, down the incline. Timothy gave a yelp as he became aware that the dray was away.

"Hey, she's moving—hang on!"

This was better than he imagined. The dray gathered momentum and began to fairly race down the slope, the three on top ceased their jiggling and held on for dear life. Timothy still astride the shafts and whooping it up as the dust flew behind. It was this scene that Arnold beheld as he checked through the window.

"My God!" He exclaimed, as he hurried to the door. "The dray's bolted with the kids on board!" As the dray sped down the rough decline, the shafts bounced awkwardly over the rocky terrain. Timothy's feet were dislodged and he ran a few metres before being pulled off balance and dragged along, he let go of the rope and rolled to a stop. The dray with the three scared brothers aboard finally ran itself out and dribbled to a standstill amongst the tall tussocks abounding at the lower reaches of the paddock. Three concerned adults rushed to the aid of a bruised and scratched Timothy, groaning as he nursed his wounds. Three apprehensive younger brothers rushed back to see what had befallen the would-be water ski champion. Their father angrily berated the errant quartet (boys will be boys) and threatened dire punishments, concluding with.

"–and no more water skiing ever again for you lot. You could have been killed getting up to a prank like that–now go to your rooms and tidy up. Don't leave the house 'til I say so!"

The three dejected boys sulkily walked back home, Patrick and David trying to comfort young Benjamin who burst into crying as the implications of what had happened, sunk in. Timothy was checked for broken bones then taken back to the house, where much liniment and sticking plaster was applied.

The mid-day meal was a solemn, quiet affair. The children were in disgrace and their punishment hung heavily on their minds.

"Patrick, David, eat your dinner!" Their mother demanded.

"I'm not hungry Mum." They choroused.

Gerry glared at the two. They picked up their forks and began nibbling.

"Dad!" Tim querulously said.

"Yes Timothy?"

"I–I'm sorry. We are all very sorry. We won't be stupid and do anything like that again. Do we really have to give up water skiing with Uncle Arnold?"

"Please Dad!" Benjamin piped up. "I like water skiing with Uncle Arnold–please, pretty please?"

Gerry found it difficult to keep a straight face as he answered.

"It is really up to Uncle Arnold, he might think you haven't enough common sense for it!"

Four pairs of questioning eyes sought the reply from Uncle Arnold. His serious face broke, a slight smile quivered at the corners of his mouth and eyes. The children had their answer and brightened, the tense atmosphere eased, the children resumed their meal.

THE END

Howard Reede-Pelling.

Brian drove the five kilometres to Leah's home in a very happy frame of mind. The elements were in his favour with a glorious showing of sunshine and a very slight, warm breeze. The forecast from the weather bureau for the day was in keeping of that of the past week; a warm to hot afternoon as the slight breeze dropped. Brian had chosen well the week end upon which to invite Leah and her family to a picnic. He was looking forwards to it with eager anticipation. Brian had just turned the panel van around in front of the gate as he arrived, when the joyous yells of Leah's two youngsters echoed down from her first floor flat.

"Brian is here, Mummy Brian is here!"

The two children raced down the steps to greet him.

"Hello, how are you two today, ready for a picnic?" Brian asked, as he picked up Ingrid and carried her back upstairs after he ruffled Philyp's hair.

"A picnic!" The two boisterous children asked. "Are we going on a picnic?"

"Well, I hope so. I made arrangements with Mum last Wednesday; I certainly hope she is prepared."

Leah was waiting at the door to welcome Brian but was still in her dressing gown.

"Hello Brian, I'm sorry, I really can't go on the picnic. I have too much work to do—just look at it—!"

She indicated the lounge room, strewn with student's papers and technical volumes.

"I really wanted to go but I must have these papers corrected for classes tomorrow and I still have that précis to do for my own studies. Could I have a rain-cheque—do you mind?"

Brian was deeply disappointed but tried not to show it, smiling his loss off with.

"Of course Leah, pity to waste such a glorious day indoors though!"

"Gee Mum!" Philyp groaned, "Can't you do that correcting tonight, we want to go with Brian."

"Me too!" Ingrid wrapped her arms about Brian's neck as she added her voice to the discussion.

"Now Philyp, you know Mum has been working all week end and it will take more than an evening to finish them. I have a large class and they are examination papers. If they were your papers you would want them corrected and marked properly, wouldn't you?"

Philyp cast his dejected features at his boots.

"I suppose so but I wanted to go with Brian, it's a rotten day to stay at home."

Brian had been thinking and came up with a suggestion.

"Tell you what Philyp. Seeing how Mum is very busy and needs to be alone, what say you run around to your little mate's place and see if he would like to come swimming with us? If you get a little mate to play with, I will take you children to the beach for the day. How does that sound?"

Brian eyed their mother questioningly. Amid a "yes please" from Philyp and a "can I go too?" From Ingrid, Leah stated.

"Oh! Would you mind? That would be a help Brian."

Phylip was away but a matter of only ten minutes, during which time Ingrid's little playmate from next door called, she had a new doll and pram to show off. Ingrid soon changed her mind about swimming with the boys and asked could she play with Cheryl instead. The two seven year olds happily ran off to play. Brian and Leah utilised the ten minutes together to have a cup of tea, with Leah promising next time they would have a whole day to themselves. At eleven years of age, Philyp and his pal Harold were quite noisy and it was not two boys who thumped up the stairs and banged through the door—it was more like the charge of a pair of rhinoceros.

"He is allowed to go Mum—Harold has come—he has his togs and a towel, but you gotta ring his Dad and say when he'll be home!"

Philyp blurted the words out as they rushed in to the kitchen.

"All right Philyp, steady down." His mother said. "You are very rude butting in like that. Come in like a gentleman next time and I do not want to hear you say 'gotta' again. You should say 'have to'. Hello Harold, do you know Mister–?"

"Just Brian will do son—how are you—I had better pop around and see your folks. Better for them to meet the one who is taking care of their son for the day. Can you swim?"

Brian reached out a hand as he spoke up. The boy took it with a bright smile as he answered.

"Yes Sir. Thanks for letting me come with Philyp!"

He was a little taller than Philyp and stockier in contrast to the slim athletic schoolmate who had been a family friend for some years, however it was the first time Brian had met Harold, even though Philyp had spoken of him often. While Leah spoke to Harold's parents over the telephone and explained with whom their son would be spending the day, Brian drove the boys back and introduced himself. When all arrangements were finalised, the trio set forth for the day at the beach. The two excited boys were keenly noting the route and Philyp piped up.

"Hey Brian, this way we pass Damien's house, could we call in and take him too, please!" Brian considered before answering. Damien was the same age as Philyp and Harold and was a member of Brian's swimming group, as was Philyp. Brian coached two classes of up to fifteen children, twice a week, at swimming. It would not hurt to take another youngster along, he supposed, although three was an awkward number of children to manage. Invariably he found, two would pair off and leave the odd one out, still, Philyp and Damien got on well and Harold did appear to be an easy-going sort of lad.

"Sure you will all behave well?" Brian asked by way of an answer.

"Sure we will, won't we Harold?" Philyp sought assurance from his mate, who replied.

"I got to; Dad said he would kill me if I did not behave!"

Brian hid a smile as he stopped at Damien's home. Philyp eagerly rushed in, with Harold somewhat cautiously lagging behind. Brian remained in the van and in a couple of minutes Damien came flying out with a towel and swimming gear fluttering, as he clambered into the back of the panel van with a hasty.

"Hi!" To Brian. "Mum's been trying to ring you!" He called.

Damien's mother came out.

"Hello Brian, I have been trying to ring you. Missus Wallers has 'phoned me. She said she can't contact you and maybe I knew where you were. Her father is ill and they have to rush up country to him, she wants to know if you can mind her brood for the day. She is desperate for a baby-sitter, I offered but she can't afford the time to bring them over and thinks they will get lost if they come by public transport. Said she will just have to take them with her. She only rang a few minutes ago, can you help her?"

Brian sighed.

"Why not. What is another four anyway? Can I use your telephone please?

The relief was evident on Missus Wallers' face as Brian and his three charges drove into her driveway. The whole family was in readiness on the veranda and the younger boys hastily climbed into the vehicle, to secure the better positions. Brian alighted and spoke with Valma and Erin.

"Sorry to hear the old Dad is not too well, Valma. When do you expect to get back?"

Both Valma and her husband Erin were quite plump dumpy little folk, as was their sixteen year old daughter, Carmen. The four boys however, were typical lithe Australian youngsters; slim and energetic. They ranged in ages from Darren at thirteen, down past Gavin and Peter to little Wayne, aged six. Brian was a bit disappointed with the older three, in that they were not responding too well with his coaching. Young Wayne was progressing quite well though even if he did swim mostly underwater; an art at which he excelled. Valma answered Brian's question rather vaguely.

"I really don't know Brian. If we get held up, would you be able to stay for the evening? Carmen will be able to manage the evening meal she will be back by then—wants to spend the day helping out at her girl friends house, the mother is a single parent and she is not in the best of health either. Well, so Carmen says. I have my doubts; I think they may have lined up a couple of boy friends!"

"Oh Mum!" Carmen blushed. "That is not fair; we will just be playing records—truly!!"

196

"That is what you would have us believe." Erin laughed, as he hurried his other two boys into Brian's van. "Can you drop us off at the Station Pal?" He asked.

"Sure." Brian replied, and then said to Valma. "Yes, that is okay, I would love to stay for dinner and don't hurry back; I can stay the night if necessary!"

The relieved and thankful Wallers were duly let off at the station and Brian and his seven little charges were motoring to the beach. Philyp asked.

"Which beach are we going to Brian—Sandringham?"

"No Philyp, that is too far out of the way."

"But it is fun climbing up the cliffs!" Philyp pleaded.

"Yeah!" Damien agreed. It was some time before the barrage of suggestions which came from all, was run out and Brian stilled their tongues with his own suggestion.

"We are going to Williamstown and then on to Altona!"

"What is at Altona—are there cliffs?" Gavin asked.

"No cliffs, just a nice safe stretch of beach—"

Groans of dissent came from the youngsters

"-but there are rock pools where you can chase crabs and there is a very high pier where you can dive into deep water!"

Brian grinned to himself as the dissent changed immediately to eager questions. He answered them as they came thick and fast. So the time elapsed as they completed the drive to the foreshore parking area. Brian managed to park near a pedestrian crossing within easy reach of the public dressing rooms. Having cautioned the boys about madly rushing across the road, he hastily brought up the rear so as to make sure they obeyed his instructions.

When all were in their swimming attire and had been warned not to go near the pier until after lunch, Brian pointed to an area in the near vicinity in which he expected them to remain. The two younger boys, Wayne and Peter, his elder brother by two years, were keen to start crab hunting. Brian went with them, realizing the older children would have more fun unsupervised. There were not as many people on this beach as could be expected on such a lovely day, possibly because this side of Melbourne was a heavily industrialised area. Also, it was a little out of the way for the majority of the population. The breeze as yet had not abated and the waves coming ashore were of an interesting size, giving those people who dared the water ample excitement, be it surfing or diving through the waves; Brian's charges were no exception. Peter had found a large shallow pool left by the receding tide, so he and Wayne began paddling in it, searching for shells. Brian entered the warm pool and noticed many small flounder flitting about. He brought the youngster's attention to them. Both boys went eagerly and somewhat unsuccessfully after the elusive fish.

"Aw gee!" Wayne grizzled. "Where do they go all the time? I see them stop but they ain't there when I go to grab them!"

"Don't say 'ain't', Wayne. You know mum does not like it; you should say 'they are not there'!" Brian corrected.

"But where do they go?" Wayne evaded the chiding.

"They quickly bury themselves in the sand–look–I will show you."

Brian had the boys walk beside him, then, when a fish was sighted, he pointed to its outline and explained how to cup the hands and scoop it up quickly. He did so and the boys were intrigued by the small fish that appeared to have a twisted, flat head. It flipped about on his hands as he passed it to Wayne, who upon feeling it wriggle, smartly dropped it back into the water.

"Ooh, it tickles." He said.

"They are called 'flounderers' aren't they Brian?"

Peter showed his superior knowledge to his young brother.

"Just flounder Peter, yes, that is their name. Now do you want to try and catch some yourselves?"

The lads eagerly set about the task but were unrewarded and soon tired of the fruitless attempts and led Brian to the rocks in search of crabs. Brian was in the habit of continually checking the whereabouts of his small charges, so it was with no qualms that he went with the two smaller boys amongst the rocks, which were some two hundred metres from the older children playing in the light surf. Having assured himself time and again that they were well and safe,

Brian lifted small boulders covered with coral and seaweed, for the benefit of the two crab hunters. Peter found a holed plastic bucket in which to house the multitude of crustaceans they expected to catch. After a slight disagreement with Wayne as to who should best carry it, eventually he let the little bloke have it; just to stop him walking off in a huff. Brian had come across a hole that was just a little deeper than those previously searched and was standing on the sandy bottom between two large boulders, with smaller ones packed into the crevices. Peter saw a couple of large crabs enter the crevices and he jumped on to the small rocks the better to see, then the one upon which he jumped, moved. As it slithered out of position and slithered down, Peter lost his balance and was quickly steadied by the ever alert Brian. The rock landed on the sandy bottom beside Brian's leg and fell against it, effectively holding him by the foot; the coral bit into his leg. Brian was trapped, the rock too heavy to move on his own! With Brian holding him steady, Peter rode the rock as it settled on the sand and as he stepped off it on to the large rocks, Brian received a slight release of pressure on his trapped leg. With leg pinned awkwardly, it was difficult for Brian to get any leverage on the heavy rock. The two boys tried to help move it but Brian made them stop, just in the event the rock may roll on to one of them; Wayne began snivelling.

"Will you drown if the water comes in, Brian?"

"The water won't come in for a long time Wayne and it would not be over my head anyway!" Brian forced a reassuring smile through the pain of the sharp coral biting into his leg.

"Now Peter, go and get an adult from along the beach, then tell the other boys to come ashore. I don't want anything happening to them while I am trapped here."

Peter hurried off, pleased to have something to do that would be a help. As he ran, he yelled to his brothers and the other boys, playing in the breakers. No doubt they could not understand what he was saying above the noise of the surf, for those that noticed him, just merrily waved back. Peter hurried to a group of people sunning themselves on the sand. His evident excitement and frantic pointing as he hurriedly explained Brian's predicament and returned with two men of the party, was noticed by his brothers and they told the others that something was doing. The boys all left the water and hastened to where Peter and the two men were heading. Between the whole mob of them, Brian was easily released. He called all the children away from the area and they were told to wash the sand off themselves and get dried. It was time for lunch. Brian bathed his lacerated leg and applied antiseptic and a large patch of lint to keep the wound clean and dry. As they did not bring any food with them, Brian decided that hot potato chips and a piece of fish each, would be just the thing to fill the hungry children. They enjoyed that sort of lunch much more than sandwiches, which more often than not, they have daily at school. Once now and again potato chips would not harm them and they needed something filling. Brian led his flock around the block to a nearby shopping centre and luckily, there was a fish shop open. As an added treat, Brian also bought some dim-sims. They retired to the grassy park between the shops and the beach to enjoy the welcome meal. Brian would have preferred a cup of tea to quench his thirst, but there was no shop open on that Saturday afternoon, to cater for it. Brian had to suffice with soft drinks for all. That suited the youngsters' fine. To let their lunch settle, Brian had the children play in the park. There were ample amusements for them, besides feeding the seagulls with the few left-over chips. There were swings, see-saws and a may-pole that clanged incessantly as the steel rings and chains slammed against the metal pole; causing irritation to many an adult. No doubt they were wishing the children to the devil, so the peace and serenity would return to the park.

An hour had elapsed and the boisterous children cheered when Brian announced it was time to return to the beach. He had to caution them a few times for running too far ahead, he was finding it difficult to keep pace with the energetic lads. His leg was becoming quite stiff and sore. When they neared the car-parking area, Brian had two of the older boys check the van and make sure it had not been tampered with.

It was really only an excuse so he could catch up with them. They returned and reported that all was well and asked could they go to the pier now? Brian agreed but warned them not to dive in until he was there, they ran ahead. The Altona pier stood a good four metres above the undulating swells that were beginning to build up as the afternoon tide came in. The railing along one side was dotted every here and there by hopeful fishermen. At the very end, where some steps led down to a landing platform, a half dozen teenagers and younger boys were diving and swimming. It was here, at the end of the pier, Brian finally caught up with his seven charges. Harold was all for diving in and having a swim, as the afternoon was by now, extremely hot. It was only through Philyp's persuasion that the new boy did not enter the water.

"You'll get into trouble and we won't be allowed to come again!" Philyp warned. "Brian is very strict; he says we are not allowed to go in until he says so."

"Well, he is here now." Harold insisted. "So I can go in—can't I Brian?" He added, as Brian arrived in time to hear this last.

"Yes, now that I am here, all in if you want to and no stupidity please!"

Six happy youngsters took to the water, all but six year old Wayne.

"Can I go in too? I—I think I am scared!" He looked at Brian. "Is it deep?"

Brian smiled.

"Yes Wayne, it is very deep. Way over my head but you can do it, you can swim the length of the baths and you do not have to swim that far here. Just dive in and swim in a circle back to the steps. Off you go!"

Wayne watched the others for a while, and then suddenly was in the water and swimming hard. He hurried back and climbed the steps.

"I did it, didn't I?" His little face broke into a huge happy smile.

Brian nodded his approval as he tried to catch what Philyp was shouting from the water.

"Can we swim to the shore please Brian?"

"Ooh yeah!" The others chorused. "Let's go!"

"Only if you all keep together, I don't want anyone racing ahead. I want to keep an eye on the younger ones." Brian gave his consent.

"I can't do it!" Wayne stated.

"Of course you can Wayne. Just pretend you are swimming in the heated pool!" Brian urged.

It was perhaps one hundred and fifty metres to the shore and only seventy five metres to where Wayne could stand up in the shallows. Brian knew the boy could swim the distance and he was not overly worried. Wayne dived in and began swimming. He had swum perhaps forty metres when the heavy swell got to him and the boy panicked. The other boys who had waited and were swimming with him, went to his assistance. Wayne grabbed Darren in desperation and they both got into difficulties. As Wayne and Darren struggled, Brian was already on his way to help them. From the high pier, the water where the boys were was too shallow to dive into, so Brian had to race twenty metres seawards along the pier before diving in, only then could he swim back to the children. Harold and Gavin were doing their best to keep the troubled pair afloat. They themselves could not quite reach the bottom but were proficient enough to pull the struggling pair apart and allow the important few seconds of respite until Brian arrived. He could stand on tip-toes just enough to take Wayne with one hand and push Darren towards one of the piles supporting the pier, with the other. Darren soon recovered as he was more suffering the effects of a mouthful of salt-water as a result of Wayne ducking him, than anything else and soon took off towards the shore again. Wayne though, was frightened of the waves. It was the first time he had been in water that fought back at him. Brian was being swamped with the endless waves and shouted to Wayne.

"Keep going Pal—you can do it—off you go. I will swim with you!"

He pushed the youngster ahead. Although not wanting to, Wayne was compelled to swim and Brian kept beside the boy, calling encouragement. When Wayne could stand easily in the shallows, Brian put an arm around his shoulders and said.

"There you are Wayne; I said you could do it and only one little ducking!"

"But I was frightened, the water was too big!" The boy complained.

"Yes, I forgot you have not been in the sea before I suppose the waves could frighten you—but I was proud of you Pal, you kept going after you got a fright. That is being big and tough that is, we will have to come to the sea more often so you can get used to it, won't we?"

Brian ruffled the boy's hair and the lad ran to tell his brothers that Brian was proud of him because he was big and tough now.

Once in the shallows, the older boys decided to catch some flounder. They were being urged on by young Peter, who was again showing his superior knowledge by instructing the other boys how to catch the fish, as Brian had demonstrated. He was quite surprised when his own efforts failed, but Damien and Philyp each managed to catch a couple.

"Argh, it is easy!" Philyp skited.

"Yair!" Damien agreed. "Do you want us to catch some for you?"

"No thanks." Peter determined. "I will catch my own!"

Unfortunately, Peter was unrewarded and rather than admit defeat, sought Brian and Wayne, who were sunning themselves dry by the concrete sea wall. They watched Peter come up to them, he sat down beside Brian.

"You know what?" He asked.

"No Peter—what?"

"Some lollies would be nice!"

He put tongue in cheek as he cheekily looked at Brian with tilted head.

"Oooh yes, they'd be beaut!" Wayne agreed.

Brian smiled, and then nonchalantly answered.

"Yes, they would be nice, wouldn't they?"

All sat in silence for a few moments. Peter put his elbow on Brian's knee and rested his chin in a cupped hand as he studied Brian's now impassive face.

"Well?" Peter queried.

"Well what?" Brian feigned surprise.

"Well what about buying us some lollies?" Wayne shouted, as he jumped up.

"Please!" Peter added.

Brian turned the fob pocket of his swim gear inside out, extracting only his car keys.

"Sorry–look, I have no money–besides, I think it is Wayne's turn to buy the lollies!"

Wayne was genuinely concerned.

"But I didn't bring my twenty cents; it's on the kitchen table at home!"

"Ooohh! You have got plenty of money Brian, you could shout us. You left your wallet under the car seat, I saw it." Peter said.

Brian slowly shook his head.

"No–sorry–I don't buy lollies for cheeky boys who ask for them. Bad luck!"

The two boys sat with downcast faces. Brian waited a little, and then said.

"But I will tell you what. If you two go and call the other boys over, we might walk around to the shops and buy an ice cream."

"Wow! Thanks Brian, come on Wayne!" Peter yelled as he jumped up and raced in pursuit of the rest of the gang.

They spent the latter part of the afternoon building sand castles until Brian called it a day and took the children to their respective homes. As the children lived in different suburbs up to twenty kilometres apart and the beach where they spent the day was another ten kilometres in a different direction, it was imperative that they leave the beach reasonably early. Damien's was the first house they came to but as Brian had to pass his house and then come back again, the boy asked could he go for the extra ride; just to be with his friends a little longer. Both Harold's parents and Leah, asked Brian in for a cuppa but he preferred to get his young passengers home as soon as possible, for all were very tired. The parents agreed, perhaps it was best, so Brian was able to have the last lot–the Wallers children–home in nice time for the evening meal.

Carmen, true to her mother's prediction, had a nice meal ready for them; ably assisted by her girl friend that came over to help. After the dishes were cleared away, the tired boys settled themselves into the lounge room and watched television. After an hour or so, Peter and Wayne were asleep and Darren and Gavin drooping. Carmen came in bearing a cup of tea and biscuits for Brian, who accepted them thankfully. Carmen jolted the four boys awake.

"Come on you sleepyheads–have a shower and get to bed–scoot!"

The grumbling boys went about their retirement placidly. As they filed to bed, each poked a head in to say goodnight and thank Brian. The house was all quiet by ten o'clock that evening when Erin and Valma returned. Carmen was still watching television; her girl friend had gone home. She put a finger to her lips as her parents entered. They beheld a tired Brian, leg stiffly out, sound asleep on the settee. Valma got a rug from her room and covered him, then switched off the television and retired to the kitchen. Valma whispered.

"Thanks Brian".

THE END

Howard Reede-Pelling.

The little red mini slewed around the elbow bend sending clouds of fine gravel, leaves and dust billowing behind it like a gossamer mushroom, as it growled in angry protest when Lana changed down for the climb up the short rugged hill, now in view. Two hours of tortuous driving along narrow bush tracks and seemingly endless and long-forgotten pitted old bitumen side roads, had passed with monotonous regularity. Her back was stiff and sore, her arms ached with the vibration of the direct-drive steering, and her throat and mouth were as dry as the countryside through which they were speeding. Natalie, her navigator, was still poring over the map and charts, ably directing them on their winning way. Yes, Lana was positive they were winning this car rally at the moment; they were third to be flagged off and passed Jim and Flo Angrage in their dinky little Austin seven, within ten minutes of the start. Jim and Flo did not really expect to get a placing, they just joined in the rally to make up the numbers and have a nice drive in the country. They would be the last to finish. It was a milestone and a windfall though, when they passed newcomers Barry and Andrew Nordic, the twin brothers who fancied they would be there amongst the first three placegetters, in their little German beetle. Unfortunately for the twins, they were jacking up their car to change a wheel when Lana and Natalie flew past. The girls cheerily waved to the disgruntled brothers and left them far behind. No one had passed them, so they must be winning.

"Natalie, got a breather to fish out a drink? I am as dry as a Scotsman's shout!"

Lana croaked, without taking her eyes off the track ahead. At the speed they were going a mishap could be fatal.

"No worries, the next turn is a right about fifteen kilometres ahead."

She fossicked in a knapsack strapped at the back of the seat.

"Looks like an orange drink—that do?"

"Yes dear, anything!" Lana accepted the opened can and took a few careful sips. "Thanks Natalie, you have the rest, I just wanted to wet the whistle; that was lovely."

They drove in silence again until Lana said.

"Fifteen coming up!"

"I see it that is it there, past the gum with the mistletoe!"

Natalie pointed as Lana prepared to again throw the trusty little mini around a corner sideways. They negotiated the corner well and 'revved her up' as the next straight stretch loomed ahead. This section became very risky after a few kilometres, as the track twisted and turned, then went up and down. In parts the track even wove in and out among the large blue-gums lining it and Lana was of a necessity, ever alert. It was just as well, for ahead and as they rounded a curve, they beheld a huge fallen tree across the track. Lana managed to swing the mini quickly enough to avoid the main trunk but the vehicle ploughed into the fine tips, which at one time were the top of the tree; fifteen or twenty metres up in the air. The mini burst through the fine leaves and branches but the wire fence bounding the roadside scratched the duco along the driving side, as Lana tried valiantly to steer away from it as she was applying the brakes. The fence was not the only worry for them, because they could not see the already fallen rotted logs on the other side of the great tree. Although Lana tried desperately to dodge between them, their size and numbers were too great. The mini leapt in the air like a bucking bronco and crashed to its side, steam hissing from the fractured radiator, the wheels spinning. The engine was still revving madly, for Lana's foot was jammed on the accelerator pedal. Her head was quite sore where it had come into violent contact with the upright of the door jamb. Dimly, through a mist that seemed to come and go in hazy brilliance as her head thumped to her heartbeats, Lana managed to turn the ignition off, before she sank into oblivion. The dust settled but a deathly stillness hung over the little blue mini as the spinning wheels one by one, ran themselves out, then they too; were still.

Lana stirred. Why did everything seem blurred? She could not for the life of her, understand what she was doing in this old wrecked car. She glanced down and noticed Natalie prone and apparently asleep. Best not to disturb her, she works hard at the office and normally comes home very tired. Through numbed eyes, Lana saw the long grass through the windscreen and mentally noting she must get the little Johnson boy in to cut it next week end, decided it was time to get up and prepare for work. Did Jamie say he was calling for her tonight? Come to think of it, what day was it? Must be Saturday, Natalie was sleeping in; she always slept in of a Saturday. Lana climbed out of the wreck and began walking down the track; she was quite unaware she had done so and soon all thought of the car and Natalie asleep in it, were lost to her. 'What a lovely day for a walk' she thought, 'was this the park Jamie took her for the picnic. Where was Jamie? He was there two minutes ago wasn't he? Wish he would not walk off like that, perhaps he went to the kiosk for cigarettes.' Lana thought it would be best to sit under this kind old tree and wait for him to return. My word she was hungry, perhaps Jamie went for sandwiches; he is a long time coming. On an impulse Lane got up and went looking for him.

Two hours passed and Lana was still wandering aimlessly through the virgin bushland, each new thing attracting her attention, be it a wallaby or a flight of galahs or perhaps a rabbit scurrying for cover. By chance she stumbled upon a clear little brook, prancing merrily over multi-coloured gravel and rocks. She drank of the soothing water then fell to collecting the pretty pebbles. Deeming to have enough to fashion a bracelet or some such, Lana crossed the little watercourse by the simple means of stepping over it, and continued her wanderings.

"Hello Lady!" A child's voice startled her.

Looking in the direction from which the voice came, Lana saw a youngster in a scouting uniform hacking at a dead branch with his hunting knife.

"Oh, hello son. Have you seen my Jamie?" Lana stopped beside the boy.

He stood erect to answer her.

"I don't remember a kid called Jamie, is he with our troop?"

"Troop?" She queried. "Oh! You mean a scout troop. No, Jamie is an adult; I have been looking for him."

"No Lady, the only adults are at the camp, I have been sent to gather firewood, so I don't know if he went to the camp or not. He may have gone to the house over there!" The boy pointed the way. Lana nodded.

"Yes, I will have a look."

She wandered off. The little scout watched her walk away. 'What a strange lady.' He thought. She looked quite dishevelled and the boy fancied he saw blood and a little bruising on her forehead. Perhaps he had better hurry back to camp and tell Skipper, just in case the lady was in trouble. Maybe she was lost! The scoutmaster knew by the lad's sincerity that he was not concocting a story, so, leaving the other adults and senior scouts to tend the camp routine Skipper took the boy and his father (who had volunteered to help with the troop on this camping exercise) on the search for this mysterious lady that young Robbie had come across. It did not take the skilled scout leader long to locate the wandering woman. She was sitting by an outcrop of granite, picking wildflowers from the small shrubs beneath it, the while she hummed merrily to herself.

"Excuse me Miss!" The scouter called as he neared Lana.

"Oh!" She exclaimed, and then quietly watched as the three came and stood awkwardly about her.

"Er–are you lost Miss?"

The scouter became very concerned as he noted there was indeed, bruising and a slight swelling with a trickle of dried blood above the young lady's temple.

Her expression was dreamy and she had a far away look upon her face. She failed to answer the question but stood looking, almost vacantly at the people who had come to her aid.

"I think she has had a knock and lost her memory." Robbie's father whispered.

"Were you with someone lady?" Skipper asked.

"She was looking for some bloke called Jamie!" Robbie interjected.

"Yes–Jamie!" Lana said, softly.

The scouter took her hand and they slowly walked back to the scouting camp. Lana docilely walking with them, smelling of her flowers and again quietly humming a tune. It was the tune she and Jamie loved most, the tune they danced to the first time that they met. It was three hours after the little blue mini overturned before a search party arrived at the scene of the mishap. Lana's boy friend Jamie, finished his mornings work early and hastened to the rally starting point, hoping to be in time to see Lana and Natalie off; he got there too late. The stewards refused to tell him the destination of the rally until the last vehicle was flagged on its way, then only if he pledged himself to secrecy. The point being that the finish line was only a half an hour drive away and the rally course was a three and a half hours run. It would be possible to intercept any of the cars and thus gain an advantage, if one was so inclined; the stewards were loathe taking the risk.

Jamie awaited the blue mini at the terminal and became worried when most of the cars arrived, but no blue mini. It was when the little Austin seven with Flo and Jim Angrage came chugging in, that Jamie knew that something was amiss. The Angrage's admitted waving the blue mini past but were adamant they never saw it again. Jamie enlisted the aid of a steward named Benny Preon and they back tracked the rally course to try and locate the errant girls and the missing mini. It was the sharp eyes of Benny that noticed the skid marks where the blue mini had spun around the fifteen kilometres turn-off.

"Look there!" He said, pointing the marks out to Jamie. "They've taken a wrong turn I'd say. A car turning normally wouldn't skid like that. I bet they have turned along that track. It is half a kilometre short of the correct turn. Let us check it out!"

It was obvious they were on the right trail because the wheel tracks were definitely those of a very small car and they were quite fresh in the dust. Even as Benny was speaking, Jamie had his sports car turned about and was speeding along the unfamiliar track. At the fallen tree the two men alighted from the sports car. The fact that there had been a mishap was evident by the freshly ruptured earth

210

and the broken tips of the fallen tree. It was obvious that something as large as a motor vehicle had ploughed through. It was with grave misgivings the men saw and approached the wreckage. The driving side wheels just discernable above the outflung branches; Jamie feared the worst as he peered into the little car. Natalie was conscious, she smiled feebly at Jamie.

"Oh! Thank God you have come at last. I have just about exhausted myself calling out. My–my leg is stuck, I think it is broken–please get me out Jamie–and be careful it hurts like hell!"

"Where is Lana?"

Jamie frantically looked about as he and Benny worked at prising the shattered and twisted flooring and superstructure from about the damaged leg.

"Is she off looking for help?"

Amid groans of pain as her leg was extracted, Natalie gasped.

"I don't know, she was not here when I became conscious–she–she may have been thrown out. Oh Jamie, do have a look for her, she must be around somewhere. Pray she is not dead–no–Heaven forbid, she, she couldn't be; she has just gone for help!"

They made Natalie comfortable, her leg was broken and it took some time to straighten and strap it to some sticks. Jamie and Benny had a quick but fairly thorough search of the area, but could find no trace of Lana. It was decided that they carry Natalie to the sports car and Benny would take her to the nearest hospital, while Jamie remained to continue the search for Lana. All three were of the opinion that Lana must have gone to get help for Natalie, when she was unable to free her navigator from the wreckage. Just in the event she may have wandered off in the wrong direction and got lost, Jamie would stay and search. It was as well that he did not know the truth of Lana's troubles, had he been aware that his loved one was lost and suffering amnesia, his frustration would have been all the more severe.

Jamie searched the immediate vicinity of the mishap once again, this time more thoroughly than the first. Nowhere was there any sign of his missing girl-friend, so Jamie became more convinced than ever that she must have gone seeking assistance. Had Lana gone back the way she had driven earlier, someone would have noticed her, especially the Angrages. It was therefore, evident she must have gone in the direction they were heading before the accident, and no doubt in the belief there was a house up ahead where she may get help. Jamie noted there were no houses the few kilometres back to the main road where the girls made the wrong turning. He walked briskly ahead now, knowing Lana would keep to the road. Two kilometres and still no sign of a farmhouse or Lana, Jamie was becoming worried. Perhaps she had gone out across country after all. He was about to retrace his steps, when he saw the road dipped up ahead, he would walk there and if no trace of his missing girl-friend could be found, he would go back to the wreckage and wait for Benny Preon to come back for him. He would decide then whether the two of them should carry on together or call for a search party. The dip in the road proved to be a ford across the small stream trickling down from the undulating hills he could see in the distance. Jamie had a drink of the clear flowing water and his worried gaze wandered upstream. What was that? Smoke! He could see smoke in the distance, perhaps it was Lana, it had to be; she was lost and had lit a signal fire! Jamie hastily ran through the shrubbery and made for the smoke. The old fence along the road was fallen and useless, so he had no trouble crossing to the paddocks and following the banks of the stream. The scrub was not very thick; in fact it was quite sparse and easy to manoeuvre. He came to an easy part of the stream where it was fairly open. As he stepped across, he noticed a small pile of coloured stones, neatly packed. He stopped to study them. Someone had been here but was it Lana. Why would Lana bother to stop and pile pebbles if she was in a hurry to find assistance? No, it could not have been Lana but someone had been here. Jamie was still of the opinion that Lana was lost and that it was her smoke signal. He pushed the pebbles aside and hastened in the direction of the smoke signal. When Jamie was within a hundred metres of the fire, he could hear the voices of many children. His faith was deflated, his hope dropped. A youth camp, a bloody youth camp! He was under a misapprehension, still, now he was here he may as well go and ask them if they happened to see a young lady seeking assistance—one never knows! As he entered the clearing and saw that it was a scouting camp, Jamie returned the polite Salutations and asked of the youngsters, where was their scoutmaster. A youngster directed him to the main tent and introduced Skipper, who was just on his way out.

"Look, I am Jamie Dently, and I wondered if—?" He began but was cut off.

"Oh, Jamie, you must be the Jamie she is looking for." Skipper stated.

"She is looking for? You mean you have found Lana, she is here?" Jamie asked, incredulously.

"Well we found a young lady but we do not know her name. You see, she seems to have lost her memory. She seems to have had a knock of some sort!" Skipper hurried Jamie into his tent where the relieved Jamie knelt beside Lana's sleeping form.

"We fed her and have only just got her to sleep; do you think it is wise to wake her?" Skipper queried with a whisper.

Jamie rose and went outside to ponder the situation. The scouter followed him.

"We were about to set out over the hill there to Doctor Meuren's house, it is only a week-end shack and we are not sure if he is there even; what do you suggest we do?"

Jamie considered awhile and concluded.

"I think it is best if we wake her. If she has got amnesia due to the bump on her head, she may snap out of it when she sees me. A familiar face may do the trick. We can always take her to see the doctor afterwards!"

Jamie dampened his handkerchief and whispered soothing words as he bathed the bruised forehead of his loved one. Her eyes flickered open, she gazed steadily at Jamie, then sitting up suddenly; exclaimed.

"Oh Jamie—the car—we hit a tree. What happened, where is Natalie, is she all right?"

Jamie embraced Lana as he soothed her.

213

"It is all right now, Pet. Natalie is fine, and it's all right now. Everything is all right now!"

He kissed her and she responded warmly. Skipper discreetly walked out, leaving them to themselves.

THE END.

Howard Reede-Pelling.

Jim Dory did not like this neighbourhood at all. The dingy little streets smelled of sewage and were littered with garbage from over-turned bins. A cat spat at him as he disturbed it from scavenging. The poor little thing was despicably thin and well in keeping with the atmosphere of this slum suburb. Jim would not have come here at all, if it were not to try and collect the outstanding debt owed to him, by a Missus D. Hird. It was not an over-large amount, but fifty dollars was fifty dollars and he was a stickler for keeping his books in order. In business one had to be firm. Missus Hird would pay her debt today or face court action, the debt had been dragging too long. As Jim passed a small lane, he heard a child sobbing and glanced in the direction from which the noise came. He saw a little girl of about six years, cramped in a doorway; hidden by the recess. He could see she had beautiful long pale yellow tresses; her small frame shook as she sobbed. Jim walked up to her and asked.

"What is the matter little girl, are you hurt–or lost?"

She turned glistening blue eyes up at him and shook her head. She was a very pretty little girl, but oh, so grubby. Her clothes were ragged and frayed, with stains here and there. Jim sat on his haunches.

"Why are you crying, Honey-bun?"

Shyly, the little girl tucked her chin into her chest and mumbled.

"'Cause the big boys pick on me and tease me. And that naughty Wayne calls me dizzy-prizzy and I don't like it!" She burst into tears again.

A slight smile touched his lips as Jim tried to cheer the little girl.

"That is not nice of him is it, tell me; what is your name, Honey-bun?"

The sobbing stopped as she studied this kindly man, she liked the way he called her 'honey-bun', it sounded so friendly.

"Priscilla." She mumbled.

Jim patted her head.

"My, that is a lovely name; I think the boys are donkeys, calling you nasty names when you have such a nice name. You know what I think? I think they are just jealous because you have a pretty name and they don't. A pretty girl with a nice name like Priscilla should not cry. Let me see a great big smile."

He put a finger under her chin and gently lifted her face to him. A coy smile rewarded his efforts.

"That is a good girl, you forget about the boys calling you nasty names and just be proud you have a beautiful name—is it a deal, Honey-bun?"

With a brighter face, little Priscilla nodded, her flaxen hair flopping about her shoulders. Jim waved goodbye with a smile as he returned to his task of debt-collecting. The house he was seeking was in the terrace bounded by the lane in which he found the little girl and the next intersection. The houses all looked alike with their meagre unkempt gardens and garish colours, painted no doubt by labourers who had no sense of colour balance and who used whatever scraps of paint they could scrounge. The gate of the tenement where Missus Hird resided was half ajar, due to the fact that the bottom hinge was broken and the gate hung at a rakish angle; firmly embedded in the dirt. Jim marched up to the front door and knocked loudly. All was quiet; it appeared that no one was at home. Jim knocked again, harder. He fancied he saw the curtain inside the one front window, move just a little. No, perhaps it was the wind, but the window was shut! 'She is probably there peering out of the window at me and refuses to open the door.' Jim thought.

He rapped yet again. Still no answer. Jim walked out of the gate then quickly turned and looked back at the window. Someone was at home, they had been peering out at him, and the curtains were again moving. As Jim walked back to thump on the door, he was aware of little Priscilla walking towards him. She stood at the gate as he banged on the door. There was still no reply. Jim turned to the little girl.

"Do you know the lady who lives here, Priscilla?" He asked.

She nodded her head vigorously.

"Do you know if the lady is at home?"

Again the golden locks scintillated as she nodded in the affirmative. The screeching voices of two young boys echoed throughout the street as the noisy urchins raced past. They stopped when they saw Priscilla at the gate.

"Yah-ha, prizzy-pants!" One called.

"Yeah, dizzy-prizzy!" The other mimicked.

"Hey! You boys, come here!" Ordered Jim, his eyes blazing under his shock of red hair.

The boys paled and would have run but Jim again demanded.

"Be quick!"

The two shuffled over.

Jim addressed them sternly.

"Aren't you ashamed of yourselves, picking on a little girl like that? You don't have to be very big and tough to pick on a little girl. You must only be babies if that is all you have to do. When I was your age I was out playing cowboys and indians with the big kids, I suppose the big kids won't let you play with them because you can only give cheek to little girls. Is that right?"

He gave them a stern look. The boys shuffled their feet and pouted.

"Argh! We was just havin' fun." The more arrogant of the two stated.

"I do not think that is much fun—making other people unhappy!" Jim suggested. "Why don't you get with the big boys and play a man's game and leave the little girls alone?"

"Yeah! C'mon Eric, let's look for Barry and Rod; she only cries anyway!"

"Arggh!" The other lad replied. "I was just sayin' that, I don't pick on girls—"

They faded into the distance. Jim turned back to his debt collecting. Priscilla was waiting at the door of the house as Jim walked forwards. She called through the letter chute.

"Mummy—there's a man—he's at the door!"

Surprised, Jim Dory awaited the outcome of the youngster's cry. The door opened almost immediately. The woman most certainly must have been in the front room and aware of Jim's presence, he was sure. But for the advent of Priscilla, she may not have answered the door. The little girl's mother was quite a good looking woman–well–she had been. The worried face had a tired expression and a little of fear was in her eyes as she asked.

"Yes, what is it you want?"

Jim introduced himself and produced a bill for the amount owing.

"I have come to demand you settle this account Missus Hird, I loathe going further but I must balance my books!"

The woman held Priscilla to her; the child wrapped her arms about her mother's legs. Missus Hird implored.

"But I pay the premiums regularly, I can only afford so much now, I have my widow's pension, couldn't you give me more time; please?"

She rubbed her eyes and forehead with a shaking hand.

"I had to have the sheets and school clothes, it was urgent!"

Jim noticed that although her own clothes were clean, they too left something to be desired. Poverty was staring him in the face. 'I mustn't weaken' he thought 'business is business.' Aloud he said.

"I am sorry Missus Hird, I can not run a business on promises."

Jim fancied Missus Hird stifled a tear as she turned, taking Priscilla with her.

"Won't you come in for a minute Mister Dory–I'll–I'll see what money I can spare. I won't be able to pay it all now!"

She ushered him into the front room where he knew she was watching him through the window, earlier.

"Please be seated, I won't be long!"

Missus Hird left the room and Priscilla came over and sat on the settee beside him. Jim smiled at her.

"Hello Honey-bun, do you go to school now?"

Again the little girl nodded, and then coyly said.

"Thank you for growling at Wayne and Eric; they are naughty, aren't they?"

"I do not think they will call you names anymore." Jim said, sympathetically.

He arose as Missus Hird returned.

"I can only find fifteen dollars that I can spare—I have twenty two—but I will have to keep some to tide us over the week!" She worried.

"If you can wait a little, I'll run next door and see if I can borrow some off Missus Williams—"

Jim could stand it no longer, the dire circumstances of the family, the unhappy mother and daughter. He felt like an ogre, a greedy monster, he should be ashamed. Bullying a mother like this—he was no better than Wayne and Eric. He glanced at Priscilla; she smiled at him, her innocence hurt.

"Missus Hird." He interrupted. "If you are willing, I could find you a casual job at my store during school hours that may settle both our problems. I am prepared to discuss it further over a cup of tea—?"

Missus Hird placed a hand at her heart.

"Oh! You would do that? I—I don't know what to say—I'll—I'll put the kettle on!"

She almost rushed out of the room. Priscilla knelt on the settee and tugged at Jim's sleeve.

"Please, could I sit on your knee?"

The pretty little face warmed his heart. He was lost.

"I think you had better ask Mummy, Honey-bun, if Mummy says it is all right I would love to have you sit on my knee!"

Priscilla ran to her mother, Jim knew what the outcome would be and felt strangely contented. Priscilla's dilemma had made him look to his own faults and he found himself wanting. People are human, in poverty or wealth. Pricilla made him feel human again.

THE END.

Howard Reede-Pelling.

The violent movement of the uppermost branches of the normally sombre weeping willow, attested to the fact that a foreign body of some substance moved within its covering foliage. Jacqueline had been seeking her brother for nearly fifteen minutes and was on the verge of giving up this one-sided game. How was it that she always seemed to be the hunter and diminutive Andrew the quarry? Of course the agitation in the tree could only be that snub-nosed little nine year old terror of a monster, who was her only play mate; a bird would not cause so many disturbances. The area, in which the Gravers children were playing, was perhaps two hundred metres from 'Glencarrigal', the weatherboard homestead in which the children were born on this magnificent property of some three thousand hectares. It was primarily sheep country but the Gravers Family also ran a few hundred head of cattle, including half a dozen milkers and some horses. Way out here in the outback of Australia, where the nearest township was one hundred and twenty five kilometres away, each station had to be, more or less; self-sufficient. An extremely large vegetable garden and a full chicken coop were set behind the covering gallery of rambling pines predominately down-wind. Here too, were the seventeen pigs and piglets, bred to enhance the ever abundant and wholesome meals of the family. Jacqueline brushed her mousey-coloured hair back from her eyes, the better to study the lay of the land and work out the best possible avenue in which to approach unseen and surprise young Andrew. There was ample cover for her behind the thick pines and as she quickly skirted them to the rear of the dividing humps of undulating rises in the sheep-mown grass, Jacqueline made her way down to the willows guarding the swift; clear creek. As yet she was sure, Andrew had not seen her. As if to verify the fact, he let out a yell which startled her.

"Jackie Gravers in a jar, she don't know where I are!"

He giggled to himself like a chattering little possum as he peered from behind a branch where he sat in a crotch of the large willow; his back towards Jacqueline. She approached the tree in which her brother tried to hide and selecting a chunky stick from the many scattered about, threw it at him. It struck the boy on the back. A surprised "ouch" as he jumped, almost upsetting him, was accompanied by Jacqueline's shout.

"You are struck, a burned out match, now it's me you have to catch!"

The girl ran helter-skelter back over the undulations and disappeared behind the shearing shed, to one side of the pines. Disgruntled, Andrew slowly made his way down from the dizzy height that proved to be nowhere near as good a hiding place as he thought. Upon reaching the safety of the ground, the boy quickly ran to the edge of the pines and climbed up to a thick branch that lay parallel to the ground about four metres high. This was his secret weapon, a vantage point from which a panoramic view was laid open to him of the farmhouse and surrounds. Andrew gazed urgently from his quick blue eyes and was rewarded by the slight movement he detected behind the shearing shed. It could only be Jacqueline's hair, fluttering in the slight autumn breeze. 'So that's it'. He thought. 'She is hiding in the sheep ramp and peeking around the corner'.

Andrew relinquished his position to the birds or whatever the branch would next support and on swift, silent feet, ran to the shearing shed and crept beneath it; making his way quietly to the ramp where his twelve year old sister hid. Jacqueline was unaware of his presence and still peered around the corner, her toes protruding through the gaps in the side of the ramp.

Andrew reached up and firmly grabbed one of her feet, sliding it down the ramp in an effort to unbalance her. She bumped a shin against an upright as the boy called.

"You are struck, a burned out match, now it's me you have to catch!" He scampered away on all fours.

Jacqueline screamed as her shin struck the upright. She was hurt by the bump but more so by the fact she was caught so soon. How did the little brute find her so quickly?

"I'm not playing anymore, you've broken my leg!" Her yells caused Andrew to stop.

'Broken her leg', he thought, 'Gee, he would cop it from Dad if he has!' Fearfully the lad came back to the ramp where his sister was grizzling as she massaged her injured member. Large blue eyes looked apprehensively through the gap in the side of the ramp at the grazed shin, where a trickle of blood oozed.

"Is it really truly broked?" Andrew asked, fearfully.

"Just about, I should rip your leg off and hit you with it. Why did you make me bang my leg?" Jacqueline too, had blue eyes, slightly paler than those of her brother. Now however, they glistened with unshed tears.

"I didn't mean to hurtcha, I only wanted you to slip." Andrew tried to pat the leg better. Jacqueline slapped his hand.

"Nick off, you've done enough damage, go play on your own!"

Andrew wrinkled his nose as he walked away.

"Yah! You're a sissy—you're only a girl—I don't want to play with girls anyway!"

Jacqueline poked her tongue out at him but he was well gone and did not see her rude gesture. Jacqueline went into the shearing shed and browsed about, looking for something to do. Her eyes beheld the open bale of wool clippings. She gathered some and began to fashion the fleece in the image of little dolls, binding them with pieces of hemp that were strung from the walls. These were used to sew the bales when full.

A pleasant hour passed and she had fashioned a whole nursery of the little dolls from the old bits of fleece, including a larger doll that would be the nursing sister who would tend her nursery. Suddenly, the mother instinct within reminded the girl she was responsible for young Andrew. He was awfully quiet; it was unusual for him not to annoy her at least once every half hour. Perhaps it would be wise to investigate and see what he was up to; more than likely he had returned to the house and was playing with one of his toys. Jacqueline moved to the window over-looking the creek where Andrew's favourite tree stood. No doubt he was playing at the creek or in the tree. A quick glance along the creek did not inform her of his presence, so she fastened her eyes upon his tree and studied it minutely. Ah yes, there he was, well up near the top. Dad had warned him many times about climbing too high. She would go down and chastise him, which would make up a little bit for him hurting her shin. Jackie stopped as she saw Andrew reach out to a thin branch for a better grip. The tree top bent alarmingly as his weight strained the thin branch, then what she feared happened. The branch broke and Andrew fell, a sharp piercing scream echoed along the waterway but was quickly cut short as the boy landed heavily on his stomach across the branch directly beneath him.

Archie Gravers was a small, quiet person. As a young man he had been a horse riding jockey of some note and had invested wisely the proceeds of his turf career. 'Glencarrigal' was the result of those investments and it was paying handsome dividends. Although not immediately involved in the racing scene these days, he still had an avid appetite for the racing game and the Saturday and mid-week meetings, were the one link with his past that he would not forego. If he were unable to attend the meetings personally, he would be glued to the radio listening to the broadcast. These were the times when the children preferred to play outdoors as their father did not take kindly to being disturbed.

Katherine was a dutiful wife and mother, so of course she always managed to do her darning or a little crochet work on race days. She felt it her duty to sit with Archie so he would have someone to sympathise with if the meeting did not go as expected. Kathy, as she preferred to be called, was a little taller than her man and it was she who wished to settle way out in the back blocks. 'Freedom for the children to grow' was her motto, and as Archie agreed, 'there's more than enough freedom out here'. They bought the property off Glen and Carrie Galling, who had to sell out and move closer to a Specialist in the big city. Carrie was ailing and only specialist treatment could help her. The Gravers liked the name of the property, so left it as it was. Kathy suggested perhaps Archie was just too lazy to think of a better name anyway. It was of course, far from the truth, Archie was a very industrious and active man. Saturday especially was his day of rest and he so looked forwards to the afternoon of bliss with the racing pages and the broadcast. It would take an emergency to move him now that he was settled. Mundane tasks would be left to Kathy and the farm could fend for itself, there was nothing so important to be done that could not wait until the broadcast was over. Had either of them been aware of the plight of their youngest, both would have become engines of activity. However, they were ignorant of the mishap that befell young Andrew, so pursued their present interests quietly.

Jacqueline raced with all her might to the stricken Andrew, expecting to see the small body bounce from branch to branch until it landed with a sickening thud–a broken heap–at the foot of the tree. Not so, for when the girl came to the tree, her brother was still balanced across the branch upon which he fell; quietly moaning as he held on grimly to the tip of the broken branch. It was this piece of branch that kept the boy from falling further, as it was caught in a fork a little away from the unfortunate Andrew and held precariously.

"Hang on Andy, I'm coming!" Jacqueline called, as she began the climb to her brother's assistance, ignoring the stiffness in her lacerated leg. The girl was not afraid to climb trees and had done so often. When one has only a younger brother as a playmate, it becomes necessary to indulge to a certain extent in his type of activities, however, Jacqueline was loathe climbing as high as the young scamp did and in truth, was a great deal afraid of the dizzy heights of the tree-tops. In this time of need she cast her fears aside, knowing that Andrew could fall further and possibly be killed if he did not have assistance. She was the only help available in a hurry.

"Stay still, I'm nearly there!" Jacqueline encouraged as she pulled herself along the rather stout branch and peered anxiously at Andrew. "Are you dead?" She worried.

"Mpft, I think so!" Gasped a very pale Andrew.

Relieved, the girl reached out and said.

"Grab my hand and I will pull you across."

"I can't move, my stomach hurts!"

"You'll have to try; you can't stay there all day. Come on, make an effort Andy–I'll balance you–I've got a good grip on this branch. While I hold you, try and get a leg over the branch you are on!"

With much coaxing and the near presence of a helping hand, the winded boy slowly managed to edge his way to the trunk of the tree. Between them, he was eased to the safety of solid earth. An immediate inspection of his abdomen showed a large overall bruise with a small indentation, slightly lacerated, beside the navel. It would appear that the stump of a broken twig had penetrated his clothing. Evidently no bones were broken and besides being winded, the only other injury was to the boy's pride as a tree-climber. Now that the danger was over, Jacqueline berated her brother, more as a warning than for revenge.

"Serves you right, you could have been killed. Dad warned you about climbing too high; you are going to cop it when he finds out."

"Aw gee Jackie, he does not have to find out; don't pimp on me please."

Andrew nursed his stomach as he cast an appealing look at the older sister who now held the trump hand.

"Why not?" She teased. "You nearly broke my leg then you almost got killed climbing too high when you know Dad said you're not to, you deserve to get into trouble!"

Jacqueline turned away, chin high, enjoying the situation. Andrew winced in pain as he humbly followed her, pleading.

"Arh, c'mon Jackie, I didn't mean to hurt your leg—I'll—I'll play dolls with you if you don't pimp. Eh Jackie—do you want to?" His little face frowned as he tugged at her arm.

"Anything you want me to do I will do, I promise!"

Jacqueline stopped and faced him.

"Anything at all?" She asked a dark gleam in her eyes. Andrew nodded.

"Long as you don't pimp on me!"

"Alright, come over to the shearing shed."

She led the way, relieved, Andrew followed.

He knew his sister would keep her word; their parents were strict in such matters. Andrew was sitting on a half full bale of wool, watching his sister adjust one of the wool classer's aprons about her. She neatly folded a towel which hung from the same peg as the apron and laid it beside the inquisitive boy.

"What is that for, what are you going to do?" He wondered.

Jacqueline gently pushed him until he lay flat on his back atop the bale.

"I'm the mother and you are the baby. I have to change your nappy and put you to bed!" Andrew sat bolt upright, wincing again as he gasped.

"You are not–I won't let you do it!"

Jacqueline stamped her foot.

"Lie down baby, you promised, I will tell Dad; remember?"

"Argh gee, it's not fair!" Andrew reluctantly lay back.

Archie and Kathy were enjoying a quiet relaxing afternoon; however fate destined a change in this idyllic setting. The change occurred with the arrival of Kathy's sister and her energetic family. Estelle did not often manage to visit her sister because of the long journey involved, so when this effort was made once or twice a year, the family would stay for a week or more. In the shearing shed, the slam of the car doors could be heard quite clearly. With a relieved shout, Andrew sprang to his feet before his ordeal began, again wincing with pain from his battered stomach and hurried to the door; Jacqueline close upon his heels.

"It is Aunty Estelle!" The boy cried. "Pudden and Emma will be with her–come on Jackie–hurry!"

Andrew was outdistanced by his sister on this occasion due to the restrictions caused by his injury and almost in the same breath, he begged.

"Oh, wait for me Jackie!"

It was with slight annoyance that Archie turned the radio down a little as he and Kathy went to welcome their relatives. Visitors were always made welcome, more so when they were kinfolk.

It was nice to have someone different about occasionally; it broke the sameness of everyday living. Estelle, like Katherine, was fairly tall in comparison to Archie and the sisters could well have been twins. They were blue eyed and fair haired as were Estelle's two children. Emily Crensy was only nine, as of course was her twin brother Paul, but there the similarity ended, for she was quite slim where Paul had put on so much weight that he was naturally nicknamed 'Pudden'. The children all got on very well together. As the boys were the same age, they also had the same interests and after salutations all around were dispensed with, the adults entered the house for refreshments while the children paired off and went their different ways. Jacqueline was three years older than her cousin Emily but that did not matter one bit, she was another girl and could play girls games. It was but a matter of a few minutes before Jacqueline was proudly showing off the newly made dolls to Emily and the boys were down at the creek by Andrew's favourite tree. Paul was part way up the tree calling to Andrew to follow him but Andrew with his sore stomach, was not up to it and declined; suggesting that they look for frogs instead. A stentorian voice calling from the house saved the day, as Archie summoned the children back for milk and biscuits. As they obeyed, Jacqueline remembered her deal with Andrew and urged him quietly aside, so that she could whisper in his ear.

"Don't you pimp on me about the nappy and I won't pimp on you about the tree—alright Andy?"

Andrew nodded as he again brought up the rear. The adults partook of their tea in the lounge room, leaving the children to themselves in the kitchen. If there were accidents, they could be more easily cleaned up on the tiled floor, by comparison to the lush carpet in the lounge room.

Estelle could see through the connecting doorway from where she was sitting and it so happened that Andrew was the one more easily seen. His slow pained approach to the business of getting settled in a chair, then reaching for a biscuit, gave his Aunt cause for concern.

"What is ailing Andrew Katherine, is he ill?" She worried.

"No, not that I know of, why do you ask?" Katherine queried.

"Oh I don't suppose it is anything at all, probably just my imagination, he seemed lethargic; that's all!"

"He is as fit as a fiddle Estelle." Archie put in. "You should have seen him racing about this morning. Playing at chasey or some such with Jackie, he is all right!"

"Must be me then. How is the farm going? Shearing all finished I suppose?"

She changed the subject.

"Yes Estelle, we are doing quite well thanks. Shearing's been over two-three weeks now. I am going to have to make a start on the fences though. Some stretches leave a lot to be desired. Have the 'roos in before long!"

They spoke of various matters for some minutes, and then a lull in the conversation gave Jacqueline the opportunity to speak. She had left the kitchen and was standing by her aunt.

"Excuse me Mummy, I've cleared the table and rinsed the things, can Emma come to my room so we can play, please?"

"Yes dear, what are the boys doing?"

"They are still in the kitchen talking about frogs–yuk!"

Amid smiles from the adults, the girls ran off to the bedroom. Katherine, concerned by Estelle's query, called Andrew to her. Paul followed as the boy slowly came, trying to look unconcerned.

"Are you well, dear?" She placed her hands on his shoulders the better to hold him steady as she studied his face.

"Mpft!" He nodded, avoiding her eyes.

"Well, you had better take Paul out and play Love." Kathy gave him a gentle squeeze.

"Ugh!" Andrew jerked convulsively.

"Well! You are touchy, what made you jump Andrew?"

Kathy poked him gently in the ribs. The boy pushed her hand away, saying.

"Please don't Mummy, my tummy hurts!"

"You haven't been at those green berries again have you? I warned you about eating green fruit!" Andrew was most uncomfortable and tried to edge away, saying.

"No, I didn't Mummy. I–I just hurt it, it's all right!"

"Andrew!" Archie demanded. "Don't you go running off just yet, let Mum have a look at it, how did you hurt yourself?"

"Argh gee Dad, I was just playing. I am all right, can I go now?"

"No. Let Mum have a look at it, go on!"

Reluctantly the boy confronted his mother; she gently lifted his clothing up under his armpits. Three adults gasped in surprise simultaneously. The skin had discoloured alarmingly since the injury occurred. The multi-coloured bruise was spread all over the entire front of the youngster's stomach and even penetrated a little around the sides. The laceration beside Andrew's navel was red and angry looking; it had been bleeding.

Archie jumped to his feet and checked for himself the extent of the injury.

"How did this happen. While you were playing this morning, was it?"

"Yes Dad. It–it doesn't hurt much!" Andrew began trembling.

His father could be very severe at times.

"Was Jacqueline with you?" He summoned his daughter. "Jacqueline, come here this instant!" The girl came, pausing as she saw Andrew's injury exposed.

"Yes Daddy?"

"Did you know Andrew was hurt?"

Guiltily hanging her head, she mumbled.

"Yes Daddy."

"I made you responsible for Andrew, why didn't you tell us he was hurt? Even if you had nothing to do with him being injured, it was your responsibility to bring him home and tell us. Now why didn't you?"

Jacqueline was shocked when she saw how the bruising had spread; Andy must have been hurt worse than she thought.

"It wasn't as bad as that when I looked at it Daddy. I–I didn't think it was much to worry about. Truly Daddy, I'm sorry!"

Her father "hrumpfed" then dismissed her with.

"I will want to know more about this later, we will tend to Andrew first. Take Emma and Paul away to play."

Andrew was made to have a luke warm bath then hop into bed, where his lacerations were tended and he could rest the soreness from his body. He deemed it better not to protest for the fear of more questions being asked. He had no desire to be banned from any more tree-climbing. The boy only hoped that Jackie would not 'dob him in'.

Jacqueline had lost the urge to play and was most fearful of the consequences when her parents spoke to her at length on the subject of Andy's misfortune, as she knew they would, more than likely after tea. If it were not for her father sending her outside, Jacqueline would have dallied until Andrew was alone in his room. She urgently desired to talk to him now, fearful that her brother may weaken and tell how he was hurt. If that happened, he could also mention why his sister did not inform their parents. Then she would really be in trouble because even though she only wanted to play at being a mother, Jacqueline knew they were not supposed to play that sort of game.

Jacqueline was a very unhappy girl as the twins urged her to play. Paul did not help matters by asking.

"Hey Jackie, how did Andy get a black tummy; what happened. Will it wash off?"

Jacqueline snapped at him.

"No Dummy, it's a bruise and he got hurt playing and I don't want to hear any more about it; go play with Emma somewhere!"

Piqued, Paul was silent, then pouted.

"Well, I don't care. I wish we hadn't come to your rotten old house anyway!"

He took Emma by the arm.

"Come on Emma, we can play on our own!"

Jacqueline realized she had been unfair, venting her frustration on her cousins. She called them back.

"Oh, come back Pudden, I am sorry; I am just worried about Andy."

The twins stopped and looked back.

"Do you want to play on the swing?"

Jacqueline set the example by running to it, the twins raced after her.

The swing was just an old motor tyre fastened by a strong rope to an outflung branch of an aged gum tree, between the house and the shearing shed. It had served its purpose well over the years and by the look of the smooth shiny surface, was still doing so. As the children played and Archie held the floor, Kathy excused herself and checked on Andrew. She caught him frowning at the ceiling looking quite worried indeed.

"Feeling better dear, is it very sore?"

She sat on the bed and brushed a wisp of hair away from his eyes as she asked. Andrew answered almost inaudibly.

"No, it does not hurt when I stay still!"

"Would you like to tell me how it happened, Love?" Kathy smiled reassuringly.

"Do I have to?" He was on the defensive, like a puppy that had been growled at.

"You would rather not tell me dear?"

"No!"

"Daddy might make you tell when he has a talk later; you were doing something you should not have, weren't you?" She held his hand, gently stroking it.

Andrew turned away, and then faced his mother.

"Yes, but I won't do it again Mummy, truly. Please don't let Daddy growl at me!"

"I can't promise Darling but I will have a talk with him!"

Kathy kissed her son on the forehead, tucked him in, and then left; smiling encouragement.

Andrew felt a little easier and closed his eyes.

While the womenfolk nattered in the kitchen, preparing the evening meal, Archie caught up on his racing results. The other children could be heard laughing as they played at the swing. Jacqueline temporarily let her worries fade into the background; after all, having playmates other than Andrew was an opportunity too good to miss. Later on could take care of itself, she would worry when the time came. Another good, wholesome meal was readily dispatched by those active and healthy enough to enjoy it, not so poor Andrew. His battered body felt swollen and no doubt was, a little. His food lay untouched on the bedside table where his mother had left it after gently waking him. Andrew would have preferred mother let him sleep on and then maybe Dad would not bother to ask him any awkward questions. But, mother deemed it better that he try to eat a little, and then perhaps he would sleep soundly throughout the night.

During the rest of the evening Jacqueline was on pins and needles, expecting at any given time that her father would embarrass her in front of her young cousins; it was not to be so. Her ordeal was not begun until Emma and Paul were well settled into bed. Jacqueline bit her lip when her father gave his 'severe look' and beckoned her over.

"Well Jacqueline, why did you not tell mum or me that Andrew was hurt; did you do it?"

"No Daddy!"

There was a slight silence and Jacqueline fidgeted awkwardly. Her parents waited expectantly.

"Well?" Archie raised his eyebrows expressively. "Must I punish you first?"

Mad plans and excuses for the events of the day had been chasing in vicious circles through her mind all day, yet still Jacqueline had arrived at no suitable explanation that would not land them both in big trouble. She recalled her pact with Andrew that they should not pimp upon each other but her father was demanding that she do just that.

"Jacqueline!" Archie growled.

"Please Daddy, I–I promised Andy I wouldn't pimp on him. It, it was not my fault!"

"Weren't you keeping an eye on him like you promised me?" Jacqueline nodded. "And yet when he did something stupid you did not stop him. Isn't that your fault?"

"Oh Archie" Kathy broke in "does it really matter how it happened? I had a talk with Andrew and he promised me that whatever caused it won't happen again. I am sure Jacqueline won't let it happen again either, couldn't we forgive them just this once?"

Jacqueline looked hopefully at her father. Archie thought for a moment, and then agreed.

"All right but I will expect better of you in the future Jacqueline. Tell me, why did you promise not to tell?"

A bombshell may as well have exploded about her, Jacqueline was stunned. Just when she thought she had got out of it, Dad asked another awkward question. She took a deep breath and told the truth.

"I wanted to play mother with Andy and I did not think you would like it if I pretended to change his nappy. So we promised not to tell on each other. I wasn't really being naughty Daddy!"

Archie kissed his daughter on the cheek.

"Don't be frightened to tell us these things Love. We know you are just growing up and we do love you, you know. Perhaps if you remind Andrew of that, he may come and be honest with us too!"

After kisses all around, Jacqueline raced up to bed, eager for tomorrow so she could talk to Andrew.

THE END.

Howard Reede-Pelling.